Botanica

Praise:

"I just finished *Botanica*. Loved the book. Kudos to the authors. Such talent! Such wisdom!! Inspiring as well."
—Sue M., teacher, book club member/organizer

"I loved reading *Botanica*! This captivating novel craftily takes a subject like plants and weaves an intriguing plot that makes you think differently about things such as electric cars, wildfires, etc. In summary, *Botanica* takes you on a wild journey that I strongly recommend!"
—Greg Davis, author, *Checkmate*

"*Botanica* is an electrifying, high-wire eco-drama that defies the lines between science and nature's wrath. It is a gripping and timely tale that will keep you hooked until the last page."
—T.K. Peoples, award-winning librarian and author

Novels by Fred Yager
The Asian Queen
Rex (middle school)
Sound from a Star (YA)
Cybersona
Just Your Everyday People (with Jan Yager)
Untimely Death (with Jan Yager)

Novels by Jeff Yager
Atom & Eve (YA)
I Like God (with Skye Bynes)
Seven Days in Virtual Reality
Stunt Double
A Ghostly Twist (forthcoming)

Botanica

A Novel

Fred Yager
Jeff Yager

Hannacroix Creek Books, Inc.
Stamford, Connecticut

Published by:
Hannacroix Creek Books, Inc.
1127 High Ridge Road, #110
Stamford, Connecticut 06905 USA
https://www.hannacroixcreekbooks.com
e-mail: hannacroix@aol.com

Library of Congress Control Number: 2024905148
ISBN: 978-1-938998-66-9 (trade paperback)
ISBN: 978-1-938998-65-2 (hardcover)

Chapter 1

The man was dressed in a white protective Hazmat suit made with a thick impermeable material that covered his entire body. It also came equipped with a clear plastic faceplate and self-contained breathing apparatus. From the expression on his face, it appeared that he was not very happy.

Jason Woods hated the Gene Gun which had the size and shape of his mother's hair dryer but weighed about five pounds. Every time he picked it up, he felt as if he was holding a hydrogen bomb in his hands and that it could go off at any moment. He knew that was a ridiculous thought, since no hydrogen was involved in this otherwise complicated process known among genetic engineers as "biolistics." Who came up with that obnoxious term? He always wondered. He guessed it was a play on ballistics, since instead of bullets and gunpowder, the Gene Gun used pellets coated with plant DNA (thus the "bio" part), and helium gas to rupture a plastic disk that was filled with the tiny, microscopic pellets that shot them into the target cells of another plant. Or at least that's what was supposed to happen if everything worked correctly.

On this Tuesday, in the R&D lab at Morabito Genetic Engineering, Inc., on the outskirts of the Chicago suburb of Evanston, Illinois, someone, unbeknownst to Jason Woods, had mistakenly overloaded the Gene Gun with way too much helium gas.

Since Jason was using both hands to hold the Gene Gun, another engineer, also dressed in a Hazmat suit, held the helium hose line connecting the gun to the helium tank, as both maneuvered Jason into a pristine, immaculate 100 percent particle-free chamber the size of a shed too small to contain more than one person at a time. Therefore, the second engineer holding the line had to remain outside while Jason entered with the Gene Gun. As soon as he did, a vacuum sealed door with a notch large enough to fit around the hose line closed behind him, sealing him inside.

Outside the chamber, the other engineer, Howard Bowde, checked some readings, paying particular attention to a round window tracking air pressure, where the reading had just hit 100 lbs/pressure. Inside the sealed area, Jason was watching the other engineer give him a thumbs up.

Jason nodded and switched off the safety lock on the Gene Gun. Then, holding it with both hands, he aimed it at the target DNA. If everything worked properly, a plastic disk holding the plant DNA cells would be fired into the target DNA. But when he pulled the trigger, the plastic disk exploded inside the gun, sending the tiny, microscopic pellets coated with plant DNA right through Jason's protective suit and directly into his body, just below his clear plastic faceplate.

To Jason, it felt like being shot by a gun firing cotton candy since the microscopic pellets made holes so small even a droplet of blood could not get through. Jason's skin turned bright red, and the wound looked more like a burn than a penetration. However, the tiny pellets carrying the plant DNA had indeed penetrated Jason's impenetrable Hazmat suit as well as his body and the various cells within it. Some even ricocheted upward, and into his eyes and the space between his eyes and eye sockets, which meant some of the plant DNA had even penetrated Jason's brain.

Jason dropped the Gene Gun on the chamber floor. "I told them this gun was a piece of shit," said Jason.

He opened the chamber door, stepped outside, and fainted.

Bowde, standing outside the glass enclosure, stared at Jason lying on the floor.

"Hey, Jason! You okay? What happened in there?"

A voice came over a hidden speaker: "An EMT unit is on its way. Stay in place. No one leave the lab until cleared. Is that understood? Just nod if you understand."

Bowde looked up at wherever the voice was coming from and nodded.

The Gene Gun accident at the Morabito lab never made the news. That's because the corporate communications department of the parent company took immediate steps to ensure that word of the mishap remained confined to the small group of technicians known as genetic engineers who had been with Jason when the Gene Gun misfired. They did as protocol directed—reported the accident to senior management, who quickly assembled the business continuity management team that included the firm's crisis communications specialists who then advised the c-suite (senior management) that in this case, no communication, external or internal, was the best strategy. If no one outside that small circle knew about the accident, then to the rest of the world, it never happened.

Morabito was a subsidiary of a larger agriculture corporation, AG-Con, that specialized in the production of genetically-modified plants and vegetables the media had nicknamed "Frankenplants." That included over-sized tomatoes, or the recently famous "ketchup and fries" creation that was both potato and tomato. Their products had made it into hundreds of top retail stores across the country, including the megastore, CostSMART.

Recently, Morabito had expanded into areas beyond food products. When this incident occurred, Jason had been attempting to combine redwood DNA with maple DNA to create a more durable wood commonly used in new home construction. It would come from a tree that grew faster than a typical redwood, thereby generating stronger lumber at a faster pace than it took to harvest similarly-sized redwoods.

A fine idea if ever there was one, thrown slightly off course when the altered maple tree DNA was accidentally fired into the body and absorbed by Jason, one of Morabito's top genetic engineers.

The accident was immediately contained inside the small laboratory since Jason was the only person affected. A medical team rushed Jason into an examination room and began running tests for his blood pressure, EKG, temperature, and pulse.

"I feel fine," insisted Jason, once he regained consciousness. "Really, this is all unnecessary. Barely felt a thing."

They treated the wound, which was basically a red blotch on his upper chest with betadine and proceeded to monitor Jason's vitals.

For the first twenty-four hours, Jason experienced no change whatsoever, other than an odd craving for pancakes and French toast, neither of which he typically ate.

The medical team eventually determined that there would probably be little to no effect from plant DNA being absorbed by a human since we eat plants every day, albeit not trees as a rule. As for the small, microscopic pellets of tungsten, they would have to wait and see how Jason's body dealt with it.

A CAT scan and several blood tests later, Jason was finally given a clean bill of health and then dismissed from the clinic.

The next day, when Jason arrived back at work, he was directed to Human Resources where he was advised by an HR specialist that he was being released from his position on the DNA transfer team. Their reason was that it must have been human error on his part that caused the Gene Gun to misfire.

"After careful review of what happened, including watching the available video, we have determined that you are the reason the gun misfired," said the HR manager.

"That's ridiculous!" Jason exclaimed. "Whoever filled the gun with helium messed up. It wasn't me. When I get the gun, it's supposed to be ready to fire. I just use the tools I'm given. You can't blame me for somebody else's mistake. If you do, I'll sue your ass."

Jason continued to sit there, angered, as he began to clean the lenses of his glasses with his T-shirt.

The HR manager disappeared for quite a few minutes, returning with a different expression on her face.

"We have reconsidered," she said. "I have received approval to remove any wording from your file that implied that the accident was your fault."

"Much better," said Jason. "Now, can I get back to work?" he asked the HR manager.

"Not exactly," she replied.

He was told to sit tight until they knew what they were going to do with him.

"We have to see if there's another position open for you in the company."

Minutes turned to hours as Jason waited on a cold chair at a desk in the human resources department, scrolling through the e-mails on his phone and reading the posters on the walls with their various slogans to boost employee morale like "Make everyday a good day" or "You are in charge of your own destiny." Finally, Jason was told he could leave the HR office and that he should check his email for a status update.

As Jason walked out of the office, heading toward the parking garage, he stopped to take in what he suddenly found on his phone. It was from someone in HR. It read, *Unfortunately, your services are no longer required. As a contingent employee, you are ineligible for severance or continued health care coverage. However, the company has agreed that after you sign the attached non-disclosure agreement, and the second document agreeing not to sue the company related to the accident, you will receive two weeks' severance pay. We would like to wish you the best with your future endeavors, and we thank you for your service here at Morabito.*

Jason blurted out, incredulously, "Two weeks! If they really want me to sign an NDA, then they'd better offer me at least six months' severance."

Jason sent an e-mail with words to that effect back to HR. And he added, *Plus, if you want me to sign that NDA and the other document, I will need a letter of recommendation addressed to Whom it May Concern."*

We will get back to you about this, the HR manager that he had originally met with e-mailed him.

It took the company lawyers roughly thirty minutes to convince senior management that it would be financially beneficial to accept Jason's counter proposal rather than risk him leaking the mishap to the media or having to bear the costs of any lawsuit.

So, Jason left Morabito with a half year's salary. He figured that it was just enough to take a month's vacation before he needed to start looking for a new job.

Jason had been dreaming of a vacation since he began working at the plant, but because he was considered a part-time or contingent employee, he could only take time off when he could afford it since he was only paid for the days he worked. Contingent workers did not have paid vacations or holidays. Also, things had started to get a bit heated between Jason and his boss, Miles. So, Jason wasn't sure how much longer he was planning on working at Morabito anyway. He felt like the company was heading in the wrong direction. He noticed it had started with Morabito partnering with more and more companies that Jason considered either corrupt or just greedy. Plus, he was starting to worry about what their gene manipulation was doing to the food supply in general. Gene-mapping and manipulation was a relatively new science. And while tests had been done to the satisfaction of the Food and Drug Administration, which deemed Morabito's product safe for human consumption, there was no long-term study yet available to determine any lasting effects.

Still, the more "Frankenfoods" they created, the more the public seemed to want them. Now that they were branching out into areas beyond food to home goods, furniture, and home building materials, Jason was starting to worry that Morabito was having too much influence on consumer goods, and more influence on the science behind it by funding most of the research being conducted into genetically modified food as well as plants used for other functions.

Managers like Miles had become company loyalists and believed Morabito could do no wrong, let alone do any harm. That was one reason Jason believed his complaints about a lack of quality control over equipment that kept failing went unanswered. The Gene Gun explosion was just the latest in a series of preventable accidents if someone had done their job of making sure the systems were operating the way they were supposed to. Miles' answer to Jason's complaint about someone over-loading the Gene Gun with too much helium was, "Isn't it your job to check that stuff out?"

As Jason left the building where he had spent the last five years of his life, he felt a sense of relief. Walking to his car, his anxiety over being unemployed was replaced with a strong sense that this departure was the best thing that could have happened to him. That this accident and his firing were all just a blessing in disguise.

"Hey, wait up," shouted Bowde, who had followed Jason into the parking lot.

"You sure you want to be seen talking to me?" asked Jason.

"Come on, man. Let's go to Papa Ralph's," said Bowde. "I'm buying."

Jason followed Bowde out of the lot and down the highway about four miles until they pulled into the gravel parking area of Papa Ralph's Roadhouse, Morabito employees' favorite watering hole.

They took the last two empty stools at the long horse-shoe shaped wooden bar. Ralph, the owner-bartender, immediately placed two drafts in front of them.

"Run me a tab, Ralph,' said Bowde, picking up his glass of lager. "To hell with them."

He drank the glass dry and nodded to Ralph to get him a refill.

Jason picked up his beer and took a sip. "When did it all go to shit?"

"You mean when did the world turn upside down?"

"That too," said Jason. "All I wanted to do was make a difference, ya know. Make life a little better for folks."

"You got a raw deal," said Bowde. "That Gene Gun should not have misfired."

"But it did, and the company says I'm responsible for not making sure the gun was operating properly."

"How were you supposed to do that?"

"Good question. I made them take it out of my separation letter though."

"How'd you do that?"

"By refusing to sign their NDA until they did."

"I had to sign one of those too just to keep my job," said Bowde.

Later that night, Jason was back at his apartment wondering about this new feeling of exhilaration that was filling his body. Freedom. For the first time in longer than he could remember there was nothing he had to do. Not nothing. He did have to eat. So, he scoured his pantry and settled on a can of cream of mushroom soup. He popped the round metal opener that allowed him to pull open the metal can and poured its contents into a paper bowl. He covered the bowl with a paper towel and placed it into his microwave, setting it on high for two minutes.

As he waited for the microwave to work its magic, he thought about his new life with no responsibilities. He could get used to this. Unfortunately, it had a time limit. Six months. Six months of income without working. He originally thought he would look for work after his one-month vacation was over, but now he was wondering if he could push that to three or four months before he had to find employment. Maybe he could last five months since it would probably take him at least one month to find a new job. And then he'd have to be vetted and investigated. So there goes another month. So, he should really start looking after four months. Okay, I'll take it, he thought.

The microwave beeped and Jason opened it up to take out his piping hot bowl of cream of mushroom soup. He brought it over to the round table in his dining room and placed it on the placemat. He grabbed an ice-cold bottle of IPA beer from the fridge and walked over to the table and took a seat in his chair. He grabbed a spoon and was about to eat when he stopped. He had an overwhelming urge to pray. He put down his spoon and bowed his head while placing his palms together. "God, thank you for this food I am about to consume, and this beer I am going to drink. But mostly, thank you for giving me four months of freedom to do whatever I want, to be who I want to be, to think what I want to think, and to live my life to the fullest. Amen."

Jason picked up the spoon and scooped up a serving of the soup, blowing on it before sucking it into his mouth. "Damn, that's good."

Chapter 2

The next morning Jason made an overdue run to CostSMART, where he always bought more of everything than he would ever need, including one of their bowling ball-sized rotisserie chickens. What did they put in it to make it so large and still so tasty? he wondered. But at $4.99, how could he not buy this giant fowl? This one bird would feed him for a week. CostSMART took a bath on these chickens but it more than made up for that loss by enticing Jason to also purchase two dozen rolls of toilet paper or eighteen rolls of paper towels, along with $50 worth of paper plates, bowls and cups. He never left CostSMART without spending less than $100 on things he did not really need, but usually he always found a way to make use of almost everything. He had enough garlic salt and cream of mushroom soup to last a lifetime.

After putting away his perishables and finding more places to hide the towers of paper plates and cups, he thought about what he wanted to eat.

Usually, he had some of the chicken that was still warm from the CostSMART ovens, but for some reason the thought of consuming the carcass of a creature that had once been walking, clucking, and breathing the same air he had was no longer all that appetizing. Instead, he opted for some of the giant spinach salad CostSMART sold with garnishes of hard-boiled egg, onions, tomatoes, bacon bits, and cranberry raisins, topped off with its thick avocado ranch salad dressing that probably added another thousand calories but made all that spinach go down so smoothly.

As he chomped on his salad, Jason thought about his life. As a single man, at the relatively young age of thirty-three, he was now free to do pretty much whatever he wanted within reason and the law. But there was something missing. Someone to share all this freedom with.

Jason's last relationship had been with an AG-Con intern who was ten years younger than him. It had ended abruptly when he balked at spending $7,190 on a one-carat diamond engagement ring. The relationship had been nearing its one-year mark, but Jason wasn't sure if he was ready to commit the rest of his life to someone from another decade. Although Jason was mesmerized by her looks, he and Paige had little in common beyond their intense physical attraction. When it came to their intimate life, Paige was insatiable, a quality Jason enjoyed in the beginning. But he soon began to resent her constant need for sexual satisfaction. To put it simply, she drained him physically as her constant demands were too much for him to handle.

Their relationship came to a thundering end in a Biloxi, Mississippi hotel, shortly after the big jewelry store debacle. Paige wanted Jason to just take her, forcefully, but he couldn't do it. He didn't have it in him. He was physically tired and, also, the spark was gone.

That was all it took. She grabbed her backpack and left the hotel room and his life forever. Since then, Jason had been living alone, and enjoying every minute of his life, up until that accident.

Now that he had the severance money in his bank account, he thought that maybe he could reconnect with one or two of his old girlfriends. His last serious relationship before Paige had been fifteen years ago, when Jason was only eighteen years old. Sally had been his high school sweetheart and one day she and her parents just packed up and moved away. He would have tried harder to find her, but he had already been accepted to college and felt obligated to go since his parents were paying for it. Still, he wondered what had happened to Sally. He tried looking her up on social media apps like FacePage, but he could never find her. He figured she probably got married and changed her name.

Forty-eight hours had passed since he absorbed the maple tree DNA. Jason figured that if nothing had happened by now, it was unlikely there would be any after-effects to the accident.

But almost to the forty-ninth hour, that thought was no longer valid as things were slowly beginning to change. He noticed that he was becoming sensitive to sunlight, and to weather changes in general. He soon discovered that he could tell if rain was coming long before it arrived, because his hands would turn over by themselves, as if they anticipated catching the drops. It was the strangest thing.

Jason felt an urge to go outside. He started walking down the street when his hand began to turn over on its own and a single large raindrop splatted in his palm.

"Whoa," Jason said to himself as another raindrop fell on his other hand.

The biggest change, however, occurred in his dreams. Jason had begun dreaming in green. One dream specifically. He remembered the entire sky turned from blue to green. He even began to think in green. All his thoughts began to have a green tint and hue. It was a bit alarming at first and he could not get the childhood saying from Sesame Street out of his head that "it's not easy being green." It also seemed that everywhere he looked, he saw green.

There was the media pumping out headlines about a Green New Deal, or the latest Green Bonds to fund clean energy utilities. He even got pulled over for running through a red light, because he thought that it had already turned green.

Within just a few days, he was starting to feel like he was losing his mind.

Then something incredibly strange happened. He was walking home from the store when he sensed someone, or better yet, *something* was trying to communicate with him. It wasn't a verbal communication but a more basic primal form of messaging that was being sent. Only the message was not auditory in that he could not hear it, or visible so he could not see it. All he could do was sense it, like a vibration rippling through his body, soaring through his veins and nerves and into his brain. His stomach began to rumble, too.

Jason looked around and found that he had walked into a park. The communication seemed to be coming from all around him, from the trees, the bushes, the grass. He had the urge to take off his running shoes and socks and walk barefoot on the grass. So, he did.

As soon as his feet touched the cool blades of grass, he felt as if some kind of connection had been made; that he had been plugged into something. It felt entirely surreal. It was coming from under the grass, from the roots.

Jason took off his shirt, laid down on the ground and began rolling around on the grass. An energy-like vibration was entering his body and sending messages to his brain in a language he could not comprehend. The grass almost looked and felt like it was evolving into a giant green ocean with waves rocking him back and forth. He felt like he knew everything and nothing all at the same time.

What in the hell is happening to me? Jason thought to himself. All he really knew was that he had suddenly become connected to a strange new world. Mentally and emotionally, he felt plugged into this other world, the world of plants. One thing was clear. Something was very wrong. It started as a feeling, a mild disturbance, that quickly grew into something resembling a panic attack.

Where's this coming from? Jason wondered. What the hell? One wave of anxiety after another washed over him as he tried to figure out what could be bothering him.

Then it hit him. It was not he who was bothered. It was everything around him. The plants.

Jason knelt and began clawing at the grass, digging into the damp topsoil, feeling the dark moist dirt between his fingers. There is where he found long, stringy networks of silky fresh mycelium fungi. He had seen a documentary about how plants communicated through the thin white filaments of mycelium.

As soon as his fingers touched the mass of mycelium, a stronger, clearer awareness filled his mind. It was like a silent alarm had awoken a part of his brain that until now had been asleep. He looked down at his hands clutching the mycelium and realized it was the tiny thin white streams that were transmitting a new message. But what did it mean? He sensed danger! That he was being warned about something. But what? What could inspire such a dire feeling of dread that now permeated his mind?

A new message then formed that seemed to say something must be done. What must be done? "I don't understand," he silently screamed. At least the free-floating anxiety he had been feeling now had a focus. He just did not know what was causing it.

Jason pulled his hand away and the connection broke, along with whatever message was streaming into him. He looked around at all the plant life that surrounded him. How could something so peaceful be so worried?

He touched the mycelium with his fingertips; despite the peaceful, serene atmosphere surrounding him, Jason sensed that the plant life was not happy. In his mind, a word began to form, one green letter at a time: B O T A N I C A.

Chapter 3

Botanica? What the hell does that mean? Botanica. He took out his phone and googled *Botanica*. The search result came back as Botanica, a small store that sells herbs and charms used by followers of Santeria. So, he proceeded to look up the word, *Santeria*. It read: a religion originating in Cuba where Yoruba gods are identified with Roman Catholic saints.

He searched *Yoruba* and learned that it was a tribe and language in southwestern Nigeria. What the hell? He went back to the search results for *Botanica* and learned that it was also the Spanish word for *Botanical* or anything pertaining to plants.

Now that made a little bit more sense. Still, he thought that maybe he should cover his bases so he looked up where he could find the nearest Botanica store in the area.

According to Google there was one less than a mile away. So, Jason brought up the GPS app on his phone and entered the Botanica's address.

He began walking down one street, then another, until he reached the end of a block-long street that stopped at the back of a large warehouse with a rugged brick exterior. But there, just a few doors from the end of the dead-end street, stood a small, single-story shop. The store had strange looking objects in its dirty windows and words in Spanish painted on the inside. But what he saw over the door grabbed Jason's attention. It was a single word in large letters that stretched the entire width of the small single-story building wedged between two five-story brownstones. That word was *Botanica*.

Jason slowly walked across the street and through the open door of the exotic little shop. Once inside, Jason stopped and took in a deep breath of musky air unlike any he had ever smelled. There was a combination of patchouli aroma—the patchouli is also known as the mint plant—and other aromatic odors such as sandal wood and cedar. Sticks of incense were burning throughout the shop.

He could now see that the objects in the window were mostly religious statues of different figures. A shiny golden Buddha sat in the window smiling at Jason as he walked into the dusty shop. An elderly woman sat on a stool behind the counter reading a newspaper. She had skin the color of dark sandpaper, and a face lined with age and deep-set, dark brown eyes. Behind her on about a dozen shelves were glass jars containing an assortment of objects from bird claws and dead flowers, to what seemed to be different shades of dirt.

Jason stepped up to the counter and the woman lowered her newspaper and looked at him.

"Botanica?" asked Jason.

"Si'," replied the woman.

"What kind of place is this?" he asked.

"It's a Botanica," said the woman.

"Why am I here?" Jason asked himself aloud, prompting the woman to respond.

"Well. What are you seeking?"

"I was hoping you could tell me, actually."

"People usually come here looking for something. Love. Money. Revenge. What it is you are looking for?" she asked again. "Do you want to put a curse on somebody?"

"I mean. Hmm. Umm. You're going to think I'm crazy," said Jason.

"Crazy people come in here all the time, trust me," said the woman. "I not judge."

"I want to be able to talk to plants," said Jason. "Well. More. I mean, I think I already am talking to plants. Or at least they're talking to me. I just don't always get what they're saying, know what I mean?"

"Not really."

"I think I need to learn how to talk to tree."

"Talk tree?"

"Yeah, sorry. You got anything like that? Something to help me talk tree, or at least to plants?"

The woman stared at Jason for a few seconds. Finally, she nodded to herself as if this was a regular request and began searching among the shelves of dusty glass jars until she came to one.

Nodding again, she pulled a jar from the shelf, dusted it off, and removed its sealed top. She inhaled deeply over the jar and nodded yet again. She returned to the counter and placed it in front of Jason.

"Here," she said. "For you only. You don't tell nobody where you got this, *comprende*?'

"Huh?" Jason said as he examined the jar that she had placed in front of him. The jar contained dried mushrooms. "What's this?"

"Eat three, wait an hour, then if nothing happens, eat three more," said the woman.

Jason could feel his senses start to tingle in his hands.

"What are they?"

"Mushrooms. Special mushrooms. Kids call them shrooms. Or Magic Mushrooms."

"These don't look very edible," he said.

"Take with ginger tea and honey. Go down better," she said. "Boil water then let cool. Too much heat will be bad for mushrooms. Kills the magic."

"I eat mushrooms all the time. What are these going to do for me?"

"They're a psychedelic. You, know, they give you, what do they call them? Halluce-something or other?

"Hallucinations?"

"Yeah, hallucinations. What we used to call tripping, back in the day. These are special. Forty dollars plus tax," said the woman.

"For this? I can buy ten times this much at the supermarket and wait until they've dried out."

"Supermarket mushrooms different. Only for eating. These are magic mushrooms. They contain something called psilocybin (she pronounced it sil-oh-sigh'-bin) but it all depends on the shroom. That's what the kids say. Each shroom is different. Just try it. I hear good things. Take a few and fall asleep. It works best that way. Takes you places you never been. You ever take a head trip?"

"No."

"Then you in for a treat," said the woman. "You find your answer in your shroom dream."

"You mean people have come back and said they were able to talk to plants after eating this stuff?" asked Jason.

"Maybe not that, talking to plants, exactly. They do different things for different people. If anything will help you talk to plants, it's this. Just try it," said the woman. "Whatta ya got to lose?"

"Forty bucks," said Jason as he took out two twenty-dollar bills and placed them on the counter. "This is all the cash I have on me."

"I'll mark 'em produce. No tax."

The woman took the money and put the glass jar in a paper bag with a rubber band to hold it closed.

"Remember, you never got this here. If you get in trouble, you never knew me, Sí?"

"Why would I get into trouble?"

"Still not sure it's legal here to sell magic mushrooms. We get ours from Canada."

"Got it," Jason responded.

She handed the bag-wrapped jar over to Jason, who shook his head in disbelief and left the store.

Back in his apartment, Jason boiled some water, then let it sit to cool a bit. He then took a ginger root out of a bag from a local grocery store, and shaved some ginger into the water, along with some black tea and three dried mushrooms. He stirred the concoction a few times as the aroma of ginger, musky earth and tea filled his apartment. He then poured the ginger, tea and mushrooms into a mug, added a tablespoon of honey and drank it down. One of the mushrooms got caught in his throat so he brought it up and started to chew it. The mushroom tasted like bitter dirty leather soaked in foot sweat, so he drank what was left of the ginger tea to wash it down.

"Aggghhh," he retched as he swallowed the last of the mushrooms.

Then Jason lay down on the sofa and waited. The time ticked by slowly, second by second. He lay there waiting for the magic to kick in, but after an hour went by, and nothing happened, he stood up. He looked at the clock and realized it was almost midnight, long past his normal bedtime. The caffeine in the tea must have been keeping him awake.

Jason wondered when the mushrooms would kick in. Just the thought of having to consume three more of the disgusting toadstool caps made him gag. Maybe if I mix them with lemonade or better yet, put them in a blender with chocolate ice cream and make a shake, he thought, as his eyes began to feel heavy. He stood to get the blender when a tingling feeling rippled through his body. Just the act of bending over and straightening up made him dizzy so he settled back down on the sofa as he grew more tired by the second. Within minutes, he started to yawn and shortly after that, he fell asleep.

The dream began right away. Only this dream was different from anything Jason had ever experienced. It was a dream, but then it wasn't. When he reached out to touch something he could feel it. He could also smell different scents, something he could never remember doing in any previous dream.

He was in a forest surrounded by different species of trees from pine to cedar to fresh fallen maple leaves, each with its own distinct scent and feel. Each tree had its own texture, and he began to tell which was what just from touching their bark. He felt the smoothness of the white birch and the rough grooves of the maple.

Jason opened his eyes. Was he awake or still dreaming? He couldn't tell. He stood up from the sofa and suddenly he was back in the forest. The dream didn't go away, so he must still be dreaming only it didn't feel like a dream. It felt real.

He looked around and he was no longer near his sofa or his apartment. He seemed to be in some sort of rainforest, and something was going on just beyond the trees and jungle growth.

"What in the world?" Jason said.

He tried to move toward the sounds he was hearing but realized he couldn't move. That's when he looked down at himself and saw that he was no longer in a human body. Instead, he was a tree. A young sapling, about 20 feet tall, standing among the giants of the rain forest. He sensed an impending fear. That danger was approaching. He wanted to flee, but as a tree, he couldn't move. Whatever was making those crashing sounds just beyond his line of sight were coming closer and there wasn't a damn thing he could do about it.

Then, as quickly as he had become a tree, Jason found himself back in his body. He immediately pushed aside some ferns and saw in the distance a scene of mass destruction as earth moving equipment was uprooting giant trees while other trees already felled were burned to make way for backhoes to begin digging up the recently-cleared land. Jason could feel the violation of what his human species was inflicting on the unprotected flora. They were raping and murdering the jungle.

No sooner had the image registered in his mind as the scene around him dissolved into a lab where technicians were genetically altering what nature had created. He recognized it as the Morabito lab where he had worked and where the accident had occurred.

The lab quickly dissolved into a different setting. He was now in another forest of giant redwoods where armies of lumberjacks were carving a huge swath out of the forest and trucks of timber barreled down a mountain highway. Workers continued to arrive to chop down more and more of these beautiful giant trees. Suddenly, an awareness filled his thoughts. This isn't good. This is an utter and total disregard for the impact all of this was having on the biodiversity of the planet and the plant world in particular. Is this what the plants were trying to tell him?

But what did it mean? Like most environmentally aware people, Jason knew that the lion's share of environmental issues these days dealt with climate change and the war on fossil fuels because of something called the greenhouse effect. He wasn't sure what that was other than it had something to do with global warming. Jason had seen the movie *An Inconvenient Truth* and saw how the polar icecaps were melting. He believed climate change was real.

But he had also read Michael Crichton's essays on how the phenomenon of global warming and climate change has been going on for millions of years, and that the real unfortunate truth was that there really wasn't much that we, meaning human beings, could do about it. All this talk and political rhetoric about getting rid of fossil fuel was just another false flag. As sources of energy go, oil, natural gas and coal may not be the cleanest ways to power the world, but until a better solution was available, it was the economically best we could come up with. Nuclear, solar, and wind might eventually replace the fossil fuels, but the transition wasn't there yet. The real reason to eliminate or minimize fossil fuels was the unhealthy air pollution they caused which led millions of people to suffer from respiratory illnesses.

The more Jason read about climate change, the more confused he became. He never quite understood the urgency with which climate crusaders preached about an impending crisis. Even climate change scientists admitted that if all carbon emissions were eliminated, the actual impact on the temperature of the planet would only be about one or two degrees Celsius over a period of 150 years.

More importantly, the scenes he had just witnessed in this magic mushroom dream had nothing to do with climate change or carbon emissions. It had to do with something else, something darker and deeper.

Chapter 4

Jason asked, "What are you trying to tell me?" Suddenly, *in his* mind, an answer appeared, not in the form of words but of an awareness. We got it wrong. No surprise there, we usually do. What did we get wrong? Pretty much everything. But mainly the real threat. The plants, it seemed, could care less about the infinitesimally small rise in the planet's temperature. Global warming, while a real phenomenon, wasn't a concern to the plant world. They know how the earth's temperature is constantly changing depending on several factors including the earth's orbit around the sun, which at times puts it closer or farther away. In either case the distance of the earth from the sun played more of a role in the planet's changing temperature than almost everything else.

In many ways, the plant world experienced global warming in a favorable manner. While climate change had become politicized to the point that science was often blurred or misconstrued to fit an agenda, plants accepted it as a natural occurrence rather than an existential threat, whatever that means. No, the world of plants and all things botanical knew the real danger lay elsewhere.

But where? What am I missing? Jason wondered.

Suddenly Jason couldn't breathe. It was if something had cut off his oxygen supply. He gasped and tried to breathe through his mouth, but his esophagus had sealed the pathway to his lungs. Just as quickly as it had occurred, the feeling disappeared. And with that, another awareness filled his mind.

Is that what you're trying to tell me? That we're all going to suffocate? Is that it? Something is depleting our atmosphere of oxygen? That's it, isn't it? Is it another meteor, like the one that supposedly killed the dinosaurs? That's wrong? What's wrong, that scientists think that a meteor hit the southern hemisphere, causing this giant dust cloud that made it impossible to breathe. No? That's wrong? What did happen?

An image of barren wastelands filled his mind. In the distance, he could see a brontosaurus nibbling on the remaining few leaves of a nearly naked tree, already stripped of most of its leaves. Elsewhere, dinosaurs were toppling over in the dust, struggling to breathe.

Slowly, the image dissolved into a rainforest where giant earth movers uprooted one tall tree after another, until the land once again lay barren. Is that what this is all about?

A soothing calm filled Jason's body. I'll be damned, he thought. I had no idea things had gotten that bad. Trees. The removal of trees. Trees are what supply the earth's atmosphere with the oxygen we need to breathe and sustain life. By eliminating the source of oxygen in our atmosphere, eventually it will no longer sustain life. Is that what you're trying to tell me? Oh, man. That's it.

You're telling me it's getting worse, isn't it? What's making it worse? What are we doing now that we didn't do so much before? We destroyed so many forests in the name of urbanization and industrial progress and that still wasn't enough to cause concern. What's happening now that has the plant world so worried?

A word was forming in his mind one letter at a time. L I T H I U M. Lithium?

Then another word began...N I C K E L.

Then C O B A L Tand M A N G A N E S E.

G R A P H I T E and A L U M I N U M.

These are minerals, right? Why them? What am I missing? Another image filled Jason's mind. Electric vehicles, millions of them, sitting idle next to charging stations. Plugs connected to rechargeable batteries. It's the batteries, isn't it? Lithium, nickel, manganese. These are the minerals used in rechargeable batteries, thought Jason. Electric vehicle batteries. Are you telling me that the push to build electric vehicles is putting the planet in jeopardy?

California. What does California mean? It started with California? Oh, right. California was the first state to say it would ban the sale of all gas-powered cars by 2035. The mandates. It prompted all the major auto makers to pledge they would produce affordable EVs to meet the demand. How does all that demand for these minerals have anything to do with the removal of trees? I don't see the connection, Jason thought.

The image of a mine filled Jason's mind, and then like a film moving backwards, the mine entrance was filled in and the entire area became filled with trees. They must remove the trees to get to the minerals. Is that it?

The movie started to move in the right direction as Jason saw forests being destroyed to clear areas where mines are dug to get to the minerals used in the batteries that power electric vehicles.

That's it, isn't it? That's the tipping point. This recent surge in demand for electric vehicles. Oh my God! The rush to save the planet from global warming by mandating the use of electric vehicles is ironically going to be what destroys life as we know it.

The feeling of calm returned and now Jason realized that the feeling of calm was the plant world's way of communicating "yes."

What can I do to help stop it? Who would ever believe me? They'd think I was a headcase. Oh, the trees told you. That's a good one.

There must be an answer. Just because we humans couldn't see the forest through the trees, to steal a pun, doesn't mean we just give up.

Jason knew that this time the problem was going to be even more dire. Politics had coopted and corrupted science to the point that no one knew what to believe anymore. Well, the plants knew. They've known for years because in the world of plants, politics does not exist. It was becoming clear to Jason what his role in all this was going to be. He would have to become their voice.

Now he just had to figure out how to make the world believe him. How was he going to convince anyone that with less plant life and fewer trees the amount of oxygen in the earth's atmosphere would drop to a level that would no longer support life because the air we breathe will no longer be breathable?

How will he convince anyone that the world was headed toward a mass extinction event sooner than predicted, and that it would be more devastating than anything global warming could ever cause?

As Jason drifted deeper into his dream, another message began to emerge. The humans who controlled the animal kingdom were not going to stop this behavior, so the plant world would have to do something about it. What that something was, however, was still being decided. Jason knew he wanted to help, to be a part of whatever solution the plant world came up with. Maybe this new dream would provide some answers.

Chapter 5

In this new mushroom-induced dream, Jason was an eagle gliding high above the forest of Sequoia redwoods searching for supper among the elevated branches of the tall old trees. Jason felt like he was flying alongside another wide-winged predator as it moved down through the whispering pines, its fine feathered span floating on the gentle breeze. While the other eagle scoured the forest for prey, it seemed oblivious to the rustling hissing sound coming from these giant thousand-year-old life forms as the planet's oldest living creatures communicated with each other, planning and strategizing.

Jason could feel the wisdom of a hundred-thousand years passed down through the centuries, not unlike the voices and data that travel through phone and cable lines to digital clouds and back. If there was an answer to what I need to do, thought Jason, it would be here. But where is here?

As Jason soared among the Sequoias, he sensed he was being led somewhere, but to where he did not know. Then a communication came out of nowhere: the General has the answers. Who was the General? All he knew was that it seemed the trees he was passing were getting taller, wider and older. Eventually he came to a giant Sequoia that stood taller than all the others. As he flew closer to the ground he could make out a wooden plaque that read: General Sherman. He had found the General.

His closeness allowed Jason to feel what the giant redwood was feeling, or at least feeling in the sense of what a feeling was like to a plant. It seemed the General was feeling the burdens of age and responsibility. While hundreds of years were still left in its normal lifespan of 3,000 plus years, Jason sensed that the massive redwood felt that it was letting down its forest family along with the planet which its species had called home for the past 240 million years.

Suddenly, Jason's mind filled with knowledge he hadn't known before. That for nearly a quarter of a billion years, the family of tree known as Sequoias had served its mission with honor and distinction, protecting and leading the earth's widely diverse and mysterious world of plant life and its collaborative connection to the two other life forms inhabiting the third sphere from the sun—fungi and animal. This ecological triumvirate formed an interdependent biosphere with one primary goal: to maintain a balance in nature that preserved an environment and ecosystem that sustained life for these three unique, carbon-based biological creations.

For as long as they existed, trees also helped provide the rest of the plant world with the information and nutrients they needed to survive. It was all part of the cycle of life in this ecosystem, where plants, animals and fungi, through their elimination of waste and deaths, would decompose and add nitrogen to the soil, while bacteria in that soil would convert the nitrogen from animals into the kind of nutrients plants could absorb to grow and thrive. This was just one element necessary to complete the cycle that preserved an environment and atmosphere that helped keep the one living planet in the solar-system alive.

Keeping the planet alive was a 24/7 endeavor. The one constant in all of nature was the struggle for survival, and threats to the planet's eco-system seemed to come every few hundred-thousand years. And now it appeared that, once again, that system was about to be disrupted.

Jason learned that that trees and their global network had detected warning signs that another global extinction event not unlike that which had erased the dinosaurs from the face of the planet was on the horizon. And despite its nearly three-thousand years of wisdom, the giant Sequoia known as General Sherman had only come up with one way to prevent the next mass extinction: do whatever was necessary to stop this disruption before it was too late.

He also learned that the General Sherman had been storing and sharing information for over two millennia and had been communicating to other trees as well as the connected plant world that something wasn't right. For several years now, the tree network had been detecting signs that the planet's balance of nature was being disturbed and the system that had sustained life for thousands of years was in jeopardy. It appeared that the cause of this disturbance was tied to the removal of more than 80 million hectares—equivalent to nearly 200 million acres—of oxygen-producing forests during the past few decades. The recent rash of wildfires had not helped much. Despite the Sequoias' thick protective bark, an estimated ten thousand of General Sherman's neighboring Sequoias had perished in a massive inferno that forced the Sequoia National Park to close for several months.

What this new dream underscored was that Jason was now indeed totally plugged into the world of plants. A communication of sorts was made and passed down through the wood of branches and thick trunks, into the roots and soil and across the fungi and onto the backs of ants and grubs that crawled up through the grass.

So far, most of the communication Jason was sensing was something Jason already knew. But there was a new sensation that was attached this time. As the message spread wide and far, all throughout the world, that there has been a disruption to the cycle in the earth's biodiverse ecosystem, the message carried a sentiment rarely expressed in the secret world of plants—the world's oldest living creatures were angry. Beyond angry. They were enraged…and when nature becomes enraged…death is sure to follow.

Then Jason sensed something he didn't know. That promises to slow the devastation of forests and jungles had been made and broken as rainforests continued to be gutted by greedy companies at an even faster pace than before. More of the earth's wilderness was being replaced by mines, cities, and farmlands. Huge tracts of once green backwoods were bulldozed into oblivion to make way for agriculture and industry.

In Jason's new dream, humans continued to focus their attention on climate change, global warming, and efforts to cut down on greenhouse gases, ignoring the more serious affect the destruction of the rainforests had in store. The message soaring down from above and into the roots of the world was that something needed to be done to get their attention before it's too late and the damage is irrevocable.

That I get, thought Jason. But how? How do we get their attention?

The climate change advocates had won the PR battle by getting enough scientists and industries to buy into the notion that carbon in the atmosphere from burning fossil fuel had caused the temperature of the globe to increase and that this rise would create all kinds of havoc from violent storms and flooding to a rising sea level from melting icecaps and glaciers.

How do we change the narrative? How do convince the world of climate changers that they got it all wrong? We convinced *you,* didn't we? There are companies out there that are preparing to speed up the process of eliminating the rainforest, causing a domino effect of cataclysmic events worldwide. If you want to help, you must start now.

Okay, thought Jason. If I'm going to do this, I'm going to need more of those magic mushrooms. I'd better get over to the Botanica before it runs out.

He suddenly realized he was no longer in a mushroom induced dream. He got up, got dressed and took a trip back to the Botanica to purchase a few more jars of the powerful hallucinogenic. He wanted a good supply to make sure he would not lose his newfound powers anytime soon.

Meanwhile, unbeknownst to Jason, the plant world had settled on a target to begin its retaliation against those responsible for the wanton destruction of huge tracts of forestry.

Chapter 6

The silver electrically-powered Porsche Taycan Turbo S sliced through the winding turns of the rain-slicked back roads of Fairfield County, Connecticut, following the serpentine route that the GPS had recommended to avoid the Merritt Parkway, which had turned into a parking lot because of a fender-bender at Exit 35.

As the eccentric CEO of Lyons Electric, Cecil Lyons had little time to enjoy the fruits of his labor including the development of electric vehicle batteries, one of which was powering his recently-purchased Porsche Turbo for just under $250,000. Ironically, because of the car's power-guzzling 522 horsepower engine, it drained the battery faster than any of its competitors, thereby limiting its distance between charges to just under two hundred miles. None of that bothered Cecil, who could care less if it meant that he had the fastest electric vehicle that money could buy.

According to his GPS, Cecil had been able to shave twelve minutes off his trip from the southern tip of Manhattan to his mansion in Greenwich, which he just purchased from the sale of $2 billion in stock in his electric vehicle battery company, which Forbes had touted as one of the fastest growing companies in the country. One reason was the recent discovery in South America of large deposits of lithium, cobalt, and nickel, the three key minerals used in the creation of electric vehicle batteries. Lyons Electric immediately acquired the land under which those minerals existed and just as quickly began clearing the area to begin mining them to fill the growing demand for affordable electric vehicles.

That demand had skyrocketed, following the federal government's electric vehicle mandate and near total shutdown of fossil fuel exploration, drilling and distribution, which in turn caused the cost of home heating oil, gasoline, and natural gas to more than double over the last year. Many Americans long dependent on gasoline-fueled cars were being forced to turn to electric or hybrid vehicles even if they could not afford them. Thus, the demand to make them more affordable.

Cecil's mobile phone received a call, which he answered through the car's voice navigation system. "Hey Honey."

"Hi dear. I was just checking to see when you'll be home. Food is on the table and it's going to get cold. I made your favorite, Shepard's Pie and Caesar salad," said Mrs. Lyons through the car speaker.

"Oh, doll. In that case, I'll turn on the turbo boost and make it home even faster. I should be there in no time, sweetheart," said Cecil.

"Okay. I'll open a bottle of Moscato and drink it slowly until you get here," his wife said.

"I'll be there as soon as I can, less than fifteen minutes, Hon."

"Okay, if you're not here by then, I'm going to eat my salad without you," said Mrs. Lyons. "Don't say I didn't warn you!"

"If I'm not there, then go for it. But I'll be there," he said.

"Okay, see you soon. Drive safe. I love you."

"I love you too. See you soon."

Cecil clicked *end call* on the large navigation screen just before he almost drove headfirst into a road sign that read "Yield."

"Shit!" he yelled after swerving his car around the sign and back into his lane. "That was a close one."

Cecil pulled out his pack of Ballyhoo red cigarettes, opened it up, and pulled one out. There were seven left in the pack. He grabbed a lighter from his center console, put the cigarette in his mouth, and sparked the lighter to it. He inhaled the tobacco causing smoke to fill his lungs. He threw the lighter onto the passenger seat and inhaled a few more times before letting out one big exhale. He began to cough because he did not smoke that often.

He rolled down the window to let out the smoke. Rain splashed up against his windshield and sprayed into his car. He took a few more puffs of the cigarette until it was about halfway done. He threw the lit cigarette out onto the road. The half-smoked butt of the cigarette bounced off the road a few times before landing in the grass next to it.

As Cecil gripped the special racing-style steering wheel he had custom built and installed, he marveled at the way the car handled each hairpin turn on his route home. The speed limit on the turns was a mere fifteen miles an hour, but he was able to take them at close to forty. He seemed oblivious to the environment around him until what had been a steady drip of rain grew stronger.

"Oh shit," said Cecil.

He put his windshield wipers on full speed as the rain picked up and his visibility diminished significantly, especially since the harder rainfall had brought with it more falling autumn leaves. The leaves not only caused the road to slicken but started to cover the car's windshield faster than the wipers could remove them. Cecil was forced to lower the driver's side window so he could reach out and remove a clump of wet leaves that had bunched up around the wipers. Only his seatbelt would not let him reach the leaves, so he unbuckled it. That allowed him to remove the leaves, which were quickly replaced by more. "Oh, god damn it!" Cecil yelled as more leaves kept landing on the windshield.

According to his GPS, he was less than a mile from the turn off to his North Street estate, which had its own gate and private road. All anyone could see from North Street was a forest of trees. Even if they got a glimpse through the gateway, all they would see was more greenery, or at this time of year, the yellows and oranges of the fall.

Cecil could just barely see the final turn at the top of a steep incline, so he gave the Porsche Turbo more power to speed up the hill. Rain continued to fall as more and more leaves gathered, blinding the CEO. The car's rear-wheel drive propelled the sports car up the incline like a rocket taking off. As he sailed toward the top, Cecil thought about how much he usually loved the fall and the changing colors of the season. But now it seemed as if the autumn was betraying him, with the falling leaves conspiring with the rain to turn an otherwise pleasant evening into a battle of man and machine against the forces of nature.

As the winding road leveled off, Cecil slowed to make the sharp left at the top of the rise. But, as the car turned, the rear wheels spun out on the wet leaves now covering the pavement. Slowly, the car revolved in a circle and Cecil found himself staring back down the steep incline he had just sped up. He tried using his brakes, but they seemed to be of little use as the car slid back down the incline which was now almost totally covered in slippery yellow and orange leaves.

The last thought Cecil had before his $250,000 car slammed into a giant oak at the foot of the hill less than a mile from his home was, "Shit, I forgot to re-buckle my seat belt."

Chapter 7

Fifteen hundred miles to the southwest, in the Texas panhandle, Calvin Cooper, the CEO who would be taking CostSMART global, was hunting quail with a few members of his management committee and two influential state and federal lawmakers that Calvin called upon whenever he needed legislation that improved his company's bottom line.

CostSMART's recent acquisitions of similar chains in China and India were poised to quadruple the size of the already trillion-dollar company. That meant it would need to vastly increase the amount of cardboard necessary to package the goods it intended to offer its additional four billion potential customers.

The company was already on the Top Ten list of companies responsible for deforestation, so this move to go global would only exacerbate an already tenuous situation sure to anger environmentalists on an equally global scale.

Calvin carried a copy of the Top Ten list in his back pocket as his assistant had printed it out and handed it to him the day before. At first, he was offended he made it onto the list, but then he found a little bit of pride in it. "Well, I guess any publicity is good publicity, right?" he said to Bill, one of the committee members. They both laughed and took a swig from their bottles of Adlerwick Light Beer.

Calvin Cooper had already foreseen this PR issue and created a foundation for sustainability that supported efforts to slow climate change by funding windfarms in Africa, India, and China. "See what an environmentally friendly company we are?" Calvin said on a recent NEDTalk put on to demonstrate his company's commitment to sustainability.

"Just let us cut down a few more trees that nobody will see anyway. We'll even plant new ones to replace the ones we've cut down. Everybody wins," he said to a crowd of likeminded consumers who began to roar enthusiastically.

The hunting party had just set up camp with state-of-the-art tents and camping equipment, all available at a discount at CostSMART stores everywhere, when the rain started. At first it was just a light drizzle, but it quickly turned into a downpour.

"Oh god damn it. The forecast said clear skies until six!" said Jim, another member of the board.

"Guess the quails get a reprieve today," snickered Calvin. "Let's all convene in the conference tent and break out the cards until this storm passes. I wouldn't mind a couple more brews before we go out, anyway."

A bolt of lightning struck nearby, startling Calvin and his friends.

"Well, shit! That one was close. Fortunately, we have these trees to protect us," said Calvin as he looked up at the big branches above them. "If anything is going to get hit by lightning, it's going to be one of them. Now let's see how much of that bonus money we've been paying you assholes that I can win back."

Calvin laughed before entering the largest of the tents to join the rest of his pals. Bill pulled up a chair for his boss around the plastic table they'd set up for cards.

"Take a seat, Cal," said Bill.

The rain continued to pour down around them as the crew settled-in to play some poker.

"I'll deal," said Jim.

Calvin guzzled his beer and replied, "I'm winning this time, Big Jim, you son-of-a—" Calvin stopped mid-sentence as another lightning bolt struck eerily close by.

Bill stood up from his seat and said, "Well, damn it guys. We might want to think about getting the hell out of here."

"Oh, come on, you pussy! Remember last winter, we went hunting in a fucking blizzard? This is nothing! Now shuffle those cards, Jim. Let's play already!" Calvin exclaimed.

Jim shuffled the cards and dealt them around to the rest of the men. Calvin walked over to the cooler and pulled out another beer. "Anybody need one?"

"I'll take one," said Bill.

"Ah, shoot. Looks like we're out."

"We got more in the cooler in the other tent," said Jim. "I'll grab one for you, boss."

"I can do it myself, dude," said Calvin as he unzipped the tent and stepped outside. Rain splashed over his face as he raced to another tent about fifteen feet away.

He reached inside for the other cooler that was full of ice and cold beers, then turned and headed back. The rain stung even harder. Calvin tried to run to the conference tent, but strong winds knocked him to the ground, spilling the cooler of beers.

"Shit!" he yelled as he struggled back onto his feet. "Screw it!" He left the cooler where it landed and sloshed through the mud to rejoin his friends.

Bill poked his head out of the tent and shouted, "You all right, boss?"

"I got this!" Calvin yelled. He powered through the wind and rain, and finally jumped through the opening of the conference tent.

"Jeesh, that was a close one," said Calvin covered in rain and mud from getting knocked to the ground.

"Dang, what happened to the beer?" asked Jim.

"Dropped them on my way in. That wind is fucking strong," said Calvin as he dried his face. Then, "Let me have that," he said, grabbing a half-drunken beer off the table.

"Hey, that's mine," said Troy, the company's top lawyer.

"You snooze, you lose," said Calvin as he took a sip.

Just then lightning struck again, this time hitting a giant spruce. It cracked the evergreen tree so that it toppled down, decimating the tent and crushing Calvin Cooper beneath its 6,000 pounds of 170-foot trunk, hundreds of branches and spiney green leaves.

The document containing the Top Ten list of CEOs that was in Calvin's back pocket fell out and flew in the wind and out into the forest. It landed on the dirt between the trees as Calvin's body lay lifeless underneath the giant evergreen trunk. No one noticed as the List continued to fly until, completely soaked, it slammed into the trunk of a 300-year-old oak. As the sodden paper slid down the side of the tree, it began to dissolve and be absorbed into the bark. Now liquified, the Top Ten list continued its absorption into the cellulite of the tree, becoming one with a network of tree roots in a forest that stretched as far as the eye could see.

Chapter 8

Jason opened his eyes in total darkness. "Where am I?" he asked himself. Something was covering his head and face which was why he couldn't see anything. He gripped the fabric and wrestled it away until he finally removed the thick blanket that was covering him. He sat up and looked around, letting out a sigh of relief as he realized he had left the sofa for his bedroom, and that he had somehow slipped beneath the blanket during the night.

"Holy shit!" he exclaimed.

Jason got out of bed and started pacing. "Was that a dream? Or something else? It felt so real. It must have been the mushrooms. They worked. The plants. They were talking to me. Well, maybe not talking … but now I know what's going on. I've got to help them. But how? I can get the word out. The world needs to know what's going to happen. I can be their liaison, their translator. Yes sir, I can speak plant. And boy you better listen."

He continued to pace back and forth. Jason stopped at the mirror in the hallway and looked at himself. He had green tint on his face and body. His face had about a week's worth of stubble that felt rough against his fingers. "Guess I forgot to shave," he muttered. "What do I have to shave for anyway, right?

"Oh boy, I must be losing it. Can this really be happening?" Jason asked himself as he stared in the mirror. He looked at a plant he had seen in the reflection, and it was glowing brighter than ever.

What amazed Jason was that he found himself in total solidarity with what the trees were telling him. He could almost understand what they were feeling. His dreams felt so real, he had no clue how to decipher what was his reality anymore.

"Wait. What if I'm slowly becoming one of them? Could that happen? Wasn't there that cheesy movie from the 1980s about a man who turned into a plant? *Swamp Guy* or *Swamp Thing*, or something like that, that later became a television series. That's what it was called. Is that happening to me?" he asked himself.

Jason looked at his hands and arms, but they didn't look any different aside from the green tints and shadows. If he was changing, he couldn't see it. However, Jason decided then and there that he would use whatever time he had left on earth to help his new family.

He opened his laptop and took a seat on his couch.

As the days and nights went on, Jason consumed more of the dried mushrooms and his dreams got even greener. The images that flickered through his REM sleep were no longer just a green tinge. The entire hue of the dreamscape had turned greener, as if someone had adjusted the color on a television to mute the blues and reds while highlighting the greens. It was, for him, the new normal. He was just trying to get used to it. Meanwhile, the stubble on his face grew a few millimeters longer.

Jason still could not believe Morabito had fired him. He had been one of their top genetic engineers, charged with overseeing a variety of experiments designed to create their super-plants. Whenever environmentalists protested saying they were unnatural and therefore evil and dangerous, it was Jason they called on to speak to the angry crowds outside the gates. He was almost their spokesperson for crying out loud. He could not believe they kicked him to the curb just like that.

Some company officials thought the accident that left Jason exposed to radioactive airborne plant DNA had been sabotage on the part of the protestors. But Jason did not think so. He blamed Morabito's push to get their "super-plants" to market way before they were ready. That pressure had caused several lab technicians to overlook some of the safety precautions necessary to prevent the kind of accident that had exposed Jason to "active" genetically altered plant molecules. In other words, someone should have pre-tested the Gene Gun before Jason used it that day.

It was during the second week after the accident that Jason awoke with a start. By now, he was no longer just sensing the message, he was feeling it. It was this feeling that jarred him awake. He was angry. He may not have been able to talk to the plants, but they had certainly been talking to him. All he wanted was a bit more clarity. The mushrooms were starting to help clear things up a bit.

Jason sat up and got out of bed. He went to the window and opened it and gazed out into his backyard. Leaves were rustling in the bushes and trees, blades of grass bent to a mild breeze.

He took in a deep breath of crisp night air, and a feeling bubbled up from the depths of his consciousness. An overwhelming feeling of sadness washed over his body, followed by feelings of anger and determination. He was not sure what his role would be, but he knew that he had to do something.

"I said I'd help. What do you want from me?" he asked the night. Did he think it, or had he said it aloud?

Jason returned to his bed, took more mushrooms, sipped some more water, and tried to sleep. As he drifted off, he could hear in his mind an old Jefferson Airplane song, *Eskimo Blue Day*, with Grace Slick singing, "the human dream doesn't mean shit to a tree."

This triggered a memory from a college lecture in Biology 101.

"Fact: The oldest living things on the planet are trees," said a bearded professor whose name Jason had long since forgotten. And then he remembered, Professor Thornton was his name. He had not thought of that name in quite some time. But he remembered that he had been one of Jason's favorite teachers.

"Fact: The largest living organism on the planet is a tree, the Quaking Aspen found in Utah. A single Quaking Aspen covers one-hundred-six acres of land and weighs more than 6,000 tons. It is a forest of trees born from a single root said to be 80,000 years old. The tallest trees, however, are the Sequoias, rising to over 275 feet, and living more than 3,000 years. Fact: without plants, there would be no oxygen and therefore no life above the land."

As Jason slept, he dreamt in green once again. Images flickered across the screen in his unconscious mind. Once again, scenes of smoke and fire, mass destruction, rainforests being gutted, mountains blowing up, factories pumping smoke and smog, industrial waste pools, oil spills, chemical spills, waste plants, dumps, fires, huge tracts of once green jungle bulldozed into oblivion, a virtual environmental Armageddon. It was an environmental nightmare.

The wasteland dreamscape dissolved, and Jason found himself in a forest of redwoods, the world's tallest, oldest, and wisest trees. In his dream, he was flying high among the branches, where he could make out a faint sound of wind whispering through the leaves of the tree's highest limbs. Listening closely, he realized the whispering was the trees talking to each other; planning, discussing, strategizing. He'd done it, with a little help from those mushrooms. It wasn't like anything Jason had ever experienced. It was an overwhelming feeling of connectedness in that he was now a part of a kingdom of living things that shared an innate drive to survive. And that this survival was being threatened—including his own existence.

Still in the dream, Jason found himself standing at the foot of a huge redwood, only now Jason had a long beard and was wearing torn up jeans and a red and black flannel shirt.

He reached out and touched the thousand-year-old bark. The first thing he noticed was how strong the exterior felt on his hand.

"I'm with you," Jason told the tree with tears in his eyes. "I can help. Wait until you see what I can do with a little deadly nightshade."

Jason still had friends at Morabito, and he knew they hung out at Papa Ralph's roadside bar. When Jason awoke, he gathered his things, left his apartment, and headed across town.

He was sitting at the bar when some genetic engineers he knew came in and grabbed the stools on both sides of him.

"Hey," said a bearded, overweight man with his name tag, Howard Bowde, still stuck on his white bib-coveralls. "Look who it is. You got the shaft, man. That's all I can say. All the guys miss ya, bud. Watcha' drinkin' there? Let me buy you another one."

"Thanks," said Jason. "I appreciate it. You still work in Morabito's supply room, right? I left some of my tools in the locker room, but they took my card, so I haven't been able to get back inside. You think you could help me get my stuff?"

"No problemo, *amigo*," said Bowde. "Just let me finish this brew."

Chapter 9

Jason decided to let his friend, Howard Bowde, drive them to the Morabito plant, since he no longer had an employee sticker on his own truck. He also decided to hide under a blanket in the back seat of Bowde's bright red Ford-350 pickup, since he also had to give back his employee key card.

Howard pulled up to the gate and swiped his keycard and waved to the guard. The gate lifted, and he pulled his truck through.

This was going to be Jason's first visit back to his old company since he was dismissed two weeks prior, and it began to bring up a bit of anxiety along with some bile. Bowde parked his pickup in his regular spot and turned to look at Jason who took off the blanket once the Ford was in park.

"Are you okay? You look a little green around the gills," said Bowde. "I like the beard though. Suits you."

"Riding in the back," said Jason, "always makes me a little car sick. Something I had since I was a kid. Nothing to worry about."

Jason almost puked before he swallowed the bile back down to his stomach.

"Then let's get your stuff," said Bowde as he turned the engine off and took the key fob from the cupholder.

Jason followed Bowde to a side door in the back that led directly to the lab where Jason used to work.

Once inside, Jason's anxiety rose to a new level and he thought he was going to vomit, so he dashed into the men's room. He was almost sure that he was going to be caught, arrested, lose his severance pay, and God knows what else would happen to him.

"Making a pitstop," said Jason. "Too much beer."

"I hear ya," replied Bowde. "I'm gonna go into the chief's office and take advantage of his luxury sofa. Just let me know when you're ready to leave, bud."

Jason nodded and rushed into the men's room just making it to a sink before his dinner flew from his mouth along with that last pitcher of beer.

He let out a deep sigh and looked at himself in the mirror. With vomit all over his shirt, he turned on the sink and began splashing water in his mouth and on his face to freshen up. He felt a little bit better after letting out the puke. But he was still rough around the edges. He grabbed some more towels and put them under the faucet to get them wet enough to clean his shirt.

"Are we really doing this?" he said to his reflection.

Jason washed his face and then dried it with even more paper towels. He took in one more deep breath and left the men's room. He stumbled out into the hallway and shut the door behind him.

First, checking to see if Bowde was on the supervisor's sofa, Jason entered the lab where he had worked the last five years of his life. He then decided to cover his tracks by turning off all the security cameras and wiping the day's recorded footage from the main database computer in the front of the lab. He used Bowde's company ID and password to log in to the system, and he remembered how to work the cameras considering he helped set them up years prior.

Once he knocked out all the footage and shut off the working cameras, he looked around at his former place of employment. This had been his second home, and he knew it better than all the other genetic engineers combined. He knew he was going to miss it. It was the only job he felt like he was born to do. During his tenure, Jason had helped give birth to over four dozen new hybrid species of plants, ranging from vegetables to orchids and other exotic flowers, to various types of building materials such as wood and pulp, as well as some top-secret plants the Department of Defense had requested.

About eighteen months prior, Morabito had won a government defense department contract for the creation of genetically modified plants that would possess a specific trait. In their own way, each GMO plant would be fatal to those it touched. The purpose: to create an army of aggressively deadly plants that could be used as weapons.

Midway through the contract, funding for the project dried up and the experiment was discontinued. However, in the nine months that Jason worked on the initiative, he had developed over a dozen different hybrids that had potential to be chosen for the project, from the human-sized carnivorous hogweed to several poisonous versions of deadly nightshades that gave off microscopic droplets which, when breathed in, caused instant death.

Jason looked around to make sure the coast was clear. He knew that they had 24-hour security that would be popping up at any minute. He went over to the area of the lab where they kept all the top-secret plants and projects. They were locked in an impenetrable sealed room that could only be accessed via secret code.

He tried to remember what his password was, because it had been so long since he had to go in there. He wasn't even sure if the code would still work. He figured they would have changed it by now. He tried to think of all his passcodes he had set over the years. There were dozens. Then, he remembered he used his grandfather's birthday. He tried plugging in the numbers, 1-1-0-7-2-5. He pressed the enter button and prayed as the access screen flickered. And then, his prayers were answered as the door slowly opened.

Jason made his way inside to find that all the projects he had been told to stop working on were still there, perfectly intact. He hurried to another section of the lab and grabbed a cart that they used for transporting materials. He brought it into the top-secret room and loaded some of his projects onto the cart. He found the carnivorous hogweed he had taken so much pride in and held it up into the light.

"Wow, this is as marvelous as I remember," Jason murmured as he placed the plant onto the cart.

He then found all his different samples of the deadly poisonous nightshades. He picked them up and placed them very carefully and slowly on the bottom rack of the cart, making sure he did not puncture any of the boxes as it would have a very terrible outcome for Jason if that were the case. He finished up and placed a tablecloth over the top of the cart, so Bowde couldn't see what he was taking.

Jason pushed the cart slowly out of the room and into the lab. He wanted to make sure nothing fell off or got tainted on its way out. Jason pushed the cart steadily as he walked past his old desk.

Then, he noticed there were six portable Gene Guns recharging on the counter that glowed green, large ones and a few miniatures. It was like something inside of Jason was telling him to gather as many Gene Guns as he could.

He grabbed all six, then opened a drawer and found two big boxes, each filled with a dozen tiny vials of the Frankenplant DNA.

"Now that's what I'm talking about," said Jason as he placed the boxes under the cloth on the cart. He shut off the lights to the lab, opened the door, and left with the cart.

Jason went into the supervisor's office and nudged Bowde who had fallen into a beer binge sleep.

"I'm ready," said Jason. "Let's go."

Bowde awoke from his slumber and sat up, "Dang, that was fast, bro."

He stood up and led Jason out of the Morabito building.

Jason looked back at the logo on the outside of the building for the company he used to work for. He looked down at his cart, and back at his old job and company. "Now this is what I'd call a real severance package," Jason said to himself.

"Huh? What you got there?" asked Bowde.

"Ah, don't worry. Just some stuff I left in the office. It's got…sentimental value to me," said Jason. "By the way, hand me the keys. I think I should drive."

"You sure?" Howard slurred. "I'm fine to drive."

"Sure, you are. You can barely stand up. Give me the keys. Some of this stuff is fragile and I'd hate to think what would happen with you weaving all over the road."

"If you insist, bud," said Bowde as he threw his keys to Jason.

Jason unlocked the truck, and Bowde hopped into the passenger side. Jason opened and lowered the tailgate and began to move everything he had on the cart into the truck bed. He looked over and saw that Bowde had already gone back to sleep in the passenger seat.

He shut the tailgate and brought the cart over to the front of the Morabito building like he was returning a shopping cart in a grocery store parking lot. But as Jason got closer to the glass window of the front of the building, he started running, pushing the cart as fast as he could. He was about to shove it through the front window, when he stopped. Instead, he left the cart next to the building and walked back to Bowde's truck.

As he climbed in, Bowde woke up. "Where are we? Is it time to go to work?"

"Go back to sleep," said Jason, as he turned on the ignition and backed out of the parking spot.

An alarm suddenly went off somewhere inside the Morabito building, so Jason gave the truck some gas and sped toward the front gate. Suddenly he realized he didn't have a key card, so he pulled over and rummaged through Bowde's pockets. "Come on, where's you employee card?"

Bowde shifted in his seat and Jason found the card. He put the truck in gear and continued toward the front gate, swiping the keycard that opened the gates. The guard looked up briefly and noticed Jason was now behind the wheel of the Ford pickup.

"Hey," said the guard.

Jason stopped the truck midway through the entrance as the guard approached. He was carrying a clipboard.

"You're supposed to sign out whenever you visit after-hours."

The guard handed Jason the clipboard, which Jason took and scribbled a name, and handed it back to the guard.

"You forgot to put down the time, Mister...."

He looked at the signature, "Morabito?"

"My family owns the company."

Jason wrote in the time and handed back the clipboard. "What's your name?"

"Peterson, James Russell Peterson, sir."

"Well, Peterson, I'll let my father know what a good job you're doing, protecting his factory."

"Just doing my job, sir."

"Keep up the good work," smiled Jason as he sped off into the night.

Shortly after Jason left, a security jeep pulled up to the gate. A window rolled down, "We just got word that an alarm has been triggered in the lab. Who was that who just left?"

"That was just the boss's son."

"What boss?"

"You know, the owner, Morabito."

"Morabito is the name of the company you idiot. It's not a person. It's a combination of three names of the founders. Morrison, Ribbetts and Ito."

Jason was driving through the night when he heard sirens speeding toward the Morabito factory. The sirens woke up Bowde.

"What's going on?"

"Must be a fire or something…"

Bowde looked in the distance and saw the flashing lights heading toward the factory. He looked over at Jason.

"Shit man. What did you just do?" asked Bowde.

"Nothing. Don't worry about it," Jason responded as he made a quick right turn onto Vine Street.

"Dude, what if you get me fired?" asked Bowde.

"You won't. If they say anything, just tell them it was me. That I went into a fit of rage because I lost my job and that I made you do it. Plus, if you do get fired from there, it wouldn't be the worst thing in the world. That place is evil as hell," said Jason.

He made another turn onto Addison Street, this time almost sideswiping the truck merging onto the road next to them.

"I promise you it will be okay, Bowde," said Jason.

Jason looked over at his friend and realized he had fallen back asleep.

Chapter 10

Once Jason got home, he helped his friend get out of the pickup and walked him to his apartment. Inside, he put Bowde, who had fallen back to sleep, on his sofa and draped a blanket over him. "Sleep tight, old friend." He then returned to the pickup truck and took everything he removed from the lab out of the back and transported it up the stairs to his apartment.

It took him fifteen trips to get everything from the F-350 into his apartment and stored away. He did not want to wake Howard and ask for help because then he would see what Jason had really taken from the Morabito lab including Gene Guns and a dozen genetically modified plants, making him an accessory to grand theft.

Jason put on a pair of thick rubber gloves and retrieved one of the containers he'd taken from the lab to make sure its contents matched the labeling on the container. He pulled out the full-grown belladonna plant, also known as deadly nightshade, from the family of Solanaceae which interestingly also included such non-lethal vegetation as tomatoes, potatoes, peppers, and eggplants. This nightshade plant had been weaponized after its DNA had been combined with that of another deadly plant, Aconitum, that went by several aliases, such as wolf's bane, devil's helmet, aconite, blue rocket, and queen of poisons. Together they produced a plant so deadly that when ingested it caused death within a matter of minutes.

This combined plant species ironically produced a beautiful purple flower that gave off a pleasant aroma designed to attract its victims. Jason heard Bowde stirring on the sofa, so he put the weaponized deadly wolf's-bane back into its container and stored it in a closet and out of sight. He then removed his gloves and made himself and his guest some tea along with a few magic mushrooms.

While the water boiled, Jason contemplated what he would tell his friend. He decided that however much he told him, it would be better if Bowde heard it while under the influence of psilocybin.

The tea seemed ready, so he poured two cups and immediately drank some as he sat down before his laptop. The mushrooms took effect much faster than they did the first time. Apparently, Jason's body had adapted to the new plant DNA more fully. But before the mushrooms kicked in, he felt grateful that he had decided to hide the rest of the weaponized plants and Gene Guns in the closet. He remembered that as he closed his closet door, it felt like the weaponized plants were trying to communicate with him. But he had some research to do first before he could play with his new toys.

"Okay, I got us some weapons. Now let's find some targets," said Jason, speaking to the computer.

"Who you talkin' to," asked Bowde who had awakened on the sofa.

"Bowde," said Jason. "How long have you been awake?"

"I just woke up and heard you talking to somebody about weapons and targets. What are you getting us involved in?"

"It's not what you think," said Jason.

"What do I think? I don't think nothin. You just got fired and now you're talking about weapons and targets. Whatta ya gonna do? Shoot up your old friends? We all know you got a raw deal, but don't take it out on us. You're really starting to scare me, Jason."

"Bowde, you got it all wrong. Yeah, I'm annoyed and even angry. But that was just a job. I can get another job. This doesn't have anything to do directly with Morabito."

"So, what are you up to?"

"I can tell you but you're probably not going to believe it."

"Try me. We create super plants for God's sake. Nobody believes what we do now anyway."

"Okay. Just let me lay it out for you and then you can ask me any questions you want."

"Sounds good. Is this gonna be a long story? If so, you got any beer? I listen better when I'm not thirsty."

"You've had enough beer. Here, I made us some tea."

"Tea? I'm not much of a tea drinker."

"Here's the thing Bowde. This tea, it's got some special mushrooms in it. The psychedelic kind. Now, I can understand if you don't want to try it. It can be a little scary at first. But in order for you to truly understand what I'm about to tell you, this is the only way it's gonna make any sense."

"Hey, if it's good enough for you, I'm game. Bring it on brother."

He handed Bowde the second cup of magic mushroom tea. Bowde took a sip and spit it out.

"You could've warned me that it tasted like shit."

"Let me add a little kick to it for ya."

Jason reheated Bowde's magic mushroom tea and then added some Irish whisky to Bowde's cup.

"Try this."

Bowde took a sip. "Much better"

"Okay, you drink your tea and I'll tell you what's going on. It all started a couple days after the accident," said Jason. "Where I absorbed that plant DNA."

"What started?"

"I started seeing things differently."

"Like what?"

"Let's just say I've become more in touch with the plant world."

"What the hell does that mean?"

"I've been communicating with them."

"Them who?"

"The plants. Trees, mostly. They seem to be in charge."

Bowde finished his tea and stood up.

"I gotta have a beer."

Bowde put down the empty teacup and walked to the refrigerator and got a bottle of beer.

"When you say you've been communicating with the trees, you mean like talking to them?"

"Sort of. Although it's not really talking like you and I are talking now. It's a different kind of communicating."

"Different how?"

"See, that's the problem. I can't think of the words to describe it," said Jason.

"So how does it work? How do they send you messages?" asked Bowde.

"I get these thoughts and images in my mind."

"How do you know it's from them and not just you? Your imagination?"

"Cause I'm not thinking about what they're trying to tell me."

"So, it's not like you had to learn to talk tree, or something like that?" Howard asked.

"It's not like that. It's more like an awareness. Let me give you an example. The plant world is really upset right now."

"They told you that? That they're upset."

"They didn't exactly tell me. It was more like they showed me."

"How did they show you?"

"With pictures. Scenes. Feelings."

"Okay, so what are they pissed at?"

"Us, I think. I think they're pissed at us, Bowde."

"You and me?"

"Humans. We're fucking things up. We're killing the planet."

"That's nothing new. How long have we been hearing about climate change and global warming, carbon dioxide from all that fossil fuel polluting the air?"

"See, that's the problem. I don't think it's about climate change."

"It's not?"

"I think that's just a distraction."

"They told you all that."

"More or less. Think about this. We just went through two years of a global pandemic, and nearly one year of lock downs. Everybody drove a lot less, and logically if carbon emissions were the problem, then the carbon in the atmosphere should have gone down, right? But it didn't. It actually went up during the pandemic. There was more carbon in our atmosphere even though we were producing fewer emissions. So, how do you explain that? You can't. All it means is that the pandemic just showed us how insignificant the impact fossil fuel is having on global warming."

"So, if climate change isn't the problem, then what is the problem? What are the plants so upset about?" asked Bowde.

"Oxygen. Or lack of oxygen, actually."

"Oxygen, huh. What is it that we're doing that's sucking up all the oxygen?"

"Nothing is sucking up the oxygen. That's not what I'm saying. It's a problem of production. Do you know where oxygen comes from?"

"Ah, the air?"

"Plants. Trees mostly. It's through a process called photosynthesis…we learned about this stuff in high school biology."

"So, are you trying to tell me that the trees aren't going to produce enough oxygen?"

"No. It's because we've been cutting them down."

"I don't know man. There seems like there's still a lot of trees around."

"Not as many as there used to be, and more are being destroyed every day, all over the planet. We've been cutting them down for centuries. Ever since humans began walking the earth. I Googled it. There are only half the number of trees left on the planet since humans arrived, and most of them were cut down in the last two hundred years, and it's not letting up. An estimated fifteen billion acres of forests are destroyed every year, mostly just for agriculture and farming. But lately something else is driving forest destruction."

"What's that?"

"This war on fossil fuel and the push to electric vehicles. They use certain minerals that must be mined and many of these mines are in land beneath the world's largest forests, like the South American rainforests. Acres of trees are now being cut down in order to fill this increased supply of metals like lithium, iridium, nickel, and copper."

"So, what's going to happen?"

"If something isn't done to stop it, it's going to be just like what happened to the dinosaurs. If we continue to remove oxygen-producing forests and wilds at the rate we're going, we'll have us another mass extinction, only this time it will be us who becomes extinct, along with every other breathing animal."

"I thought some meteor killed the dinosaurs," said Bowde.

"That's what we've been led to believe, but from the chatter I've picked up from the plant world, I've learned that as the dinosaur population grew, they ate the plants faster than they could be replaced, like what's happening now.

Jason continued. "It's been going on for a couple thousand years. Here's what I found out. About two thousand years ago, eighty percent of Western Europe was all forest. Well, today. It's only thirty-four percent. Here, in North America, in the East between the 1600s to around 1870, we cut down half of the forests for timber and agriculture. In China, it's even worse. China has removed all but twenty percent of its forests.

"The crazy thing now is that the climate change army that's trying to force everyone to stop using gasoline and buy electric vehicles are driving more companies to destroy the oxygen-producing forests in order to mine for the minerals needed for the batteries in all those electric vehicles."

"So, what do you plan on doing about it?"

"I gotta help the plants get the word out."

"Like you're gonna be their PR guy? What's that go to do with weapons and targets?"

"I see it as more like helping them shape the narrative. Sort of like the colonists did when they had that Boston Tea Party. That was basically a PR stunt to let Britain know they weren't going to pay the Tea Tax anymore."

Bowde did not know if it was the strength of Jason's argument or the magic mushroom's effect on his brain doing the thinking or the talking. But he found himself going along with Jason's theory about the current revolt by the plant universe.

"So, you're gonna have a Tea Party, are ya?"

"Well, maybe not a Tea Party, but something to get their attention."

"Count me in buddy."

Chapter 11

Jason sat down before his computer. "Let me show you something."

He turned it on, called up Google, and typed in into the search engine "Top 10 companies responsible for destroying the most forests on the planet."

In less than a second, the search engine came back with over 20 million results and first on the list was associated with the Earth website's "Top companies responsible for deforestation." The article had recently gone viral, so it was the first result.

Jason quickly scanned the list that the website had put together as well as what the Botanical Society of London, Scotland, Ireland, and South Africa had to say about what had been happening to the world's forests.

At the same time, the mushroom tea that Jason and Bowde had consumed was setting in even deeper, and the walls began to blur for both. Jason especially glowed greener and greener as the psilocybin from the fungi took over their bodies and consciousness.

"What's happening?" asked Bowde.

"That's just the mushrooms kicking in," said Jason.

"Right. Okay, what am I supposed to do?"

"Just go with the flow. Anything that doesn't seem right, it's probably the mushrooms. And it will pass, believe me."

"This is some strange shit man."

"Enjoy the ride, Howard. It's time to open your consciousness."

Just then the apartment ceiling seemed to vibrate, almost like a popcorn kernel about to pop. Jason wiped his eyes to unblur his vision so he could see his computer screen better. He could almost hear faint different voices coming from the closet where he had stored the lab projects that he had taken from Morabito.

Jason continued to read on his screen. According to several sites on Google, forests only cover about 31% of the world's land area as they continue to vanish at what the Botanical Society called "an alarming rate." One article went on to say that since 1990, 1.3 million square kilometers of forest had been destroyed as companies removed trees for commercial agriculture and other reasons. This development, they say, threatens every inhabitant of the planet: human, animal, and plant. And while there are many organizations doing this, there are twenty-three companies that are primarily responsible for this massive deforestation on a global scale.

"Well, damn," said Jason.

He looked around and noticed the colors on the walls of his apartment seeming to dance with each other before blending to create different colors, all of which ended up fading back to green moments later. Jason wiped his eyes and scrolled down to see the list of the different companies.

"Take a look at these."

"What are we looking at here?"

"The targets. Let's start with number eleven"

"Why are you skipping the top ten?"

"Take a look at those names. Those are major corporations, which means they'll have the strongest security to stop any attacks. I'm starting with number eleven because I've never heard of that company."

"Ponderosa Corporation" said Bowde. "Me neither. Says it's a U.S.-based company that turns forests into farmland throughout South America to produce soybeans and beef. It also buys cocoa and palm oil from companies that illegally clear rainforests in Africa, Indonesia, and Malaysia. Ponderosa's customers include all the fast-food chains as well as CostSMART and CASHMart. I can see why it's on the list."

"Look at number twelve," said Jason. "It's an investment management firm. RocketAssets."

"Why would they be destroying the forests?"

"Because it's going to sell all its investments that it considers having high environmental risks, including thermal coal, oil, and natural gas. They also said that they would launch new investment products that screen for fossil fuels. Ironically, what that didn't include were a host of companies with a high degree of deforestation risk. In fact, RocketAssets invested in these companies, companies responsible for deforestation, more than any other asset management firm."

Howard asked, "So, it's funding the companies that are killing the trees, while acting like its environmentally friendly for not investing in fossil fuels? What's next?"

"A new company called Lyons Electric that focuses on the creation of batteries used in electric vehicles," said Jason. "Look at this. As soon as it went public, it started an aggressive forest-clearing operation in Central and South American rain forests just to mine the minerals used in the batteries. I saw their mission statement. It says Lyons Electric intends to be the top provider of rechargeable batteries in the new world."

"I kinda like rechargeable batteries," said Bowde.

"Who doesn't. But you're missing the point. These are batteries used in electric vehicles and the world simply isn't ready for them yet."

"Why not?"

"Because they need to be recharged and that takes electricity," said Jason. "Most cars and trucks run on gasoline but if they ran on batteries that needed to be recharged every few hundred miles, that would require charging stations and more electricity than exists in the world today. You want to hear the real irony?

"What's that?"

"Most of the world's electricity comes from turbines and electric grids that depend on coal, so all those charging stations used by electric vehicles are in reality powered by a fossil fuel. They put the cart before the horse. That's how stupid this whole war on fossil fuel is. All it's going to do is cause inflation, drain people's pocketbooks, and cause another recession and probably even a depression."

"So why are they doing it?"

"Good question. If we figure that out, then maybe we can stop it. But first we have to get the attention of people who can do something about it."

"Like who?"

"Well, you must figure politics has taken over the climate change argument, so right now, those in charge are focused on eliminating fossil fuel as the primary culprit in global warming. We must either make them aware of the error of their ways or vote them out of office. The only problem with the second solution is that we may not have that much time."

"So, what are we gonna do?"

"Get their attention," said Jason. Now, let's look at the next few companies on this list so I can figure out a plan."

"Here's one that's pretty close by," said Bowde. "Shinua International Ltd. It's the world's largest refinery and trader of palm oil, and one of the world's largest palm oil plantation owners and processors. It also has a global soybean crushing capacity of 36 million metric tons per year, the majority of which are in China."

"China's not that close, man," said Jason.

"No, but Shinua International has a branch right here in Evanston. So does the next company on the list. KTJ, which it says is one of Argentina's leading exporters of beef and one of the more known deforestation companies, operating over two-hundred production facilities worldwide, processing many tens of thousands of cattle per day. In addition to beef, it uses soy in its animal feed in cattle feedlots, poultry, and swine farms. It's been linked to illegal deforestation in the Brazilian Amazon five times this year."

"Where have I heard about this company before?" asked Jason.

He got up and went to the closet where the stolen plants were stored. He returned with a piece of paper in his hand.

"Look at this."

Bowde read the invoice from Morabito to KTJ for DNA enhancement.

"That's not all," said Jason, as he revealed a stack of invoices to other companies.

"Take a look at these and see if any match up with companies on this list."

"Here's one," said Bowde. "KEEPup, the largest producer of wooden furniture in the world. Morabito sent them an invoice, too. While it says it doesn't use illegally logged wood in its furniture products, investigators found that it did manufacture products that have used logs from illegally chopped trees from the forests in Ukraine and Siberia."

"I found another one," said Jason. "PULP-IT, an Indonesian-based company that destroys wildlife habitats and forests to sell its timber, plywood, pulpwood, biomass, and newsprint to Southeast Asian and Australian paper companies. And here's two more. CafeOLE, the largest chain of coffee shops in the world that also sells products using palm oil, soy, beef, and paper, making it one of the companies that caused deforestation. Although it claims ninety-nine percent of its coffee is now ethically sourced, it does not have similar restrictions on the palm oil in its baked goods.

"You're not going to believe this last one. BurgerMeister, the fast-food chain with more than eleven thousand locations in over one hundred countries. Its burgers, sandwiches, sides, and beverages involve significant amounts of beef, soy, and palm oil, as well as paper in packaging. Getting its soy from Ponderosa, one of the most renowned deforestation companies. I'm not eating there anymore."

"And Morabito has been doing business with all these clowns," says Bowde. "Maybe I should submit my resignation."

"No," said Jason. "You can be more helpful if you're still there."

"Like a spy, or maybe a whistleblower."

"I'm not sure yet," said Jason. "What's important is that now we have somewhere to start. These companies represent billions of dollars' worth of business all around the world. There are hundreds of other firms that do the same thing causing massive deforestation. If we can just shine a light on them, to show the world what's happening and who's responsible, it just might make a difference."

"Whatta you gonna do? Teach the CEOs of these companies a lesson?"

"That's what I have to figure out," said Jason. "Now that I have the weapons and know who the targets are, maybe I can scare them into backing off from destroying the planet."

"That's a pretty big maybe," said Bowde. "Especially if you plan on doing this all by yourself."

"I have you, right," said Jason. "Maybe I can recruit a few more folks along the way."

The mushrooms had made their way through Jason and Bowde's bodies. Jason felt completely connected to the world around him. He kept hearing the plants whisper and murmur from the closet.

"Can you hear that?" Jason asked Bowde.

"Hear what?" Bowde responded.

"They're talking to each other," said Jason. "In the closet."

"Who's in the closet?"

"The plants. The ones I took from the factory."

"The plants are talking to each other?" asked Bowde. "What are they saying?"

Jason stood up, placed his computer on his coffee table, and walked over to the closet. The closer he got, the louder the voices got.

"Okay, I'm coming," Jason said as he made his way to the closet. Once he got there, he took a deep breath. The green was shining bright through the cracks of the door.

"What in the world?" said Bowde as he saw Jason standing before the closet door, where a green light was coming through the space under and around the door.

Jason pulled open the door of the closet as the green light illuminated him. Inside the closet, the plants Jason had brought home were shimmering in their containers. Some were all perked up, weaving back and forth, giving off a shining bright green. Deep inside the closet came a noise that sounded like a laugh.

"What was that?" asked Bowde, who remained transfixed on the sofa.

Jason moved some of the plants aside and looked deeper into the darkness of the closet. Out of the darkness came a carnivorous hogweed plant, dancing back and forth in front of Jason when it opened its leaf and let out what sounded like a sinister laugh.

He backed out of the closet and stared down at the army of weaponized plants looking spiky, green, and some full of poisonous thorns.

"Whoa, that was intense," said Jason as he looked around at these magical talking and dancing plants.

"Jason, what's going on?" Bowde asked.

"No one will ever believe us if we tell them about this."

"Yeah, well, what exactly is this, cause I'm having trouble believing it myself," said Bowde.

"But you heard it, right?" asked Jason.

"I heard *something*," said Bowde. "You tell me. What did I hear?"

"That was the plants talking," said Jason.

"It just sounded like noise to me," said Bowde.

"No, they were talking."

"You could understand what they were saying?"

"Loud and clear," said Jason.

"What did they say?"

"You're one of us, now," said Jason.

"What's that mean?"

"I think it means that somehow, I'm connected to the plant world and that to them, I'm one of them."

"They think you're a plant?"

"Maybe. I think it's more than that. You know plants have been using animals like forever to spread their seeds, and lots of other stuff in nature. I think what it means is that they know they can use me now."

"Well, they certainly got that right. What else did they tell you?"

"That they need my help, before those corporations destroy us all."

Chapter 12

Carter Wiseman, FBI Special Agent in Charge, read the most recent directive from FBI Headquarters in Washington, D.C. He just wasn't sure what he was reading, or what they expected him to do about it. Apparently, an FBI mainframe supercomputer had detected an unusual pattern among a half-dozen seemingly unrelated high-profile deaths in five different regions of the country, including one where Carter was the Special Agent in Charge of the FBI's field office. According to the email memo, he was supposed to investigate the recent death of a CEO in Turner Falls, a mere twenty-five miles from his office in Davis, Oklahoma and near the Texas panhandle.

Wiseman reread the part of the memo related to the death of Calvin Cooper. His was the sixth death in the past week.

At first, the local police departments reported each of the deaths as accidents, but when the fifth CEO of an industrial firm died within days of the others, an algorithm in the FBI's super-computer connected some dots that had never been connected before. The deaths had two things in common: first, all the victims were either the CEO, founder, or a high-ranking official of an industrial company; and second, a plant of some kind seemed to have played a role, either directly or indirectly, in all six deaths.

The detective's eyes widened as he perused the details included in the email. In one case, that of Cecil Lyons, the CEO's car had skidded on wet leaves that seemed to have just fallen during a heavy rain shower, causing the car to go off the road and down a steep incline, crashing into a tree.

In another death, the wife of the founder of a lumber company had just returned from a shopping trip where she purchased several plants, including a large round cactus. She set the cactus on the dining room table and during dinner with her husband, it exploded as millions of scorpion eggs that had been laid inside all hatched at the same time, spraying the couple with tiny but angry scorpions, whose bite, while not deadly, caused needle-like pain. This in turn caused the 79-year-old founder to have a heart attack.

A third instance was the most unusual in that it seemed a vine had grown overnight into the bedroom of a senior vice president at a mail order company. It had attached itself to the man's neck as he slept. As the vine grew, it constricted and, in effect, choked him in his sleep. The man's horrified and shocked family found him dead the next morning.

The fourth and fifth deaths involved the poisoning of a CEO, the first one somehow ingested deadly nightshade, also known as Solanaceae, with his after-dinner brandy. He was the Chief Financial Officer of one of Morabito's competitors.

The second CEO, unaware of his severe allergy to poison ivy, somehow tripped going out to get the mail and fell face first into a patch of the stuff. The oily resin on the poison ivy's leaves immediately caused the man's skin to blister so harshly that it covered his nostrils and mouth, cutting off oxygen so that the cause of death was determined to be suffocation.

Since the five deaths occurred in different states, jurisdiction for their investigation fell to the FBI, which immediately fed the information into its mainframe computer to detect any anomalies. By the time the sixth death occurred involving Calvin Cooper, the CEO of CostSMART, the computer had already detected the two variables—plant life and being a CEO of a major Fortune 500 corporation.

Wiseman sat back and scratched his head. Plants? This had to be a coincidence. If not, there must be more to this than just plants, he pondered.

Soon another email appeared. The computer had found a third variable. All the victims were apparently connected to some kind of list through the company or organization they belonged to.

A list. Now that's something Wiseman could get a handle on. Let's look at this list, thought Wiseman.

According to the computer, the list was created by a conservation group called simply "Earth" and it had a related website. At the website, Wiseman was able to pull up Earth's list of the top ten major companies responsible for deforestation. *Well, there you go*, he thought to himself. *The killers must be a bunch of crazy environmentalists.*

Except Wiseman knew that, in general, environmentalists were not particularly violent. In his experience of having to break up a demonstration or two, the protests usually involved nothing more than someone sitting in a tree that was about to be chopped down. But to use a tree as a weapon? Not their style. It must be something else.

The thought crossed his mind that it could have been some sort of anarchist coalition fighting against capitalist tyranny, but groups like the Weathermen had long ago been disbanded. Today's troublemakers were other groups, and they were mostly a disorganized bunch of spoiled rich kids who looked for any excuse to break stuff and turn peaceful protests into riots. Then there were those somewhat disorganized groups that seemed to be concerned with social justice and injustice but that had nothing to do with plants.

Realizing that he knew next to nothing about plants, Carter Wiseman looked up the nearest universities to his office that would be within driving distance and that also offered courses in botany, which is how he came to meet Botany Professor, Dr. Julie Green, at Texas A&M.

Detective Wiseman knocked on the door of the science faculty breakroom, which is where he was told he could find Dr. Green. An older gentleman with glasses and white hair opened the door and let Agent Wiseman in.

"FBI Special Agent Carter Wiseman. I am looking for Dr. Julie Green. I was told I could find her here between classes."

"Ah yes, Dr. Green. She's just over there," said the professor as he pointed to the couch. An attractive woman dressed in business casual attire looked up from her paperwork and saw Carter standing by the doorway. She stood up and walked over to him.

"The FBI," said Dr. Green, as she examined Carter's credentials. "How can I help you?"

"I'm not sure, Professor, but I thought I should check in with someone who knows about plants better than, well, we do," said Carter.

Wiseman sat down at a table near the couch and Dr. Green sat beside him.

"What is it that you'd like to know?" asked Dr. Green.

"Well, I know this is going to sound a little crazy but are plants capable of murder?" asked the FBI agent.

Dr. Green burst out in laughter although it sounded a bit forced.

"Is this a joke? Did someone put you up to this? Was it our chairman? He's still annoyed because we didn't all vote for him to be department chair. It's supposed to be an anonymous poll, but I think he figured out that I was one of the three who didn't vote for him."

"No Ma'am," said Carter. "I'm afraid this is real."

"You think a plant committed murder?"

"Plants, actually. And murders. There was more than one murder. Six to be exact that we know of. And all the deaths involved some sort of plant life."

"Wow. You realize how crazy you sound right now, right?"

"Believe me, I do. So, you're saying it's impossible? That's okay if you are. I just needed to check off this box to say that I went to the experts, and that they said no way is that a possibility."

"I never said it was impossible," said Dr. Green. "Let's go into my office to discuss this further. Follow me."

She gathered her files, and they walked a short distance from the breakroom to Dr. Green's small private office. She sat down behind her Formica desk and let out a deep sigh. "And you know what? I'm not going to say that."

"You're not going to say what?"

"I'm not going to say it's impossible. In fact, I think it's more than possible. It's probably already happened more than we're aware of, so if you say six deaths involved plants, then you might be on to something, detective."

"Agent. I'm a Special Agent with the FBI. We don't have detectives as such. But you think it's possible?" he asked before he took a big gulp from his water bottle.

"Yes, I think it's very possible. Absolutely. I believe I owe you an apology."

"You do?"

"My initial reaction," she continued. "I was wrong to laugh like that. I've been studying plants most of my adult life and I can assure you, they have more power than almost anything else on the planet. Let me put it another way. If a plant wanted to kill someone, it could probably figure out a few ways to do it. They, plants I mean, just don't usually act so aggressively. Well, I shouldn't say that. Some plants are every aggressive. Vines for example. But murder? With an intent to do harm? That's rare. They'd have to have a damn good reason, I would imagine. Six you say. Wow. What did the victims have in common?"

"They were either CEOs or high-ranking senior officers of the companies they worked for," said Wiseman.

"You know when it comes to the world of plants, anything is possible. I obviously must get more information, but yes, plants sort of see things in life-or-death terms. Which means they must have felt threatened in some way."

"So now you're suggesting that plants may have actually killed one or even all of these men?" asked Wiseman. "Then why did you initially say I sounded crazy?"

"Well, because you said *murder* which implies the tree or plant had a motive. Trees falling on a house in a storm have killed people. Certain kinds of plants when eaten can cause death. So, I have to say that yes, plants can kill humans. But I wouldn't call it murder. More like accidents or if we wanted to use a term that's closer to your world in the FBI, more like manslaughter, or like I mentioned before, self-defense in that they felt threatened in some way. The difference between someone who's sober and loses control of their car because they're just a bad driver and kills someone versus someone who uses their car as a weapon, purposely driving into someone to kill that person. But you think these plants did it on purpose, right?"

"Yes, and I know how crazy that sounds. But we have six men, all high-ranking corporate officers. who have died. And while taken individually their deaths seem like accidents, taken together these six deaths point to something more sinister. A conspiracy of sorts. But you don't think that's possible?"

"Now, not necessarily. You mentioned conspiracy, which implies some kind of communication has occurred and we do know that plants communicate with each other. And they can become aggressive when irritated. But, to think of them as potential murderers, I don't know. All I know is that the more I learn about the world of plants, the less I seem to know. Also, the more I learn, the more amazed I am at how we have underestimated the power of plants all these centuries."

"What are you getting at?"

"Time to expand your horizon, Agent Wiseman," said Professor Green as she picked up a flower from a vase on her desk. "What do you see?" as she held it out to him.

"A rose?"

"A rose, yes, but a rose is not just a rose. It's a beautiful flower that lures you in, so you fail to see the thorns on its stem, until you feel the pain they inflict when you try to grab them."

"A rose didn't kill these men."

"Tell me about the deaths and the men who died?"

"Okay," said Agent Wiseman as he tried to get comfortable in the hard wooden chair facing Dr. Green's desk.

About ten minutes later, after Agent Wiseman finished detailing how each executive died, Professor Green nodded to herself. Then she said, "Seems like they may have had some help in a couple of instances. But the others, like the wet leaves, the vine and the poison ivy, that's sophisticated. So is the exploding cactus and deadly nightshades, but someone had to deliver those plants to their intended victim. What about the men? What's their common thread?"

"They were all senior executives in large corporations. Our computer determined their companies were all on a list of the top ten companies responsible for the most deforestation on the planet."

"That's interesting," said Julie. "Give me their names and companies and I'll ask Summit. That's the new supercomputer at the Oak Ridge National Laboratory. All the top schools have access to it. I'm sure the FBI computer is good, but this could be better. If nothing else, it will at least corroborate what we already know," Julie explained.

Carter gave her the names of the victims and their companies, and she typed them into the computer's search engine ... which immediately spit out a list.

"Holy shit," said Julie. "Look at this."

Carter looked down at the list which not only included his list of top ten companies responsible for deforestation of the planet but added about fifty more. "Is this for real?"

"Looks like it," said Julie.

"All six were either working for companies on your list or companies those companies do business with. How much more of a connection do you need?" asked Carter after he took a long deep breath.

"We'd better start warning the folks on this list," said Dr. Green.

"That's going to be a lot of people. You're looking at some large companies," he replied.

"But you said it was just the CEOs who were killed."

"So far, but I don't think we should rule out other senior leaders," said Carter.

"We're missing something," said Julie.

"What?"

"Deforestation. That's it."

"That's what?"

"Trees. It's the trees.".

"You think? What are you saying? That the trees are angry?"

"I'd say they're a bit more than angry," said Julie. "Let me pose a theory. Science now knows that plants communicate and express their feelings. That includes trees. In fact, in a forest, it pretty much starts with trees."

"What does?" he asked.

"Communicating," said Julie.

"You're losing me."

"Here's my theory as crazy as it may sound. Something has trees and the plant world in general very concerned. It's always been up to them to maintain a balance in nature. So, if we've done something to disrupt that balance, they may be reacting in the only way they know how. They're protecting the planet. So, they've formed an army of sorts to fight for the survival of the world, or at least their world."

"Now who sounds crazy, Professor Green?" asked Agent Wiseman as he stood to leave.

"You saw the list! What do you think is going on?" she asked.

"I think maybe there's a psycho out there using plants to kill people."

"Does that psycho control the weather? We're talking about forces of nature here and the plant world is very much a force of nature."

"How is that possible?" Carter asked.

"Follow me."

Julie led the agent outside her office, the faculty breakroom, past her classroom and the botany lab and into a small area behind the college. They walked across a lawn and down a bank to a pond. Wiseman looked around at all the students around the campus and back at Julie. One student walked by and said, "Hey Professor Green! Great lecture yesterday!"

"Thanks, Percy!" she replied as she guided Wiseman to sit on a rock by the pond.

The lily pond looked like a Monet painting in motion, peaceful, and bucolic. Out of the water and onto a leaf leaped a lopsided frog. It seemed to tilt to the left and for good reason. It only had three legs. This incapacitation was made up partially by the fact that the frog had six eyes and could see in 360 degrees at the same time, meaning that nothing could sneak up on it.

It did not have a clear sightline to what was happening overhead, however, so it failed to see the net falling over it before Julie scooped it up.

Dr. Green and Agent Wiseman walked back to her lab.

Once back in her lab, Professor Green examined the frog closely with a magnifying glass.

"Take a look at this," she said to Agent Wiseman.

"What exactly am I looking at?" he asked.

Professor Green scraped something from under the frog's belly and put it on a slide.

"Try this," she said letting Wiseman peer through the lens to see cells fighting each other. He was not sure what he was looking at.

"What is it?" he asked.

"We're not sure."

"Looks like pond scum to me."

"See the cells banging into each other?"

"What about them?"

"They're not supposed to do that. It's some kind of mutation and we believe it's responsible for causing the mutations in the frogs that swim in this pond," Julie explained.

"How?" said Wiseman.

"That's what we're still trying to find out. What we do know is that those cells are plant cells, and they're not supposed to be moving like that. They're agitated."

"Agitated plant cells are quite a leap to plants committing murder," said Wiseman.

"Not when you consider who died. Didn't each person have something to do with destroying the environment?" Professor Green asked.

Wiseman paused for a moment, and then he said, "If I bring this to my superiors, I'll be laughed out of the bureau."

"Welcome to my world. I get laughed at all the time. It's something I've learned to live with. Still, it's something I believe in. In fact, I'm presenting on it next week at a Conference in Kyoto, Japan."

"You said that the plants communicate with one another. How does that happen?"

"Well, what we've discovered is that they have their own kind of internet of sorts," said Julie. "Mainly it involves mycelium fibers, or fungi."

"Fungi? Like mushrooms?"

"Fungus is kind of its own lifeform. Somewhere between plant and animal."

"Fungus, as in 'there's a fungus among us?'" said Carter before laughing.

"As in mushrooms, although most fungi are in the form of masses of thin threads, known as a mycelium. One scientist, Professor Martin Rodriguez from Princeton, is doing some exceptional research on this whole area of study, now that I think about it. Maybe he might be a good person to consult with on these matters. We now know that these threads act as a kind of underground internet, linking the roots of different plants. For example, that oak tree in your front yard could be linked to another tree next door, or even your neighbor's shrubbery, all by mycelium or mycelia to be more accurate," Dr. Green explained.

"That's how they communicate, through mycelia?" asked Wiseman.

"Seems so. Some scientists think the entire plant world is connected. We're learning more about these underground networks every day. It's giving us a whole new respect for the plant world. For example, older trees can feed nutrients to young saplings through mycelium."

"So, they distribute more than just information."

"There's so much we're still learning about all of this. It's one of the reasons I decided to study botany instead of zoology, or anatomy. Plants are so much more than just food or pretty things to look at. They supply most of the medicine we use in virtually every illness, either organically or synthetically, by chemically replicating the active elements found by genetic re-engineering various plants.

"Ever since I started studying plants" Dr. Green continued, "I've come to see them differently than when I started out. I've learned that they're not just sitting around passively. Now that we know they're connected, we can try to explain how one plant can help another by sharing nutrients and even information. We've seen some amazing things like warding off invading plants and even animals by using the network to spread toxic chemicals, like the pond scum and its effect on frogs," said Julie.

"Got it," said Agent Wiseman. "Wow, it's a lot to take in Professor Green."

"We're just scratching the surface. I'm afraid that's all the time I have for today. There's a Climate Change conference coming up in Japan, and I'm presenting. I have to get back to working on my speech and getting packed."

"I may call on you again when you're back from that conference," said Wiseman.

"Please do. Keep me informed about the case and if any more people from that list have accidents or worse," said Julie. "I'll do whatever I can to help with the case. Just a thought here, and you probably thought about this yourself as well, but have you considered the plants are getting some help?

"How so?"

"The surge in buying plants during the pandemic lockdowns was well-documented since, for many of us, our trees and houseplants became constant companions and sources of comfort during a difficult time."

"So, you think someone might be helping the plants with these deaths?"

"Relationships between humans and their plants is well-documented," said the professor. "There's a website on trees that recently did a survey and it found that out of some 1,250 plant owners, nearly half actually talked to their trees and plants."

"Half?"

"Forty-eight percent, so nearly half. And out of those 48 percent, one out of five talked to their plants every single day. So, statistically the possibility that the plants are getting help is a pretty good bet."

Wiseman sat back down in that uncomfortable chair in front of Dr. Green's desk as he ran his hands through his hair. "That puts everything in a whole different light," said Agent Wiseman.

"Want me to go on?"

"What do you mean?"

"That same survey claimed 25 percent of those who talk to their plants have also kissed their plants."

"Do they say why?"

"Most say they think the talking and kissing helps their plants to grow," said Julie. "But there are many others who do it just to maintain a strong connection to their plants, and some say it helps with their own mental health."

Agent Carter Wiseman stood up, shook the professor's hand, thanked her, and headed back to his vehicle.

"Looks like I've got a lot more work to do," Carter said to himself as he pulled out his phone and called headquarters.

Chapter 13

COP27 Was the official name of the annual conference in Kyoto, Japan. COP was short for Conference Of the Parties of the UNFCC or the United Nations Framework Convention on Climate Change. The "27" referred to the twenty-seventh year this conference had taken place, always in a different location. The previous year it occurred in Glasgow, Scotland. It was Professor Julie Green's third visit to what ostensibly was a two week-long event aimed at discussing all that was needed to slow the rise in global temperature.

Over the years it had grown into the largest forum for the heads of state, policy makers, and negotiators, as well as corporations, investors, scientists, activists, NGOs or non-governmental organizations as well as a large number of youth leaders to gather together in a common goal, namely, to drive the global climate agenda forward. Approximately 45,000 people from 196 countries poured into the many session halls to hear a variety of new investment vehicles and initiatives all designed to reduce carbon emissions that reportedly contributed to the globe's rising temperature.

The major conundrum rippling through this year's conference was how to explain the cogent fact that despite a significant reduction in carbon emissions during the COVID 19 lockdowns, the amount of carbon in the atmosphere had risen, implying that human activity could not possibly be causing the increase. If true, this threatened a multinational campaign involving billions of dollars to stop the use of fossil fuels and instead put all the world's financial resources into alternative energy sources such as wind, solar, or electric vehicles.

On the other hand, this could cost a lot of people, a lot of money. If gas guzzling cars or coal burning factories weren't responsible for the increase in carbon in the atmosphere, then what was?

Professor Green's presentation suggested the culprit was the increased deforestation, in that fewer trees to remove carbon from the atmosphere during photosynthesis could result in an increase. She even began to get climate change advocates to believe her, but never enough to combat the powerful anti-fossil fuel lobby. They were determined to prove the increase during COVID had been an anomaly. But Julie had never seen any reliable scientific evidence to support that theory.

In fact, one of her more controversial slides showing on the large projector in front of the crowd of a few hundred attendees showed the true dangers of rain forest destruction, and how the shift in the balance of nature was depleting the atmosphere of something we all needed, oxygen. That had nothing to do with melting glaciers and rising ocean levels that was theoretically going to cause global flooding.

Since her lecture was scheduled on the second to last day of the conference, she could tell the crowd in front of her was full of environmentalists who were burnt out from their attendance at the dozens of previous lectures. They had already listened to too many boring lectures where people and panels were basically repeating the same mantra repeatedly— that the burning of fossil fuels was destroying the planet by causing the earth's temperature to rise which was supposedly causing polar icecaps to melt, thereby drowning civilizations around the globe.

While Professor Green was very respected among this community, her lecture was the one right after lunch and the crowd, with their hunger now sated, just seemed to want to nap. In fact, many had dozed off in their chairs. Still, she did her best to present the information in the clearest and most interesting way possible because to her it was extremely important.

She went over how the lack of oxygen in the air now being created by photosynthesis could pose a serious health threat to all breathing creatures, and how this was a more immediate problem that needed to be dealt with than how carbon dioxide from burning oil and coal contributes to the overall greenhouse effect. She also discussed her theory that the rise in carbon in the atmosphere during

COVID was due to deforestation and the reduction in trees that pulled carbon from the atmosphere during photosynthesis.

No one seemed to care about that. So, she re-emphasized the danger in reduced oxygen.

"Yes, the oceans may rise an eighth of an inch in three hundred or four hundred years, but by then we'll all be dead or living in bubble communities as we breathe from oxygen tanks," she said, only somewhat sarcastically.

Not that any of that mattered since when she looked out into the audience, she could see that most of the people that were left in the crowd had either fallen asleep or had turned to their phones to check messages or for entertainment. *I guess it beats them laughing at me*, she thought. Except one. A young man in the back in a dark blue suit who was recording every word she said. He had a sketchy vibe to him, and it kind of spooked Professor Green out as she tried to continue her presentation.

"Let me talk to you about trees," said Julie. "Did you know that none of us would be alive today if it weren't for trees? Trees create the oxygen in the air that we breathe. Without it we would die. Literally. They also create the medicines we use to heal us when we're sick. In Japan, thousands of people bathe in forests every day. We all feel better when we walk in the forest. In Japan, they call it forest bathing. In the medicinal atmosphere, there is a chemical explanation. Trees produce one of the most complex chemical reactions, sending chemical aerosols into the atmosphere helping the immune system," the professor went on.

"Trees are the secret to our existence. They are a key player in the manufacturing and distribution of chemicals that maintain the balance in nature. There has been significant destruction and deforestation in the name of progress that today threatens to deplete our atmosphere of the oxygen we need to breathe," Julie pleaded to the crowd of uninspired environmentalists.

"Many tree species are disappearing at an alarming rate. Human need and greed are threatening our very existence! And those who are trying to eliminate fossil fuels are among the main culprits. The redwood is the largest carbon bearing organism on earth. Kings of the forests. In Japan, the forests feed the fish. Forests and oceans are connected. But we're destroying our forests at an alarming rate. For example, only five percent of the coastal rain forest on Vancouver Island remains. Can you believe that? Only five percent!

"In Ireland, the Irish were a woodland culture, yet today the oak forests are nearly gone. Ireland was left with less than one percent forest cover due to wars over thousands of years. The druids believed the forest was an almost perfect society. You all know who the druids are, right? The druids were the elite educated class of Ireland who understood the forests and its place in the balance of nature. And let me tell you, the druids were right. The forests absorb carbon dioxide out of the atmosphere. They have been doing that for four hundred million years. The carbon is absorbed into the tree and the oxygen floats out into the atmosphere. But too much of the earth's forests have been removed."

As Julie scanned her audience, she again felt like no one was really listening to what she was saying except for one man in the back in a dark blue suit. He had Asian features and she guessed he was probably of Chinese origin.

If I can convince at least one person here today, it's better than nothing, Julie thought. So, she focused her attention on the man in the back who was looking directly at her.

"Germany has managed to keep thirty percent of its forest land through sustainable forest management. They are aware of how important forests are for clean water. But is thirty percent going to be enough to continue producing oxygen? The truth is we just don't know.

"The largest forest system in the world is in Canada, the Boreal Forest. It goes all the way from Newfoundland and Labrador to British Columbia and the Yukon. All we really need to do is preserve it. So, what I'm trying to say is that the answer to climate change is not the elimination of fossil fuels. It's the restoration of our lost forests. We need to plant more native trees. And fast. If everyone planted one native tree into native spaces, we could potentially legitimately reverse this attack on our environment and restore the depletion of much-needed oxygen to our atmosphere.

"But to do that we need to get support from the world's leader nations, who up to this point have done virtually nothing to stop or even slow deforestation. I'm talking about the U.S., China, India, and Russia.

"If nothing else, let me leave you with this reminder. For every breath you take, thank a tree. Once you connect with the land, you will do anything to fight for it. We need to start putting them—the trees— first! Thank you."

Professor Green ended her lecture and headed off the stage. A couple members of the crowd clapped while others were too busy on their cell phones to realize she had finished speaking. She looked to the back of the auditorium to see how the man in the dark suit had reacted, but he was no longer there.

Later that day, in an office building in downtown Kyoto, the same young man in the back of Dr. Green's audience, the man in the blue suit, entered an office and closed the door.

"We may have a problem," he said to someone sitting at a desk.

"Why is that? I'm told nothing puts a climate change conference to sleep faster than global warming," the person behind the desk replied.

"That was the case until one botanist who knows what's going on started talking about trees and she presented a slideshow that got the attention of a few corporate sponsors. However, things could get messy down the line depending upon how loud she gets about this. We may have to shut her up if she doesn't stop herself first. It was clear that this crowd wasn't really listening, but the next crowd might."

"Get our PR department on it. You know the drill. Find a way to discredit or distract what she had to say. We must keep controlling the narrative to keep the focus on fossil fuel. And if that doesn't work, we'll find another way to discredit her. I don't think we need to take her out just yet. Just remember. Whenever we do take such extreme measures, there are always repercussions. Remember the death of that novelist? He had quite a following and when he showed how global warming was a natural phenomenon and not caused by the burning of fossil fuel, people listened. A lot of people believed him."

"That's why he had to go," said the man in the dark suit.

"Don't be ridiculous. He was in his late 60s and had already been diagnosed with Stage 4 pancreatic cancer."

"I'm talking nonsense. Forget I said that. You're right. We'd never have helped his demise along a little faster so his death wasn't considered suspicious. It all worked out naturally to our advantage. That's not going to be the case with a thirty-five-year-old scientist in good health."

"Understood."

"That said, I still want you to keep an eye on her. See if you can get close to her. If she's unattached, she may be looking for a partner."

"Yes, sir."

Chapter 14

A few thousand miles away, in his Evanston, Illinois apartment, Jason was asleep and deep in a mushroom-enhanced dream. In the dream, Jason was at the foot of a giant redwood, which seemed to have become his go-to place when communicating with the plant world. It was now entirely a world of green. Everything was in a different shade of green, and it was getting to be a bit much. At first, it was hard for Jason to adjust, but as he got more and more comfortable with it, the mushroom dreams continued to progress in ways Jason had yet to understand.

Slowly, images flickered through his REM sleep to the recent past. In the dream, he was back at the Morabito factory, his recent employer, the creator of "super-plants," vitamin enhanced, enriched, and improved. Bigger, tastier, riper, juicier, better. Signs on the wall read, "God may have created vegetables, but at Morabito, we make them better."

Jason hated that sign so much.

This was the tenth time Jason had that dream which was always a slightly different replay of the accident that got him fired. In the last version of the dream, Jason was checking a gauge when the Gene Gun exploded, firing microscopic pellets coated with maple tree DNA into his body. The scene replayed in his dreams repeatedly, making him relive one of the worst days of his life.

In the recurring dream this time, Jason decided not to check the gauge, and filled the gun with the new upgraded weaponized plant DNA and pointed it at his boss, Miles Walsh. Miles threw his hands up and said, "Now wait just a second, Jason. We can talk about this. How about I give you that raise we were discussing the other day?"

In the dream, Jason continued to point the Gene Gun at Miles, and then back at a few of his other coworkers.

"Get back!" Jason shouted as he waved the Gene Gun around.

"Calm down, my friend. Put the gun down. Nobody has to get hurt here," said Miles.

As Jason held the Gene Gun on the Morabito boss, he realized that for the first couple of years that he worked at Morabito, he had very little interaction with the owners of the company, including Miles, his immediate supervisor. Miles knew who Jason was, but Miles was always very busy and only saw Jason in passing, during his weekly walk through the labs, making sure everyone was carrying out their assignments.

Over the last two years at the company, Jason had gotten involved in more projects and Miles had become more aware of the work his top genetic engineer was doing.

Miles took it upon himself to task Jason with some of the most secret, complex, and dangerous projects the company was working on. Jason's attention to detail and his ability to identify errors which saved the company from many potential accidents helped Jason to become Miles' favorite up-and-coming contingent employee. Jason would receive quarterly raises while most of the other employees only received annual raises.

Up until the accident, Miles had only praise for Jason's engineering work for the company. That all changed with the accident, and it was if none of Jason's prior good work had ever occurred. Suddenly, to Miles, Jason was just another fuckup, someone he never wanted to see or hear about ever again. Jason wondered what Miles would think now when he found out that Jason had stolen some of the most top secret and deadly plants that Morabito had in its facility.

Jason tossed and turned in his troubled sleep as he dreamt in greener vision. The shift in his bed caused the lab to disappear as a leaf fell onto his face. He must have returned to the forest, thought Jason as his eyes opened up wide. It was only when he looked around his bedroom, he instead found himself awake in the woods.

Was this part of the dream, or was he awake and hallucinating from the psilocybin? He couldn't tell. Could he have been sleepwalking and ended up here? Either way, he realized he was no longer in his bed. He brushed the leaf from his face and stood up.

Nodding to the tree, he started walking through the forest until he came to a yellow minivan. He opened the rear doors and looked inside. In the rear of the van were boxes of plants, each one containing a different species of carnivorous plant, and each one genetically altered with a variety of extremely aggressive vines, poisonous ivies, thorny briars, and deadly nightshade.

"How did these get here?" Jason asked himself. *This is insane*, he thought. I can't leave the van here. Someone might see it.

Jason got inside and found the keys were in the ignition. As Jason drove the van down the tree-covered street, he passed a sign that said Morrison Street. There was Morrison Street on the outskirts of Evanston so he wasn't far from home. This was a more affluent suburb.

As he moved on down the street, the GPS began to flash. A voice came from somewhere. "You are about to arrive at your destination." Jason looked at the GPS in the dashboard of the van. It said that his destination was 175 feet ahead on the right.

"Who's destination? I don't remember plugging in a destination on this GPS," thought Jason.

Jason stopped in front of a ranch house which had sprinklers going off all over the front lawn. He could sense the joy of the grass as it soaked up life-giving water.

He got out of the van and ran over to the grass being sprayed by the sprinklers. Then he took off his shoes and stepped onto the wet grass with his bare feet. It felt amazing underneath his feet.

Jason looked at the house and saw movement inside one of the windows. "What am I doing here?"

Just then, the front door opened and an elderly woman in a bathrobe stepped out.

"You from the plant store?" she asked Jason.

"Plant store?" asked Jason, who then noticed the writing on the side of the van. It read: "The Botanical Garden of Exotic Plants."

"I guess I am," said Jason. "Can I just ask, what did you order?"

"One of them fly catchers. You know, one of them bug eating plants."

"A carnivorous plant," said Jason. "I'll be right back."

Jason went over to the rear of the van and opened the double doors. He looked inside and saw that it was filled with a variety of carnivorous plants as well as other DNA-enhanced plants from Morabito. He climbed in and picked out a large plant wrapped in plastic and carried it over to the front door of the home, where the woman was holding the door open.

"Hurry it up will ya. We're letting in more flies," said the woman, who looked at the large plant Jason was carrying. "Although, I got a feeling this fella is gonna gobble them up for me, aren't you, big guy?"

She reached out and tried to pet the plant as Jason carried it inside.

"Just put it over there, behind the recliner," said the woman.

Jason carried the strange-looking plant into the living room.

"Venus Carnivorous," said Jason.

"Isn't it beautiful?" smiled the woman. "I'm gonna call her Venus, for short."

Jason put it down as the woman reached out to touch it.

"I wouldn't do that," warned Jason. "The one time I've seen these bad boys in action, it was not a pretty sight, I must say."

The large leaf began to open slightly as the woman pulled her hand away.

"Oh my gosh. That is magnificent."

"Has she eaten yet?" asked the woman.

"I'm not sure," Jason said smiling.

The plant glowed bright florescent green as Jason stroked the fly-trap's top leaf to calm it down.

"What does it eat?" asked the woman.

"Pretty much anything," said Jason. "Except for plants, that is."

"You said you've seen it in action," said the lady as she stared at the plant, mesmerized in amazement. She had never seen anything like it.

Jason had worked with the Venus Carnivorous, or better known as the Venus Fly Trap, a couple of times in the past at Morabito. He recalled the last time they were tasked to inject it with the Gene Gun, when one of his fellow co-workers, Keith, was nearly eaten alive. The plant was a combination Venus Carnivorous combined with a fast-growing vine that required constant feeding. Keith had gotten too close to one of the pincher leaves when it latched on to one of his legs. Suddenly two other leaves wrapped around his arms and began to lift him up to an even larger leaf that had developed at the top.

Jason and two other engineers had to use axes to chop off the leaves before Keith became the plant's breakfast.

It was one of the most terrifying things that Jason had ever witnessed. Keith was one of Jason's closest acquaintances at Morabito. He could not believe that the plant tried to eat him, and to eat him whole. That was the last time the company did any more research using the Venus Carnivorous.

"Ah, yeah, I have. So, my advice. Don't get too close. And if you have any pets, you may want to keep them away from it as well."

"It doesn't look big enough to hurt no animal," said the woman.

"Right now, it isn't. But these things can grow big real fast," said Jason.

"I've got a cat," said the woman. "A big old tabby. He'll be okay, won't he?"

"For now, but like I said, as the plant grows, its leaves get bigger. I'd put it somewhere the cat can't get close to it."

Jason did not know who this woman was, but it seemed that the plants had guided him there in this van. It was like they were using Jason as their own vessel.

He wondered what she had done to aggravate them.

"You know, Ma'am, I didn't get your name," said Jason.

"I'm Mrs. Jacobs," said the woman. "You might have heard of my son. Ethan Jacobs? He makes them electric cars."

"Got it," said Jason. "Does your son visit you often?"

"I wish. But he's supposed to come by this weekend, if he doesn't cancel. He's always canceling, you know."

"Okay, well you take care."

"How about watering? Does it need any water?"

Jason put his hands in the soil around the base. "Seems moist enough. These things usually don't require much watering or much care of anything for that matter. They're self-sufficient. Probably get enough fluids from the insects they eat."

"That's good," said the woman. "I'm not much good with plants. Always forgetting to water them and ending up tossing out their dead carcasses."

"Good luck with this one," said Jason.

He climbed back into the van and drove away and as he did, the van disappeared from the old woman and her street, and Jason found himself back in the forest of tall trees, old trees, and wise trees.

Jason was now moving through the high branches where he could hear the aching creaking painful sound of living wood bending against the wind. The world's oldest living creatures were mad. A communication was made and passed down through the trunks, into the roots, along the grass, throughout the secret world of plants. They were all in agreement that they had had enough of the destruction that humans were causing the planet and the plant world and they must be stopped once and for all.

A few days later, at the house where Jason left the carnivorous plant, the leaves of grass on the front lawn bent in the breeze that seemed to carry an extra sensory communication in through the screens of the open window. It was as if this would be a homebase for communication for the plants to send and receive messages.

The carnivorous houseplant began to vibrate, then opened its pincher leaf. A large orange and white tabby cat entered the living room and saw the plant, its sticky leaf dripping and beckoning. The cat hissed and raised its back when the plant reached out.

Curious at why the plant was moving, the cat moved closer. Maybe a small animal or even a mouse was hiding behind the leaf, making it move. From where it stood, the cat couldn't see inside the leaf's opening.

It edged a little closer, curious to know what was inside and making the plant quiver. Perhaps it was the mouse that the cat had been chasing for weeks?

As the cat got within a few inches, it sniffed the air, and then the plant opened wide, and a third leaf, glistening with a sticky substance, emerged like a tongue and snapped out until it stuck to the cat's fur.

The cat tried to pull away but could not. It pawed at the leaf, as it began to wrap itself around the cat's body. The tabby hissed and screeched as loud as it could. Then the carnivorous flytrap picked up the screeching feline, now wrapped like a blanket and glued to the sticky substance on the surface of the leaf.

The traumatized cat tried to break free but the more it struggled the tighter the leaf wrapped around its body. The leaf with the sticky glue-like substance carried the still struggling cat in between two other leaves, as they closed around the squirming animal. The cat continued to whimper as the leaves closed over it.

Outside, a pickup truck pulled up and Jason jumped out. He ran to the rear of the house where the woman had placed the Venus flytrap. Through the large plate glass window, Jason could see two of the giant leaves had wrapped themselves around something about the size of a small animal. Jason slid open the glass door and rushed to the plant where he gripped the two leaves and pried them apart. Inside he found the large sticky leaf wrapped around the squirming feline inside. Jason pulled the sticky leaf open and removed the cat now covered with glue from the carnivorous plant.

As soon as the cat hit the floor, he scrambled from the room just as the woman entered.

"Oh, it's you," she said when she saw Jason. "I thought it was my son, Ethan. He's supposed to arrive any minute."

Jason picked up the large carnivorous plant and started walking toward the glass door.

"What are you doing?"

"I'm sorry ma'am, I just don't think it's wise to have one of these in a house that has pets. I'll make sure you get a refund."

With that, Jason carried the plant out to his truck, put it in the back and drove off just as taxi was pulling up. A young man climbed out and the taxi pulled away.

"Hi Mom, I'm home," shouted Ethan Jacobs.

Chapter 15

Robert Flint was suiting up to go snorkeling in the kelp forest in the Pacific Ocean off the coast of San Diego with his mistress, Chelsea Sandler, just as the waves were getting stronger. "Are you sure this is a good idea?" asked Chelsea.

"This is what we trained for, baby!" said Robert, as he put on his high-tech scuba gear.

Flint was the Chairman and CEO of GD Oil and Gas Company, one of the top gasoline distributors in the United States. A few years prior, his company was in a media firestorm when one of their ships transporting oil leaked into the Pacific Ocean, causing several years' worth of damage of catastrophic levels. Now, ironically, the GD Chairman was out snorkeling and scuba diving only a couple hundred miles away from where the incident took place. The company faced a large fine and had to sign all sorts of promissory notes that they would never let it happen again.

"Once we get under the water, you won't even notice the waves on the surface," he said, as he adjusted the straps holding the oxygen tank on Chelsea's back. "Take my hand. We're going to jump in together."

Once in the water, Robert helped Chelsea with her mouthpiece and then guided her below the surface and into the dense forest of kelp that grew along the California coast. They swam down through the tree-like underwater forest that formed giant kelp canopies over the ocean floor.

Chelsea's long legs allowed her to kick past Flint, who tried to grab a foot as she slipped by.

Flint began to kick harder to catch up as they swam lower and lower around the larger kelp trees, some of which grew to almost two hundred feet tall.

As they got closer to the bottom of the ocean, the trees gave way to fields of kelp stretching out as far as they could see. It was not too deep, maybe three hundred feet. But it was still lower than the two had ever dived before. They thought they were good enough divers to do it alone and without supervision from a professional.

Robert gave a thumbs up to Chelsea as they looked around at all the wonderous and beautiful formations of underwater plant life and coral reefs that lined the bottom of the ocean along with some of the strangest looking fish nature had to offer.

Chelsea mouthed the words, "This is amazing."

Robert nodded his head in agreement.

After a while, Chelsea began to swim away to search for more oceanic discoveries. Robert followed her as she swam into a tunnel and then quickly exited, followed by a giant eel.

Robert laughed and was about to follow her when his scuba suit got caught on a sharp underwater plant. It looked like a porcupine with sharp spikes sticking out in all directions. One of the spikes had torn his wet suit, and while he was trying to get a better look at the tear, he backed into another strange plant, where, unbeknownst to Robert, one of the longer spikes had pierced a hole in his oxygen tank.

Moments later, air bubbles began pouring from the tiny hole in the tank. As air poured out, water poured in where the oxygen used to be, eventually filling the tank.

Suddenly, Robert knew something was wrong. He was no longer able to suck in air from his mouthpiece. Instead, his mouth filled with water.

Robert realized he would have to hold his breath until he got back up to the surface. As he began kicking in that direction, he tried to wave down Chelsea who had continued to swim away.

It was then that Robert realized he was probably not going to be able to make it all the way up to the ocean's surface before he ran out of oxygen. Unfortunately, he could not get Chelsea's attention, since he figured they could share her oxygen tank, passing her mouthpiece back and forth, until they both reached the surface. Alternatively, he tried to kick faster while also trying to unstrap the oxygen tank that was now filled with water and holding him back.

As he struggled with the straps, he found himself in a kelp field. With his lungs about to burst, he tried once again to kick upward toward the surface, but as he did, his legs became entangled in the long leaves of kelp, which had somehow wrapped around both his feet and ankles.

Robert looked down and realized he was trapped. He tried to wave again to get Chelsea's attention, but she continued swimming around the coral reef, oblivious to Robert's gestures. Unable to hold his breath any longer, Robert Flint opened his mouth and drank water into his lungs. He stopped struggling to fight off the seaweed and kelp. Instead, he spit out the mouthpiece and mouthed one last word: "Fuck!" as bubbles left his breath.

Within seconds, his mouth dropped open and Robert stared out at the ocean floor through his now lifeless eyes.

The kelp field seemed to close in on his body which stood transfixed between two large kelp plants that now bound him.

When Chelsea finally swam back to him, he was lifeless. She screamed into the scuba tank and cried while she tried to pull Robert out of the kelp field, but she couldn't pull him loose. Finally, giving up, she began swimming toward the surface leaving Robert's unresponsive body behind.

By the time Chelsea was able to get aboard their yacht and radio for help, she had drifted nearly half a mile from where they had been scuba diving. The Coast Guard initiated a search for Robert's body, but he was never found, lost forever at sea.

Chapter 16

Agent Carter Wiseman was sitting in his office reviewing the latest reports on plant-related deaths when he received word about a CEO who had been scuba diving off the coast of California when he became entangled in a forest of seaweed and kelp and drowned.

Other plant-related deaths included a logging supervisor electrocuted by a downed powerline caused by a large tree that had become uprooted during a freak wind and rainstorm, and the president of a company that used fracking who apparently ate some deadly nightshade that had made its way into his kale salad.

Agent Wiseman tossed the latest reports aside and turned on the television. He surfed through channels until he got to the Environmental Network where he found Professor Julie Green being interviewed about the strange patterns of migrating trees. She said, "It appears certain forms of plants seem to be getting more aggressive."

After Carter's meeting with Dr. Green, he was still digesting what she had told him about how plants can communicate, not only with each other but with humans.

He especially was intrigued to learn that plants responded to emotion and music and that plant life had gone through an evolutionary process like animal life, which meant there could be a more intelligent form of plant life among today's greenery, although this was still just a theory. Plus, she had pointed out how plants have something most humans only wish they had, ESP. She had learned this during many different peer-reviewed experiments that she conducted at her university with some of the brightest botanists in the field.

Wiseman searched around his desk until he found Julie's card and decided that she must be back from that conference in Kyoto. He waited until she was finished with her television interview and gave her a call.

The phone rang as he sat patiently waiting for her to answer. It rang a few more times until he heard, "Hello?"

"You're back from your conference," he said. "I just saw you on TV."

"You did?"

"Migrating trees getting more aggressive?"

"Oh yeah. That was taped last week."

"Dr. Green, I need to see you again."

"What happened?" Professor Green asked.

"Since we met, there have been three more plant-related deaths," said Carter. "So far, they seem more like accidents than actual homicides. There's no evidence any humans were involved. But I want to explore what you said about plants getting help from humans, as well as getting more aggressive, and what that might look like."

"Sure," said Julie. "We've identified a few known environmental terrorist groups."

"For research purposes, have you made contact with any yourself, by chance?"

"Not really. They keep to themselves, and so far, none have ever been accused of murder or of harming anyone. They usually do stupid stuff to get attention, like throw soup on priceless paintings which fortunately till now have had a glass cover providing protection. Nuisance stuff mostly.".

"I'd still like your help, if that's okay."

"Of course. Meet me in my office tomorrow after three," Julie said. "My classes will be over by then, and we can get to work."

The next day, Agent Wiseman showed up at Julie's classroom fifteen minutes early, just as she was wrapping up her last lecture. The students were mesmerized by a large screen showing a dense forest. Unlike the lecture she gave in Kyoto, her students actually paid attention to every word their beloved professor said. She always scored high on her student's evaluations at the end of every semester. The pay was not that great for professors in her field, but she was not in it for the money. She taught for the sheer love of science and being able to earn enough that she could conduct her original research during the summer months that she had off from teaching.

"What we have here is a typical forest, anywhere in North America," said Julie in her loud professorial voice.

"Looks peaceful, right? And it is, on the surface. But just under the soil, and under the surface, something else is going on. Something sinister. This is where fungi live, and fungi are made up of tiny threads called *mycelium*. Fungi is nature's version of the internet. They connect the roots of different plants and trees. What this connection provides among other things is a way for the plants to communicate. It was in the nineteenth century when German biologist and botanist Albert Bernard Frank discovered a symbiotic relationship between fungi and the roots of plants."

Her students looked on in amazement as different slides of various mushrooms and plants captivated the class.

"Today we know that approximately ninety percent of all land-based plants are connected by networks of these fungi threads," she continued. "Since the 1960s, we've known that fungi aid in plant growth. Since then, scientists have learned that they also help plants locate water and provide certain nutrients through mycelia strands around their roots. The fungal networks protect the plants from infection too, by providing protective compounds, stored in the roots, which are triggered if the plant is attacked. This phenomenon, called 'priming,' makes the immune system of the plant far more effective. In return, plants feed their fungi carbohydrates on a consistent basis.

"In 1983, two studies proved that poplars and sugar maple trees warn each other about worrisome insects. This is truly fascinating. When one tree becomes infested, it warns others who begin producing anti-insect chemicals, to

130

protect against an attack. These signals are sent through the air. Now, I want you to all think about what you learned today. That's all for today. Tomorrow we'll talk about a monster plant that terrorized a town in upstate New York. Make sure you're here on time tomorrow, and yes, I'm looking at you, Winston."

"Yes, ma'am," said Winston. "I won't be late again tomorrow, Professor Green. I promise."

Agent Wiseman made his way to the front of the lecture hall as the dozens of students filed out through the rear exits of the classroom. He finally reached Julie just as she was closing her backpack.

"A monster plant, you say?" asked Agent Carter Wiseman.

"According to the Associated Press, it makes the largest Venus Fly Trap look like a houseplant," said Julie.

"Sounds like fake news to me."

"You tell me," she said, pulling out a large photo to present to the detective. "Its flowers are as large as an umbrella, and its sap not only causes burning blisters that leave scars that last years, but it also causes blindness and, according to the Department of Environmental Conservation, it's spreading across upstate New York as we speak."

"Jesus, they have a name for it?"

"The Giant Hogweed," said Julia as she smiled. "Not a very original, or sweet, name but it gets the point across. It's an invasive species, which means it came from somewhere else, and the Environmental Protection Agency is trying to locate fresh outbreaks so they can send in crews to, pardon the pun, nip it in the bud."

"When you say it came from somewhere else, what do you mean exactly?"

"Just that. It's not an indigenous plant. Someone or something brought it there," Julie said.

"So, what are they doing about it?" asked Carter.

"The EPA set up a hotline so anyone who sees the plant can report it. They want to get the word out before too many people mistake it for a friendly flower and touch it."

"One touch? And then what?"

"Within fifteen minutes, you'll have a serious inflammation of the skin," Julie explained. "It's the sap. It contains something called *photosensitizing furanocoumarins*. It basically prevents the skin from protecting itself from sunlight, and the result is a very bad sunburn. If you put water on it, it gets even worse."

"That's unfortunate! So, how do you get rid of it?" he asked.

"You have to cut it off at the root, and then dump a heap of herbicide around where it was growing so it doesn't come back," Julie replied.

"And this is growing in upstate New York right now?"

"Oh, it's growing in at least eight states. New York is just the latest. Last week around thirty of these towering plants were seen in Virginia," she explained.

"Thanks for mentioning that. It reminds me that I brought that list of companies with me," said Carter. "I was hoping maybe we could go through it to try to figure out where the plants will strike next."

He pulled out the list of companies and the write-ups on each one. It was the same list Jason and Calvin, the CEO of CostSMART, had in their possession before Calvin met his deplorable fate in the forest.

"According to the report that accompanied this list, these companies conduct billions of dollars' worth of business all around the world," said Carter. "It covers the plants and whoever is helping them feel that they should not be allowed to continue their acts against the environment, deforestation or otherwise. Unfortunately for us, they also employ hundreds of thousands of people around the world. We can't protect all of them."

Carter put down the list. "What do you think?"

"I think I need a drink," said Julie.

"Hey, listen. I was going to wait until the case was over to ask you this. But I figure…screw it. We only live once, right?"

"What are you trying to say?"

"So, I was going to say, would you maybe let me buy you that drink?"

"Only if you let me buy you one, too."

"Maybe we can get something to eat as well."

"Let's have those drinks and see what happens, okay?"

"Sounds like a plan. You know, behind this suit tie, I'm really kind of a fun guy," said Carter.

"Okay?"

"Fun-guy, get it? Like how the plants communicate? With fungi?"

Julie rolled her eyes before letting out a slight laugh and said, "Okay, but you have to promise me something."

"Anything."

"Don't give up your day job. You know I used to appreciate the occasional science pun, but I think you've cured me," said Julie, laughing to herself.

Chapter 17

Jason awoke to the ringing of his iPhone alarm. Crawling out of bed, he reached the source of the sound and touched the screen on his phone. The ringing stopped as Jason rubbed his eyes to see the digital time on the phone's screen, 5:45 A.M.

Jason unplugged his mobile and let himself fall backwards into his bed. He immediately deleted the auto-saved 5:45 A.M. wake up alarm which he had set by habit. "Don't need that anymore," he said aloud, realizing that he no longer needed to get up so early at least for the next five months. But he was awake now so he might as well get up.

Shuffling to the kitchen to get some coffee, he realized he forgot to set up the coffee maker the night before. He looked for a silver can for coffee beans and found it empty. He returned to his bedroom to get dressed.

As he walked through the front door of his apartment building lobby, he tried to remember where the nearest Starbucks was located. There were three Starbucks in different directions away from where he lived, but he could not remember which one was closest. Since he moved in three years ago, he had taken the same route from his apartment to Morabito every day that he worked there. For those three years, he would get in his truck and head east to the outskirts of Evanston, near the shore of Lake Michigan, where it got so cold in winter that waves would freeze before having a chance to crash onto the rocky beach.

Today, he stepped outside, took a deep breath of air, and turned left instead of right in search of that much-needed first cup of coffee.

As he strolled along the tree-lined street, he sensed something was going on all around him. Jason looked up at the maple and elm trees whose branches covered the sidewalk and part of the street. A morning breeze rustled through the leaves making them appear as if they were dancing. A hissing sound surrounded him as he wandered along. It sounded like the trees were whispering. He stopped to look around to make sure someone was not behind him, and saw that he was alone on the sidewalk. Jason felt his phone vibrate in his pocket. He took it out and saw that it was his friend, Bowde.

"What's goin' on?"

"Jason, my man. You got a second?"

Jason looked around at all the green that he could see in the neighborhood. "Yeah, dude. I'm all ears. Ain't got nothing but time these days."

"Well. It's Miles. He's got us working on another one of those Frankenplants. And guess what? We had another accident. Happened yesterday. But you know

Morabito. This shit will just get swept under the rug, just like everything else," said Bowde.

"How bad was it?" asked Jason as he continued to walk down the street toward the corner where he hoped to find one of the Starbucks.

"Bad. Wasn't the Gene Gun this time. The tank exploded. It's Tony. We lost Tony," Bowde said.

"No. How could something like that happen? What were you working on?"

"Miles had us working in the new lab. We were trying to create one of these new Alpha Tacca Chantrieri, you know, the Black Bat Flower or the Devil Flower. We were tasked with dosing one with rose DNA and the shit just went completely sideways, man."

"Rose DNA? What were they expecting to create?" asked Jason.

"A sweet-smelling killing machine, if you ask me," said Bowde. "The tank containing the rose DNA somehow leaked into the vacuum-sealed container holding the Devil Flower and sparked a fire."

"Don't tell me Tony burned up."

"It wasn't the fire that killed him. It was the smoke that he inhaled and then something crazy happened that no one can figure out. Seems the Devil Flower had some sort of strange side effect reaction, and it started growing. As it grew, it made this piercing screeching noise and wrapped its petals around Tony's neck. Tony was dead just thirty seconds later. We couldn't save him. The damn thing instantly grew ten feet tall. Nearly filled the lab. We still haven't killed the damn thing. We had to wrestle it into a secure contamination room so it couldn't kill anyone else. But damn, Tony was a good man," said Bowde.

"What the hell were they thinking?" asked Jason as he put his phone to his side for a second and looked up toward the green sky.

Jason continued, "Who the fuck thought combining Black Bat and Devil flowers was a good idea? And then to add Rose. I'm surprised the thorns didn't kill him. They probably would have if the petals hadn't smothered him first. This is one mean motherfucker of a plant."

"So, who ordered it?" Jason asked.

"Who do you think?"

"Miles?"

"Yup. He put a rush on it, too, so ten-to-one this was a military order, right?"

"Wouldn't be the first plant we'd weaponized," said Jason. "When's the funeral?"

"There's gonna be an autopsy, so probably not for a few days or even a week or so. Whenever it is there's gonna be a closed casket after what that Devil Flower did to Tony's face."

"What did it do?"

"Some kind of excretion on the petals caused his face to blow up into one giant pus blister. You wouldn't recognize him. It must have been a shock to his family when they identified him."

"Guess I got off lucky. Wonder how Morabito is going to explain this one to his family or to the police. A guy died so they just can't cover it up like they did with me."

"They're calling it another industrial accident caused by equipment malfunction."

"I can't believe Morabito is still up to this shit. What's Miles thinking? He's gone too far. Somebody's gotta stop him," said Jason.

"I know, man. I've had just about enough. This place isn't what it used to be. Management has gone to shit. Miles is out of his damned rocker. I think I'm at the point where I gotta start looking for another job," said Bowde.

"Look. I've been thinking about what I told you the other night when we took those mushrooms. You know, about helping the plants, but I still haven't figured out the right way to do it. I guess, what I'm asking is, are you still willing to help me?"

"Hell yes," said Bowde. "Especially after what happened to Tony."

"Good. When's your next day off?"

"Not till the weekend."

"So let's get together then and work out a plan. I feel the plants are really getting restless. I can't walk by a tree without feeling guilty that I haven't done anything yet."

"Well, try to hold off until the weekend," said Bowde. "Have you even picked out a target yet?"

"No."

"Or what you even plan on doing?" asked Bowde.

"Not that either. Whatever we come up with, I think we should try it out on Morabito first. I mean, they're involved in all those companies on the list I showed you."

"Then that's what we should do."

"You'd tell me if this was crazy, right?" asked Jason.

"I already did that my friend," said Bowde. "It's the craziest damn thing I ever heard. But I've known you for a long time and if you say you can communicate with plants and trees or whatever, then I believe you. You don't have any more of them mushrooms, do you?"

"Actually, I do," said Jason. "The mushrooms make it easier for me to communicate with the plant world."

"Okay then. Just because they didn't work that way for me, doesn't matter. If you can still do it, we should be good. But what if you run out of mushrooms?"

"I'll have to go back to that Botanica and get some more," said Jason. "Right now, I simply must get a cup of coffee. So, let's talk later, okay."

"Later," said Bowde, and he hung up as Jason continued his search for the elusive Starbucks.

Jason walked a few more blocks but didn't see a Starbucks. Then across the street he spotted a corner store that he knew sold coffee by the cup. He crossed the street and went inside. Raul the clerk waved to Jason and Jason waved back.

"Hey Raul. How fresh is the coffee today?"

"I wouldn't chance it, Jason. I just got in and haven't had a chance to make a fresh pot."

"Sounds like a soda day then," said Jason as he walked down the aisle toward the back of the store where refrigerators lined the back wall.

"What'll it be today," Jason asked himself.

He stopped in front of one of the refrigerator doors, opened it, and took out an ice-cold bottle of root beer.

On the way back to the front of the store, Jason grabbed some BBQ chips and Ranch flavored sunflower seeds. "How much?"

"Looks like about $4.75," said Raul.

Jason handed him a five-dollar bill and said, "Keep the change, Raul."

Jason walked out of the corner store and back onto the street just as his iPhone rang again. He checked the number. It was Bowde. "Hey."

"Listen, Jason, I was just thinking and there's something I forgot to mention the other night when you first told me about what's going on, you know with the plants and stuff."

"What's that?"

"I just don't want you to take this the wrong way because I already said I'd help you."

"What are you saying, Bowde?"

"I just know it must have been tough after the layoff. I'm sure of it. But you're telling me you're taking mushrooms and talking to plants and shit. Sounds like you are going through an existential crisis. Well, at least that's what my therapist would tell me," Bowde said.

"Wait, you see a therapist?" asked Jason.

"Shit, yeah. My old lady says it makes me a more, quote, 'considerate partner,' unquote, or some shit."

"Wow, I would never expect you to go to a shrink."

"And I would never expect you to tell me you're talking to plants, but here we are," said Bowde.

"You just thought of this now? After telling me how you can't wait to help me?"

"I think I'm just really pissed about Tony," said Bowde.

"No, you might be on to something. You know, maybe I should give your therapist a call. Is he a good therapist?" asked Jason.

"It's a she. And yes, she is a great therapist."

"Hmm, I guess it couldn't hurt letting somebody help me figure out what's going on with me. Maybe it is all in my mind. I don't even know anymore."

"It can't hurt. I'll text you over Dr. Kurtzman's number. Dr. Mariah Kurtzman. She is the best you can find. If anyone can tell you why you're thinking and seeing in green, and talking to trees, it would be her," said Bowde.

Jason looked around when he thought he heard a group of people talking from the corner, but it appeared to be just a couple of bushes.

"Yeah, man. That sounds good," Jason responded. "And listen. Let me know when you find out when Tony's memorial service is, and I'll make sure to be there."

"Will do. And I'll send you that text now. Keep in touch, my friend. And don't go too crazy on me, now," said Bowde.

"I'll try my best," Jason replied.

Jason walked back towards his apartment as he got the text from Bowde with his therapist's phone number attached.

Chapter 18

On his journey back toward his apartment, Jason finished off his root beer soda and the bag of chips. As he walked along, he could feel what he called his "plant powers" traveling through his veins.

He found himself walking down 22nd Street and suddenly had an urge for vegetables. Up ahead, he saw Jose's Market, a convenience store he frequented only a few blocks from his apartment. He stepped inside, realizing he did need some groceries. Ever since the accident, he had been having a craving for vegetables. Mostly the green ones, but really anything that came from the earth.

Jason grabbed a basket and walked down the fresh produce aisle. He began filling the basket up with all sorts of greens like broccoli, Brussel sprouts, green beans, lettuce, and zucchini, as well as some root vegetables like beets, ginger and carrots. He picked up a cabbage and held it to his nose. He took a big whiff of the delicately pungent smell. "Ahh," Jason said to himself.

What was amazing, thought Jason, was that before the accident, he hardly ever ate a vegetable that was not fried like French fries or deep-friend onion rings. He used to hate broccoli and cringed at the thought of Brussel sprouts or cabbage.

He looked up at all the bins of green vegetables as they now appeared to be dancing and swaying back and forth. He put his basket down on the floor and rubbed his eyes. He then continued to fill his basket up with as many vegetables as it would hold. It was now almost too heavy to carry, so he used both hands to lift it up to the counter.

As Jose began ringing up his purchases, Jason gazed around the small store which seemed to carry anything anyone would ever need, from foot powder to pharmaceuticals. The major difference now was that every item in the store was a different shade of green. Everything that was already green was an even brighter green and stood out.

Jason never felt so close to the planet and nature. He had been to that convenience store hundreds of times, but this was his first extended visit to the produce section. He leaned closer to his basket of marvelous plants that he would consume later. He felt stronger with them close to him. He felt like they were murmuring quietly as Jose took them from his basket and stuffed them into paper bags. Jason wondered what they were talking about. Were they trying to talk to him? He could not make out what they were saying. It was just murmurs and whispers.

He felt happier and more motivated than ever. Jason felt stronger. Despite his chips and root beer breakfast, he now only wanted to eat healthy food, which was a first for him. He was used to eating fast food regularly. He did not have anyone to cook for, so he did not make it a big part of his life. Now, he just wanted to ingest healthy, non-processed food. The kind that came directly from the ground.

While Jose filled bag after bag with all the vegetables, Jason walked around the store some more. On the snacks aisle, he noticed a man in his mid-thirties in a black hoodie and red baseball cap on. He had his hands in both of his pockets. Jason thought he looked suspicious but then so did a lot of people in that neighborhood. He decided not to say anything and continued walking around the store. He passed by another man who was picking out a bouquet of roses. Jason gave him a nod as he walked by. The guy nodded back, and so did the roses he was holding. *What the hell?* Jason thought to himself.

He went to the cooler and picked out a few different kinds of water bottles. He usually only drank soda but lately he was craving water like he was a plant himself. He grabbed six bottles and put them into the basket. He took out one more bottle from the cooler and opened it right there before chugging it down.

"Hey, you need to pay for that first," said Jose from behind the counter.

"Of course, I'm going to pay for it. I'm just thirsty," Jason replied.

"All right. You're fine, Jason. Just busting your chops."

Jason laughed and took another sip from the water bottle. He grabbed a few boxes of instant noodles and headed to the cash register. Jose added them to what he had already rung up as the man with the bouquet of roses got in line behind Jason.

"Gotta eats your greens, huh?" said the man with the roses, nodding at all the bags of vegetables.

"You sure do," Jason responded.

Jason began to sense something when the man in the hoodie and baseball cap started powerwalking towards the front of the store. He was heading right toward Jose when he pulled out a black pistol from his pocket and pointed it right at Jose, the store owner.

"Don't fucking move. I just want all the money in the cash register. Don't make this difficult. Just throw all the cash you have in this bag!" the hooded man said as he handed Jose a plastic bag.

"Okay, okay, just be cool," Jose said as he slowly opened the cash drawer in the register.

Jason stood back a little bit and assessed the situation as it unfolded in front of him. He looked around as the redwood DNA inside him gave him a new awareness. He just needed to tap into it. From somewhere deep inside his mind, new information appeared. *Bullets cannot kill me. What, am I suddenly superman? More like super plant. Plants get shot, but they just grow back whatever got shot. If I don't get shot in the head, I should be okay. Why not the head? Rejuvenating brain cells could be a little iffy. Good to know. How do I even know any of this? It's the plant in you, baby. Get used to it.*

Jason suddenly felt worried for Jose, as he did not know how crazy this man with the gun really was.

Jose reached into the cash register and began to empty out all the twenty- and ten-dollar bills.

The hooded man looked around and said, "Nobody fucking move! This will all be over soon!"

Jason looked down at his bags of veggies as they were all leaning toward the other man in line holding the flowers. It was as if they were pointed towards the roses in the man's hand. That's when Jason made his decision. He took a step forward and everything felt like it turned into slow motion as he reached for the man's bouquet of roses.

With no plan in mind, he grabbed two roses from the bouquet. He put one in each hand and lunged toward the man the with gun. The man turned around and pointed the gun at Jason. Jason whipped the rose in his right hand as it wrapped around the man's gun. Jason pulled tight, flinging the gun out of the man's hand, sending it flying across the store.

"You fucking dumb fuck!" said the man in the hoodie as he punched Jason so hard, he flew back and slammed up against the soda fountain. The impact caused the machine to pour orange soda on top of Jason's head.

"Now you're done," the robber said as he went to stomp Jason in the face.

Jason moved away at the last second. The robber's foot splashed into a puddle of orange soda.

As Jason rolled out of the way, he reached up and grabbed a bag of vegetables and used it to whack the criminal across the side of his head. As all the vegetables went flying, Jason managed to catch a cucumber in mid-air. Just as the man regained his balance and was ready to make another lunge at Jason, he plunged the cucumber into the man's right eye.

The robber screamed as he fell back. Jason then took another rose and wrapped it around the man's neck as the rose's thorns cut into the man's skin. The robber looked down at the thorns and was about to rise when Jason pushed him back down and said, "Don't move. If you move, those thorns are going to puncture the artery in your neck, and you'll bleed out before the EMT's can get here. Trust me on this. Rose thorns can be vicious."

The robber stared down at the rose stem with its thorns wrapped around his neck.

"I think I'll take my chances," said the robber as he lunged toward Jason.

"In that case," said Jason, as he picked up the wooden stool Jose had been sitting on behind the counter, and slammed it down on the man's head, knocking him unconscious as he slid to the floor.

The robber in the hoodie was lying still in front of the counter. He was out cold. Jose grabbed the phone and dialed 9-1-1 to call the police. A crowd had entered the grocery store and began to clap and cheer, praising Jason for stopping the robbery and assault.

"I hear sirens," said a girl near the doorway. "The police are on the way."

"Thank you so much," said Jose.

"You're welcome," Jason replied as he picked up his scattered groceries and put them in a new bag since his old bag was torn to shreds.

"Those are on the house today," Jose said.

"Thank you," said Jason before he threw two twenty-dollar bills on the counter. "But I'm going to politely decline. I'm just glad I could help," he said before he walked towards the front door of the store.

Jason added, "Be safe. Cops should be here soon."

Jason left the store and headed back towards his apartment, thinking, *Did I just do that?* He'd made sure to leave the scene before police arrived. He did not want to have to explain everything he was going through. They'd probably lock him up so the government could run experiments on him.

When he got back to his apartment, Jason grabbed his laptop and took a seat on the couch. He opened it up and pulled up the internet browser. He decided to do a quick search on Morabito in the online message board forums to try to find any links to how they were planning to use their new Frankenplants that were in production.

After a bit of tedious research for an hour or so, Jason came to a document posted by an anonymous user on a tech message board. It had some leaked prototypes for some super hybrid redwood Frankenplants that could grow ten times faster and much larger than any tree alive today. These would be modified with new products through CostSMART, and consumers would soon be able to buy some of their favorite brands in "mega-bulk" and save money in the long run. But this was all at the cost of a certain forest in Brazil that would wipe out several remote villages for the resources and materials needed to make the process cost-effective. Jason could not believe or even understand what he was reading, but the overall consensus on the internet was that Morabito would inflict irreversible damage on the environment for capital gains.

This was just the sort of thing the plant world had been warning against. Morabito had to be stopped at all costs.

Jason thought, *what if I could scare Miles and the company enough to make them back off on any Frankenplant production going forward?*

He stood up and started pacing. What if I send Miles a box of Indian Lotus with some Frankenplant DNA to his mansion? Jason wondered.

He scratched his chin as he looked at himself in the mirror. Jason's eyes glowed bright green.

He walked to the closet where he kept the stolen Frankenplants. They seemed to be sleeping when he opened the closet door. He could hear the exotic plants snoring, or at least that is what it sounded like. Even the deadliest plants in the world looked harmless when sleeping, thought Jason. He found it oddly pleasing and kind of cute. He wondered if plants dreamed and if they did, what did they dream about? Many ideas started to form in Jason's mind about what he could do with this army of deadly flora.

Chapter 19

The day after Jason stopped the robbery in the grocery store, he had decided to sleep in until a dinging sound woke him up. What was making that sound? It was not his phone. Not the alarm. The dinging continued until he got out of bed and followed the sound to the door to his apartment. The doorbell? It had not rung in so long that Jason had forgotten what it sounded like. He looked through the peep hole.

A young boy stood in the hallway. He looked to be anywhere between twelve and fourteen, but kids seemed to grow so much faster these days so he could be younger.

Jason quickly pulled on a pair of sweatpants that were hanging on a hook near the door. He removed the inside chain lock and opened the door. "Can I help you?"

"Are you Jason Woods?" the boy asked.

Now that he was standing face to face with the boy Jason realized he was kind of tall to be twelve, maybe fifteen.

"Yes, I am. And who are you if you don't mind me asking?" said Jason as he scratched his head.

"I know this is hard to believe but, well, I believe that I'm your son."

"You must have me confused with some other Jason Woods. I don't have a son. I've never been married. I've never even been engaged."

"My mother told me she never married you."

Jason felt a wave of tension flow through his body.

"Who, ah who is your mother?"

"Was. She was Sally Johnson. She just died."

Jason felt his heart racing and he suddenly felt faint and as if he was about to pass out. He grabbed onto the door handle to keep himself from falling.

"Sally's dead?"

"Yes. She told me to look you up before she passed. She had cancer that spread to her brain," said the young man.

The boy stepped inside to help Jason get his balance.

"I'm okay," said Jason. "Sally Johnson. I knew a Sally Johnson in high school, but she moved away. Are you sure you don't have me confused with someone else?"

"Nope," said the boy as he pulled out a photo.

"That's my senior photo," said Jason. "From when I was in high school."

"My Mom kept it," said the boy. "I guess for a time like this."

"I don't understand," said Jason. "I never…I mean, Wait. Your mother was Sally Johnson?"

"That's right."

"And she told you I was your father. I don't understand. She wasn't pregnant when she left, was she?"

"That I couldn't tell you since I wasn't born yet," said the boy. "She said you were sweethearts in high school."

"Sally Johnson? You're kidding. Did she tell you that she dumped me? She just disappeared. We were supposed to go to the prom but when I went to pick her up, she was gone. Her whole family was gone. I remember driving up to their house and saw a 'For Sale' sign on the lawn. No one seemed to know where your mother and her family went or why."

"I guess you could say I'm the answer to that question," said the boy.

"You're telling me that my high school sweetheart, the one that got away, Sally Johnson, was pregnant her senior year? Pregnant by me and that her parents decided to move because of that?"

"That's what she told me. They even moved to another state to avoid any embarrassment. Tennessee. They also wanted to get their daughter away from you because they considered you a bad influence on her. You did get her pregnant, after all."

"Why didn't she tell me?"

"She wanted to, but she says her parents wouldn't let her. Originally, they were going to have Sally give me up for adoption. But when I was born, she wouldn't do it. She said she instantly fell in love with me and could not imagine being separated from me. So, her parents gave in and let her keep her newborn son if she didn't get in touch with you or tell you that you had a son. She went along with their demands because she didn't want to upset her parents, my grandparents, and she also did not think you'd even want to raise a child with her at such a young age. Toward the end, when she told me all this for the first time, she said that you were the one that got away. But she had to force herself to forget about you as time went on and she married someone else a few years later. My stepfather. Although I always thought of him as my father, till recently."

"When did your mother die?" Jason asked as he brought the boy inside and they sat on the couch.

"She died of cancer earlier this year and my grandma and grandpa took care of me after that."

"What about Sally's husband, your father?"

"The marriage didn't last very long, and we lost touch after a few years. But my mother didn't tell me about you till the very end. That's when she gave me your high school picture."

"Do your grandparents know you're here? They must be worried about you."

"I doubt it. I'm sort of the black sheep of the family. I never got along with my grandparents, so they were happy to see me go."

Jason took a deep breath and then he said, "Would you be okay with me giving you a quick DNA test just to check out your story?"

"I would expect you to say that. Of course. Sure. I would ask someone who claimed to be my son the same thing if our positions were reversed. You say you're going to give me the test?"

"I've been working with DNA for years, so yeah, I think I can do a simple DNA test right here in the kitchens. It may not be as extensive as sending it to a lab, but I'll be able to tell right away if we're related."

"Sounds good to me," said Sal.

"You seem very mature for twelve."

"I'm fifteen. I haven't had my growth spurt yet. My Mom reassured me that I should get taller."

Jason's face turned sadder when he thought about Sally and all those lost years they could have spent together. She was the love of his life, and he never really got over her.

"Wow. I'm so sorry to hear about your mother. I always wondered what happened to Sally. I couldn't believe she would just leave me like that. She broke my heart. So, that's why she moved away? Because she got pregnant? That is making so much sense. I couldn't understand how she could just leave me like that. I really felt that she loved me as well. Now, she's gone. I can't believe she passed away. I'm so sorry to hear that."

"Yeah. She was a really good Mother," said the boy.

Jason felt himself choking up with emotion as the magnitude of what had happened started to sink in. Sally, the love of his life, was dead. And they had a child together. A boy who is now fifteen years old.

"I'm a father," said Jason. "Oh, man. You couldn't have picked a worse time to reunite with your dad, kid. I hate to tell you. My life is a big old mess right now, I must say. I lost my job two weeks ago, for starters. But anyway, enough about me. What's your name?"

"Salvatore, but I go by Sal. You know, after my Mom."

"Sal. I'm Jason, or you could call me Dad, I guess, although that's gonna get hard to get used to."

"For me too," said Sal. "How about I call you Jason for now, and we'll see if it turns into Dad. Sound fair?"

"Sounds fair to me," said Jason.

The two stood up, and Jason opened his arms as Sal came in for a somewhat awkward hug. You might say it was the type of hug that a father would give his fifteen-year-old son after meeting him for the first time. They both managed to smile uncomfortable smiles afterward.

Sal looked around Jason's apartment and frowned.

"What's the matter?"

"I thought you would have a larger place to live."

"Sorry about that. I guess you grew up in a house, right."

"Yeah, my mom lived with her parents after her divorce, and I always had my own room. I don't suppose you have a second bedroom?"

"Sorry kid. But the sofa pulls out so you can sleep there at least for now."

"Besides losing your job, why is this a bad time for you?"

"Now you better sit down, because I have to fill you in on what you just walked in on."

"Is there somebody else living here?" Sal asked as he looking around.

"No, just me, and now you, I guess. But I've been.... How can I put this? I'm not sure where to start. First off, as I told you, I just lost my job."

"What did you do?"

"I'm a bioengineer specializing in genetics."

"Okay, what does a bioengineer do?"

"They do lots of things, but my specialty was gene splicing and creating new life forms."

"No shit. How'd you lose your job?"

"There was an accident in the lab, and they blamed me for it," said Jason. "But that's not all that's going on."

"What else?"

"I'm sort of getting involved in something that you may find hard to understand. In fact, when I tell you what it is, you're going to think I'm crazy."

"Hey, I'm getting into crazy shit all the time. How bad can it be?" said Sal, as he took a seat on the only sofa in the room.

Jason sat down in his recliner and tried to begin to explain what happened to him in the accident, his body absorbed an abnormal amount of plant DNA and how he began communicating with the plant world, and, since the accident, what he had been doing to help the plant world save the planet or at least life as we know it. He also told him about the Botanica store and how he had been taking magic mushrooms to help ease him into his effects from the plant DNA.

After about ten minutes of trying to get his son to comprehend, Sal just stared at him and then he said, "You sure this isn't just some kind of midlife crisis thing? I mean, that's what it sounds like to me."

"You may be right, but everything I told you really happened so you can call it a midlife crisis or whatever, but that doesn't really change much. You're here and you should know what I've gotten myself into. My best friend, Bowde, doesn't even believe me either. So don't worry if you don't believe it. You just must understand one thing. I believe it. And I'm the one it's happening to."

Jason went over to his closet, opened it up, and pulled out one of the Gene Guns. "This is just one of the many tools I used at my old job."

"How come you still have it?" asked Sal.

"Because I broke into the lab and stole it," said Jason. "I also stole a bunch of other stuff including some exotic plants that can be used as weapons."

Jason suddenly realized he was confessing to his fifteen-year-old son that he just learned he had that he had stolen from his previous employer.

"I'm not used to this parenting stuff so let's follow the maxim, 'Do what I say, not what I do,' so don't ever steal. Stealing is bad."

He handed Sal one of the Gene Guns. His son could not believe what he was looking at. "This is sick," said Sal.

"That Gene Gun right there with just one shot of DNA can turn any ordinary plant into what they call a Frankenplant," Jason explained.

"Frankenplant. You mean like Frankenstein, the monster?"

"They can be monsters, or they can be food, or wood for building, you name it. Weapons even."

This immediately gave Sal a few new ideas.

"That's really cool, Jason. Show me more," said Sal as he pointed the Gene Gun out the window and made the noise, "pew-pew."

Jason reached down and took the Gene Gun away from his son, and put it away. "It's not a toy."

"Sorry."

"Well, if you really are my son like you're saying you are, then I guess you can stay here for a little while we sort all of this out. I probably need to speak to your grandparents. Even though you didn't get along with them, I'm sure they want to know you are okay. And they're still your legal guardians so I need to get permission for you to stay here with me. You're still a minor."

"Pshh. They probably don't even realize I'm gone," said Sal as he opened up his backpack and pulled out a bag of beef jerky.

"You hungry, Pops?" said the boy as he handed him some of the teriyaki flavored jerky.

"What's this?" asked Jason.

"Jerky. Don't tell me you've never had jerky before."

"Actually, I do. It's just not part of my regular diet."

"Guess you're not on the road much. Ever since Mom died, I've been pretty much taking care of myself. We had caregivers for Mom in the last few months and they'd make enough food for me and Mom. Since she died, besides going to school, I've mostly been trying to decide if I should come to see you or not. I practically lived on this stuff for the last few months. It's just dried beef. Try it."

Jason took a bite and began to chew. And chew, and chew.

"Not that easy to eat, is it? I prefer the jerky rolls. They're easier on the teeth."

"That's part of its charm. It lasts longer than a burger that you can wolf down in a couple of bites. Jerky takes a while to chew before you can swallow it."

"I'm afraid it's not for me," said Jason. "But why don't we grab a real breakfast. My treat."

"Can I unpack first?" asked Sal.

"Sure. Make yourself at home. And like I said, you can use the sofa for a bed/ I'll need your grandparents' phone number and also the name of your school. I'll need to call them and figure out the procedure to transfer you to a school near here. You don't want to lose the year."

Sal went into his backpack again. This time, he pulled out a Z-Gear 4000, the newest next-generation gaming system. Then he took out a couple of wires and plugs that went with it and a couple of controllers. "You play?" he asked.

"Man, that looks neat. I haven't played video games in years," said Jason.

"Well, then. I guess today is the day," said Sal as he walked over to the high-definition flat screen television mounted to the wall. "You mind if I hook this up so we can play when we get back from breakfast?"

"Be my guest."

Sal smiled and brought the gaming console over and set it underneath the television. He took the HDMI cord and plugged one side into the Z-Gear 4000, and the other side into the back of the television. Then he plugged another cable into the back of the console and the other side into one of the outlets on the wall. He plugged the controllers into the console to let them charge up as the game booted up.

The HD TV turned on. Sal went to the side of the TV and pressed the input button a few times until the correct screen showed just as the Z-Gear logo displayed on the screen.

"You know. I'm not all that hungry," said Sal. "Could we play something first and then go eat?"

"Sure," said Jason. "What game are we going to play?" asked Jason as he looked at the superb graphics of the images on the main menu. An array of different games came up.

"Whatever you like," said Sal. "I got dozens to choose from."

"You pick," said Jason as he became overwhelmed with choices.

"Okay, fine. How about *Monster Valley*?" asked Jason.

"What the hell is that?"

"It's this dope first person shooter where you go around in an open-world apocalyptic setting killing these creatures and shit. It's pretty fun," said Sal as he scrolled through the list of games on the home screen before finding *Monster Valley*. He selected the game as it began to load up. It took a few moments. Sal handed Jason one of the controllers that were charging.

After the game finished loading, Sal selected the multiplayer option, logged in the second controller, and pushed the Start Game button. Jason looked down at the controller, which had way more buttons than any controller he remembered playing on when he was growing up.

"This might take some getting used to," said Jason as he tried to learn the buttons. He had no idea what the Y button meant, or the A button, or the square or the triangle. He was beyond confused. But he looked over at Sal and realized he was experiencing a special moment with his son. A son he did not know he had until now. All of this while still seeing green. It was all a lot for him to take in. But for now, he was enjoying the moment. He had no clue what tomorrow would bring.

The game loaded up and two screens were split down the center of the TV. Sal's screen was on top as he was player one, and Jason's player two screen was on the bottom.

The screen then read: "Round One," and the match began.

"Follow me, Pops," said Sal as he moved his character in first person from the team's base and started to make his way towards the center of the map.

"I'm not even sure how to do that. Where are you?" said Jason.

He could not figure out how to move his avatar and ended up pointing down, staring at the ground.

"Well, first. You're going to need to use both joysticks. The one on the left controls your legs and how you walk, the joystick on the right will control what you are looking at, so think of that as your eyes. Then, the left trigger button is to aim your weapon, and the right trigger will fire. The Y button throws grenades. And the B button is used to melee your opponent. Knock them down if they get too close to you," Sal explained.

Sal then saw an opponent from across the way hiding behind a barrel. He took out his plasma sniper rifle and aimed at the player from the other team. "Watch this," he said as he pressed the right trigger, shooting the enemy player directly in the head from across the map.

"Damn, nice shot," said Jason as he tried to figure out the controls. It took him a little bit of time, but he started to get the hang of it. He was not great at shooting at first, but he managed to learn how to walk around. The graphics were much clearer than any game Jason had remembered playing, considering it had been quite a long time since he gamed himself.

"This is insane," Jason said as he pressed random buttons hoping they would do something. "The graphics are so crisp."

"I know, and to think the Z-Gear 5000 is coming out this Christmas. Now, that one is going to be even cooler."

The two played Monster Valley on the couch for a couple hours until Jason said he was starving and ordered some breakfast from Uber Eats. They both got pancakes and sausages from IHOP and kept on playing.

After playing *Monster Valley* for a while, Sal ended up showing Jason a couple of other games, a racing game and another fighting game. The two stopped playing briefly when their pancakes arrived and then they continued through the afternoon and into the night, playing different video games, drinking soda, eating popcorn, and eventually watching a couple of movies.

Jason decided to show Sal one of his favorite movies of all time, *Madman Mark*. It was a slasher flick from the late 80s that he and his father watched when Jason was growing up. At first, Sal thought it was a bit cheesy, but the two found it to be rather amusing by the time they were halfway through it. They both fell asleep on the couch after a long night of games and movies.

Chapter 20

The next day, Jason stared into his bathroom mirror. His beard had grown even fuller and the world reflecting back at him was various shades of green. It was like looking at a black and white television picture, only it was green and white instead of black and white. The shades of green were getting to him, as he began to forget what the other colors even looked like. It was like when the color control on his television was off and everything turned a different shade of the same color, in this case green. His anxiety and stress were increasing daily, and now he had a long-lost son that he was trying to welcome into his life. Everything was happening so fast. He remembered what Bowde had said about seeing a therapist. Maybe it wasn't such a bad idea.

Jason went into his bedroom and found the email with her number. He called Dr. Kurtzman and set up a consultation appointment. Maybe she could help him figure out what was going on with him. Perhaps this was all just in his head.

She called him back after he left her a voicemail, and told him to come in the following day at 2 P.M.

In the meantime, Jason figured he would continue to prepare the package that he would mail to Miles, his former boss. Jason saw that Sal was playing on his phone in Jason's living room so he went into his bedroom.

Jason did not show him all the exotic plants he took from the lab. He did not want to scare his son away so soon after meeting him; he did not know what Sal would think of him if he knew what he was planning for his old boss. But to Jason, his plans seemed justified and not the least bit sinister. He felt as if he had been drafted to serve as a warrior fighting to save and preserve life as we know it. Unfortunately, he did not think most people would understand where he was coming from. Especially if he was the only one that was able to communicate with the world of plants and understand their concerns. He would be branded as insane, another crazy environmental terrorist that needed to be put down.

Sal was unaware that Jason had seen him as he texted one of his friends, Pete. He wanted to tell him all about his new dad. But before he could, Pete texted him back asking Sal if he could sell him a small bag of marijuana, which Sal had been dealing to his friends at the high school.

He texted him back saying he was out of that business and that he was not even in town anymore, and to try to see if Dylan could help him out. Dylan had taken over from Sal as their small circle of friends' main supplier. Sal had only sold enough so he could smoke for free. He always kept his supply under a pound, so it never looked like he was dealing.

Pete's text made Sal want to smoke right now, so he went into Jason's bathroom and began to roll a tiny joint. After he was done twisting it up, Sal exited the bathroom and walked into the living room.

On his way out onto the porch of the apartment, Sal saw one of the Gene Guns his father had taken from Morabito. This gave Sal an idea. *If my dad is telling the truth, maybe this gun can make my weed ten times stronger. Then, I wouldn't have to buy weed as often, and I'd make much more money if I wanted to sell weed again.*

Meanwhile, in the main bedroom, Jason was trying to tame an excited and feisty Corpse Flower. He was trying to put together a contraption that would shoot Ivy DNA from the smallest of the Gene Guns into the Corpse Flower, which is native to Indonesia, but Morabito had imported for use in a Department of Defense order involving the weaponization of certain plants. Jason's plan was to create a way for the plant infused with fast-growing ivy DNA to grow in Miles' house once he opened his mail. The mere opening of the package would fire the DNA capsule into the Corpse Flower and would scare the life out of Miles, and hopefully encourage him to rethink the company's goals of turning plants into military grade weapons, moving forward.

Jason looked at the plant and looked back at one of the Gene Guns and said aloud, "I got it." He began to drill the side of a metal box in which he would place the plant with a device connected to the Gene Gun on top.

This is going to work, Jason said to himself as he continued to drill.

While Jason prepared his package, Sal walked out onto the porch and pulled his lighter out of his pocket. He took the joint out from behind his ear and lit the twisted end. Taking a deep drag, his lungs filled with smoke. He looked inside through the glass to make sure Jason was not watching him. He did not know how Jason would feel about him smoking marijuana. It was just one joint, and he needed it to calm his nerves.

He did not know what to expect when he met his father for the first time. It turned out it was nothing he could have prepared for. On the one hand, he seemed normal enough, but, on the other hand, this story about the plants and how he can talk to them. *That was just batshit crazy.*

Sal was beginning to think that maybe he was making a mistake tracking down his father and would come up with some excuse to leave.

After a few tokes he began to zone out and he felt less anxious. Sal decided he would give it a couple of days and then decide. What's the rush, right?

Chapter 21

The next day, on his way to the consultation with Dr. Kurtzman Jason pulled up to a post office a few miles from his apartment, grabbed a giftwrapped package from the back seat and went inside. He bought a priority mailbox and put the package inside and stuck a label with Miles' address on the side of the box. After attesting that the box did not contain anything liquid, fragile, or explosive, Jason paid the $16.75 and received a receipt with a tracking code that he could access to find out when the package arrived.

Back in his car, Jason looked at the receipt and said out loud to himself, "Work your magic, my friends. Let's see what Miles has to say about this."

Jason took a backpack from his passenger seat and threw it in the back seat. The backpack contained a few top-secret materials, Frankenplant DNA vials, and two Gene Guns. He put it on the back seat and even buckled it up with the seatbelt to make sure it didn't fly around the back as he drove.

An hour later, Jason found himself in a waiting room on the other side of town. He was a few minutes early for his appointment, so he walked around the waiting room and played with the smiling ferns that decorated the windowsill. As he stroked the flat leaves, the palms of his hands began to sweat, leaving the leaves damp. *What am I so worried about?* Jason wondered as he wiped the sweat off on his jeans and took a sip from his bottle of water. Wet hands, dry throat. A typical anxiety reaction, but to what?

Finally, a woman in her late 50s entered the waiting room and said, "Hello, Jason. My name is Dr. Kurtzman. Why don't you follow me into my office."

Jason nodded, and said, "Wanna bet you've never had a patient like me before? You're in for a real treat."

He followed her behind the reception desk and into the back area.

"I'm sure you're quite special," said the doctor.

"Until the last few weeks, I would say 'hell no.' But since that time. Maybe, maybe I am, actually."

The two walked through the hall and arrived at room 4. Dr. Kurtzman opened the door and Jason walked in behind her.

"Take a seat," she said.

Jason nodded and sat down on the single sofa in the corner of the room.

"My friend Howard Bowde spoke very highly of you," said Jason.

"Mr. Bowde is a sweet man," Dr. Kurtzman replied.

"Not sure if sweet is the word I would use for Bowde, but sure, let's go with that."

They both laughed.

'So, Jason. I really want to learn about your life, and your backstory. But first, I wanted to ask…well…what brings you into my office today?"

"You're just going to tell me I'm crazy."

"Try me."

"Okay. Well, it all started a couple of weeks ago, when I still working for my former employer, Morabito. There was an accident. One thing led to another, and well, I was ultimately fired," Jason explained.

"Oh dear. I'm sorry to hear that. That has got to have been quite tough on you."

"Yeah, well. I kinda grew to hate the place anyway. So, that isn't the reason I'm here, per se. But it was what happened after the accident. At first, I wasn't in any pain or nothing. But over time, I've had these crazy side effects that are pretty unbelievable."

"I'm listening," said the doctor as she picked up her notepad. Jason scratched his head as he tried to gather his thoughts.

"Well. The accident involved this Gene Gun. It shoots microscopic pellets of plant DNA directly into another plant to make a hybrid plant. They use the process to create different kinds of genetically modified foods, mostly vegetables or sometimes wood products that have enhanced properties, such as being fire retardant. In this incident, we had been trying to make a hard wood grow faster and larger. The gun exploded because of some dumbass that didn't know how to properly prepare the gun that day. Some of the redwood and maple plant DNA we

173

were working with shot through my protective lab suit and into my body."

Jason stopped talking, suddenly.

"Go on," said Dr. Kurtzman.

"At the time, I didn't know it went inside me. At first, I didn't feel anything. Then a day or two later, I started to feel connected to the plant world and trees. I know it sounds crazy as hell. But it's true. Then, one thing led to another, and I met a strange woman at this Botanica shop who sold me these magic mushrooms, which I have been taking since that time to help me communicate better with the plant world. And well, it's been working. I have been pretty much communicating with plants ever since. I know it sounds nutty as shit. I told you it would."

He stopped to breathe deeply before taking a sip from his water bottle to ease his tension. He had no clue what the doctor was going to say.

"You probably think I'm crazy," Jason repeated.

Dr. Kurtzman continued to take notes even after Jason finished talking. She looked up and said, "You're wrong. I don't think you're crazy. I just think you are troubled. And who knows? Maybe you are communicating with these plants? Who am I to tell you what is real or what is not real? However, you did tell me you have been using recreational drugs. What was that, mushrooms, you say?"

"I wouldn't call it recreational, but yes, I have been taking psilocybin mushrooms and it has only made the messages clearer and the visions more vivid," said Jason.

"Have you considered the idea that this is all hallucinations in your mind stemming from the mushroom use?" asked the doctor. "Psilocybin is a powerful psychedelic. Some say it helps alleviate anxiety. It can also make you more anxious."

"I can attest to that. Sometimes my anxiety is off the charts. Other times it's non-existent," said Jason.

"How do you mean?"

"I recently stopped a robbery in a bodega near my apartment. Normally I would have done nothing especially since the guy had a gun. But I just didn't worry. In my mind, I was invincible. At least to a bullet. I thought that it was because of the plant DNA, making me feel like a plant in that if I got shot, I'd just grow back whatever the bullet blew away. But maybe it was the mushrooms."

"You realize the danger you're putting yourself in, then?" asked the therapist.

"But it can't all be a hallucination because I was communicating with plants *before* I took the mushrooms. They just make it easier to understand what the plants are trying to tell me. I have mostly been taking the mushrooms in smaller doses before I go to sleep. That is what the woman told me to do for the best results. And she was right. It's not like I'm just taking them and trying to fly or some shit. I wake up, and it's like my third eye has opened and gets greener and greener every day. Oh, and did I mention that I see in pretty much all green now. Every shade of green. Instead of black and white, it's black, white, and green. It is intense as hell," Jason explained.

175

"This is all a lot to take in," said Dr. Kurtzman. "Very interesting stuff."

"I don't know what to do. If I should try to stop the messages and cut off all communication. Or if I should lean in and help them out as much as I can."

"Help them out in what way?" she asked.

"They are fed up with humans who think they can control nature but continue doing the wrong things that will eventually lead to a massive extinction event, similar to the end of the dinosaurs."

"And what do they want you to do about it?"

"That's why I'm here. I'm not sure. I get the feeling they want me to help eliminate the problem."

"What does that mean?"

"Stop those responsible."

"You said eliminate?"

"I think they want me to kill them."

"You may not know this but as a licensed therapist, I have a duty to report anything I hear that could lead to the harm of others. Are you telling me that you plan on killing someone?"

"I just told you that I'm here because I'm conflicted about all this. I feel a strong connection to the world of plants and feel their concern over impending doom, but I also don't want to hurt let alone kill anyone. I need your help Doc. What do I do?"

Dr. Kurtzman stopped taking notes and looked up at her patient.

"Don't kill anyone. That would be my immediate advice," said Dr. Kurtzman. "But do you have to do anything? Is there a reason you need to do anything now?"

"They seem pretty upset," said Jason. "*They* being the plants, trees mostly."

"Trees?"

"It seems the trees are in charge," said Jason.

Dr. Kurtzman stood up. It was her cue that the session was about to end.

"I guess that means our session is over."

"I'm sorry, but I have another patient coming in," said Dr. Kurtzman.

"Damn, I didn't even get to tell you about Sal and Sally. I just learned I have a fifteen-year-old son and he's come to live with me. His mother Sally was an old girlfriend who died."

"I wish we had more time. But this was only supposed to be a quick consultation. However, I am going to want to see you more often. I think we should set up a session for two or even three times a week minimum. We need to monitor you and this situation closely. Decide if you would like me to prescribe a medication that could help you while you are going through this."

"I don't want to take any meds, but I'll come back again if you think you can help me."

"I do," she responded. "Come back and see me on Friday. We'll figure out different ways for you to cope with what you are feeling. In the meantime, don't take any action until we come up with something that's not going to lead to you hurting or killing anyone. How does that sound?"

"Sounds good, doc," said Jason.

He stood up from the sofa chair. "See ya on Friday," he said as he waved goodbye and walked out of the door.

Back at Jason's apartment, Sal was just getting started with the day's science experiments. He spent some time researching videos online on how to use the Gene Gun, and once he felt like he was ready, he filled the Gene Gun with one of the tanks containing a fast-growing plant DNA. He placed a nugget of cannabis on the table. Sal turned on the Gene Gun and let it heat up. After a couple of minutes, Sal picked up the Gene Gun and pointed it at the smokable dried plant. He pulled back on the trigger, sending a charge of air and plant DNA out and into the marijuana. He sat back and waited to see what would happen. "Well, that was cool as shit," said Sal. "Now let's see if it made a difference."

Sal waited a few moments as the clock on the wall ticked. Nothing seemed to happen right away.

He got up and went to use the bathroom. When he came back out, he noticed the nugget of cannabis on the table had grown to the size of a football. "No way," he said to himself as he ran over and picked it up. It felt way heavier, like maybe a half-pound. "This is insane," he said as he put it in his arms and held it like a baby.

"This thing is going to make me rich. Just wait until the homies get a load of this."

He took a big whiff of the plant and said, "Ahh."

"I wonder how big this thing is going to get," Sal said to himself as he placed the giant marijuana bud back on his dad's coffee table. "I wonder how it smokes." He ripped off a chunk of the bud from the corner and broke some of it up on the table. He was not sure when his father would be home, so he tried to make it fast. He pulled out a rolling paper and proceeded to twist up a joint from some of his new Frankenweed. Once he was done, he went on the porch to try it out. He lit the end of the joint with his lighter and took a puff. Sal immediately let out a big cough followed by many more coughs. "Shit, this stuff is strong."

He took a few more puffs before he could not take it anymore and put the rest of the joint out.

Sal stood on the porch and let the effects of the altered marijuana run through his system. It felt better than any weed he had ever smoked before. It hit him nearly immediately. Then, the weirdest thing happened. Sal began to start to see in slight shades of green, almost like his father. Perhaps smoking the altered marijuana plant produced similar effects to what his dad was getting after being injected with the plant DNA straight from the Gene Gun.

Just then, Sal began to rock back and forth as the effects came quicker and stronger. He grabbed the rail before he lost his step and was able to catch himself. He looked down to the ground from the third floor that his father's apartment was on. "Phew, that was a close one," said Sal as he quickly opened the porch door and went back inside. He went over and picked up the Gene Gun from the coffee table. "What the hell is my Dad planning to do with this thing?" he said as he held the gun up in the air.

Chapter 22

Jason was driving home from his therapy appointment when he got a call from Howard Bowde. He immediately picked it up.

"What's going on, man?" asked Jason as he put his phone on speaker and continued to drive. He came to a stop light and stopped the car. He looked at the traffic signal light and saw that all of them were a shade of green. Fortunately, he could tell the light was red because the red light was on top and that was the light that was brighter than the rest. The green light was on the bottom and when that brightened, he drove on through.

"Listen, Jason. They found out you took that shit from the lab. They just fired my ass after one of the security guards told management that I stopped by that one night. Apparently, all the cameras were shut off that night so they couldn't prove definitively that it was us. But I guess they somehow figured it out. Must have been on account of my key card. Anyway, I got fired this morning. And if I were you, I would get home fast and hide everything you took from Morabito. I'm sure they'll be coming to find you at any moment," said a panicked Bowde through the phone speaker.

Jason came to another stoplight which was also red and stopped his car. *How am I going to move everything I took,* he wondered.

"Damn. I guess it was only a matter of time," Jason replied as the light turned green. He pressed down on the gas pedal of his bright red 2016 Toyota Tacoma truck and began accelerating even faster towards his apartment a few miles away.

"Miles seemed really fucking pissed, man," said Bowde as he breathed heavier and heavier into the phone.

"I'm sure he is, just wait until he opens up his mail in a few days."

"Look, I don't know what you're up to, bro," said Bowde. "But whatever it is, stay safe. I was planning on leaving Morabito this year anyway, so I guess this was meant to happen. I just hope this wasn't for nothing. Whatever you are doing, Jay, good luck. Take care of yourself."

"I will. And you too. Keep in touch, Bowde. Thanks for looking out," said Jason.

"We'll talk soon," said Bowde.

"Later." Jason hung up the phone and sped his car up to seventy miles per hour to get home faster.

Jason arrived back at his apartment. He parked his car in his designated parking spot in the lot. He took the key out of the ignition, got out of the car, locked the doors, and ran through the front lobby of his apartment complex.

He ran up the stairs as fast as he could until he got to the third floor. He ran down the hallway to his apartment and put his key into the lock before opening the door. He swung the door wide open and yelled, "Sal!"

No one answered. Jason made his way into his apartment to notice that it was a mess. His furniture was all torn up. Files and papers were all over the floor. His kitchen was covered in broken dishes and glasses. Food from the refrigerator tossed on the floor.

What the hell happened here? he asked himself.

He continued to search through the apartment and shouted, "Sal!" one more time. He ran through the hallway and into his bedroom. He noticed his blanket and pillows were all ripped up with feathers still floating in the air.

"They must have just left," he said to himself. Jason walked over to the closet and flung it open. Just as he figured, everything was gone. "Damn," Jason said. He'd lost most of the sensitive materials he stole from his former place of work, except for the two Gene Guns, a box of the Frankenplant DNA vials, and three of the exotic plants he'd stashed in the back of his truck.

Jason texted Sal, "Hey, where are you?"

After he waited a few moments for a reply, he decided to call him. It went straight to voicemail. Jason then started packing a couple of duffle bags with some clothes, a few necessities, and some money he had hidden in a box in his cabinet that the people who broke in must have overlooked. "Thank god," Jason said as he put the box of money in one of the duffle bags.

He finished packing, looked around at the mess in his apartment before looking in the mirror on his wall. His eyes lit up bright green, like he was sensing something big was about to happen. He picked up the two duffle bags and made his way out the front door of his apartment.

When Jason got to his car, he pulled out his phone and dialed Bowde's number.

"What's up, Jay?"

"Listen, Bowde. I think Miles sent someone to my place. It was a disaster when I got home. Plus, they took the classified projects," said Jason in a panic.

He looked around in the parking lot of the apartment complex to make sure that the coast was clear, and nobody was following him.

Jason unlocked the trunk before throwing the two duffle bags in there next to the rest of the classified materials he had left. Then, he shut the trunk, put the key in the front door, opened it up and hopped in as fast as he could. "They ransacked the place."

"No shit, bro. I told you that they might be going over there," said Bowde. "Where are you now?"

"I'm just leaving my place."

"Anybody following you?"

"I don't think so, but I guess I can't be too sure," said Jason as he put the key into the ignition and placed the car into reverse before skidding out of the parking lot and onto the main road.

Jason's eyes became a bit blurred as he took off his glasses. They were dirty so he wiped them with his shirt so he could see a bit better.

"You gotta go somewhere and hide, dude," said Bowde. "Shit, they're probably gonna come after me thinking I took some shit too."

"I know man. I'm sorry I got you into all of this. Also, my son is gone. I'm not sure, but they might have taken my son. Would Miles stoop that low?" asked Jason.

"Wait a second. Back the fuck up. You have a kid?" Bowde asked in disbelief.

"Yeah, actually. I kinda forgot to tell you. He pretty much just showed up a few days ago on my doorstep. His name is Sal. He's actually a pretty cool kid. He's fifteen. Seems my high school girlfriend who suddenly up and left me was actually pregnant but she was forced to keep it a secret from me all these years. I really hope they didn't take him."

"Well, congrats on having a son. Why did he show up on your doorstep now?" Bowde asked.

"My girlfriend, his mother, died. Before she died, she told him about me and he decided to look me up rather than live with his grandparents."

"I see. And yeah, I hope he's okay too. I'm not sure if Miles would go that far. Then again, he seemed pretty damned pissed," said Bowde.

"Hmm. Yeah, I don't know," said Jason.

As he continued to drive down the road, he had no clue which direction to go in. As he drove down Parson

Street at fifty miles an hour, he was running through various red lights that he thought were green. Thankfully there were not many cops on that side of town that night. Then, the oddest thing happened to him. He could not figure out which way to go until he looked up and could see the trees on the side of the road began to lean to the right and pointed towards Rockland Way.

Jason followed the tree's directions and turned right onto Rockland Way.

The trees continued to lean, pointing Jason down the road and towards the highway. It was as if they were trying to guide him somewhere. He just wasn't really sure where. But he was trusting the process.

"Listen, man. You there? Jason?" said Bowde through the phone.

"Yeah, I'm here," he said.

Jason looked around at the trees pointing him in the right direction. Just then, a call came in on the other line. "Bowde, I'm getting a call. I gotta go. I'll catch up with you later."

"All right, dude. Stay safe," said Bowde.

"You too," said Jason before he clicked over to the other call and answered, "Hello?"

He looked down and saw that the caller ID read Chicago PD.

"Sal. What the hell is going on?"

"Dad!" Sal yelled through the speaker.

"Dad. Don't be mad but...I'm in jail. It's a long story, but I just need you to come and get me," said Sal.

Jason could hear a police officer in the background say, "Give me the phone."

"Mr. Woods," said the officer.

"Yes?" Jason replied.

"Mr. Woods, your son was arrested for possession of marijuana," the cop explained.

"Marijuana? Sal was caught with weed?" Jason came to a full stop once he realized the traffic light must have been red because all the other cars were not moving.

"Yes. But it's not that simple. Your son was caught with what may be the largest bud of cannabis of all time. The biggest one any of us have ever seen."

Jason then realized why he thought he was missing one of the Gene Guns the other day. He tried to think of what to say.

"I'm very sorry, Officer. I'm on my way right now to pick him up," Jason said as the light turned green and the car in front of him began to drive.

"What we are wondering is how in the world he was able to get the plant that big."

"I believe he may have used a plant-altering device I brought home that I use at my job. It's not his fault. I'll explain it all when I get there," said Jason.

Jason hung up the phone and turned onto a dark side street to take a short cut to Chestnut Road. He must have gone from zero to eighty miles an hour in just a few seconds. He made a sharp left turn, followed by another right. A few more miles later, and Jason pulled his car into the parking lot behind the police station.

He got out and ran up to the front doors of the police station. Once inside, he checked in and waited until they brought Sal forward.

Jason had to fill out a pile of paperwork and he had to promise Sal would appear in court since Illinois had become a no cash bail state. Instead, it now had a pretrial release system.

When the police officer escorted Sal to the front desk, Jason gave him a big hug.

"What in the world were you thinking?" he asked.

"I guess I wasn't," Sal answered. "Sorry I used your things without asking."

"We'll talk about that later," said Jason.

"Mr. Woods, Officer Josh Bradshaw," said the man.

Jason shook his hand and said, "I'm so sorry that Sal put you through this. I'm sure you guys have real criminals out there to catch."

"Yeah, sure. Drugs are bad. Don't do drugs. Of course. But what we wanted to know is how the hell he did it. You said it was with a device from your work?"

"Well yeah. I don't have it anymore," Jason said as he tried to keep a straight face knowing that he had two more stored in the back of his truck.

"How did he do it?" asked Officer Bradshaw.

"Well, long story short, Sal injected the marijuana with Frankenplant DNA making it grow exponentially bigger and faster. He should have known better than to experiment with it and drugs. That was just dumb," said Jason as he looked over at Sal. "But I'm sure he has learned his lesson and will make sure it never happens again, right, son?"

"Right, Dad," Sal said with bloodshot eyes. It appeared that the effects of the gigantic marijuana bud had not worn off Sal just yet. He looked at his father, wondering how disappointed he was with his newly acquainted son.

"All right, well we expect him in court a month from today, is that clear?" said the officer. "Seeing this is his first offence, and that he's only fifteen, he'll probably get probation."

"Yes, sir. We will be there," said Jason. "Right, son?"

"We will be there," Sal said in agreement.

"Okay, you two are free to go. But we're keeping the plant. The guys and I want to frame it on the wall. Maybe get it into the world records or something," Officer Bradshaw said before laughing.

"Knock yourselves out," said Jason.

They returned Sal's belongings, including his wallet and phone.

Jason and Sal left the front of the police station, got in the car and backed out of the parking lot.

"Where are we going?" asked Sal as he looked out the window. He was still seeing in faint green, as the effects of the Frankenweed were still in his system.

"I'm not too sure yet," Jason replied.

He drove up to the stop sign, stopped the car, before making a left onto 16th Street.

"Please don't be mad at me," said Sal.

"I'm not mad. I'm actually quite impressed. Looks like you've been messing with the Gene Gun, I see. I'm more disappointed in the fact that you used the Gene Gun without telling me first. You could have gotten really hurt."

"I'm sorry, Pops," said Sal.

"It's okay. Just don't do it again," said Jason.

He continued down the road, following the directions of the trees as they guided him through the night.

Jason got the idea to hop on the highway and head towards the next town over and get a hotel for the night. He had enough cash and he still had some money available through his debit card. He figured Morabito might cut off his severance because of the theft, if they had not already. He was also wondering when Miles was going to try to contact him.

He had an eerie feeling that they were being followed. But every time he looked back, no one was around.

Jason pulled onto the highway as it grew dark. Both Jason and Sal were seeing in dark shades of green in the night sky. The trees on the highway bent over to point

Jason in the direction that he was supposed to be heading, which was west.

He continued for miles down the highway until Jason saw an exit for a two-star motel which was all he could afford at the moment. He pulled off at Exit 29 and pulled into the motel parking lot.

Chapter 23

Jason parked his car in the remaining parking spot near the entrance to the Starlight Motel.

"What are we doing here?" asked Sal.

"I'm afraid we can't go back to my apartment," said Jason.

"Why not?"

"Let me check us in and I'll tell you once we get settled," said Jason. "You wait in the car."

Jason got out and went inside to a small reception area. No one was on duty, so he hit a round bell that was on the partition in front of the check-in desk.

An elderly man in a white T-shirt and suspenders holding up a pair of gray slacks that seemed about four sizes too large for his skinny frame, appeared from behind a curtain leading to another room.

"Can I help you?" he asked.

"I'd like a room for one night," said Jason.

"Just for you?"

"Me and my son, so two beds would be great if you have something like that."

"Thirty-five dollars," said the man. "Just sign the top card, your name, make of auto and license plate. Check out is at 11 A.M."

Jason gave the man two twenty-dollar bills, and the man just looked at the cash as if he had not seen any in a long time.

"Don't have any change on me," said the man.

"That's okay," said Jason. "You can give me the change when I check out."

"Won't have no change then neither."

"Oh well, then I guess it's forty dollars for the night then."

"You could put it on a credit card or a debit card like most folks."

"I like to use cash," said Jason.

"You some kind of criminal?"

"Why would you say that?"

"Far as I know only drug dealers and mobsters use cash. Everybody else uses a credit or debit card. Says you got nothing to hide."

"Not me. I just like paying with cash," said Jason.

"Just so you know. It raises a red flag."

"Thanks for the tip. Can I just get my key and go to my room? I'm tired."

Jason and Sal were staying in room B23, at the end of the second floor and next to the neon sign that read *Starlight Motel*. It was the dingiest motel that Jason stayed in. But it would have to do for the time being while he figured out their next move.

After they entered their room, Sal peeked through the curtains by the window to see if anybody had followed them. "Looks like the coast is clear, Dad."

"What?" said Jason as he paced back and forth next to the twin beds in the center of the room.

"It doesn't look like anyone was following us," said Sal.

"Right, good to hear. Why don't you watch TV or something. I must make a call."

Sal turned on the television while Jason went into the bathroom and called Bowde.

The phone kept ringing and then going to voicemail. Finally, after his fourth attempt, Bowde answered. "Yeah? What's up, Jay?"

"Hey, listen. Sal and I are staying at a motel, hiding out. I thought I'd just check in for any updates," said Jason. "How are you holding up?"

"Well. I'm all right, all things considered. Just filling out a couple of job applications online," said Bowde.

"Man. Again, I'm sorry."

"Don't even sweat it. After all the time I spent working at Morabito, my resume is a bit more beefed up and I am eligible for a much higher salary than I ever would have had if I stayed there. So, I guess, this really was both a gift and a curse you could say," Bowde explained as he typed away in the background.

"I don't know what to do, Howard. My son and I are literally on the run because I have no clue what the hell Miles is up to. He had my house torn apart and searched. He's probably going to try to have me locked up for all the stuff I took."

"Didn't you say they tore your place apart and took it all back?"

"They did, but I still have some stuff," said Jason. "Maybe I should just give it all back."

"Man, fuck Miles. Have any of the guys sent you this leaked document yet?" asked Bowde.

Jason's senses lit up even greener when he heard that. "Huh? What are you talking about?"

"Yeah, have Peter or Jim sent you anything? I just got an email a couple of hours ago."

"I have no idea what you're talking about."

"Okay, so listen. You were right all along. Miles is the piece of shit you always had the feeling he was," said Bowde. "You should check your email."

"I just did," said Jason. "I didn't get anything."

"I'm sure you will."

"Go on," said Jason, eager to find out what Bowde was trying to tell him. "What got leaked?"

"Well. The email was leaked by someone in management apparently. Jim got a hold of it first and forwarded it to me. Apparently, and this is all just hearsay, but I wouldn't doubt it. But apparently, Miles has signed a deal with Richard Adler."

"Richard Adler, hmm. Why does that name sound so familiar?" said Jason as he scratched his chin.

"He's the CEO of Evergreen Smart."

"Wait, Evergreen Smart? Evergreen Smart Phones? Like the billion-dollar smart phone company?" asked Jason.

"Yes, *that* Richard Adler. And the leaked document I got emailed to me went into full depth on the deal between Morabito and Evergreen Smart Phone. Apparently, we were going to lease our patent for the Frankenplants and use our Gene Guns to alter the lithium in the batteries that Evergreen Smart Phone uses to power their smart phones," Bowde tried to explain. "Look at me, saying we, like I still work there. Damn, we were there far too long."

"Wait a second. So, Miles is going to use the Frankenplant DNA process to help Evergreen Smart Phone make their lithium batteries stronger?"

"That would be one application."

"Maybe this is why the plants have been communicating with me," said Jason.

He suddenly started to get a headache, so he sat down on his twin bed. Thoughts were beginning to form in his head as the puzzle pieces were coming together.

"Yeah, umm, Jay. I'm not exactly sure why the plants are communicating with you. I'm not even sure if they really are. That sounds bonkers as shit, my friend. But I'm not one to judge," said Bowde before he let out a laugh. "But yeah, the email was weird. It looks like Evergreen

Smart is planning to do some demolition somewhere to get access to lithium from some sort of unknown location."

"Can you forward me that email, like right now," said Jason.

"Of course, sending it right now," said Howard. "Check your inbox."

Jason opened his email app on his phone to see that a new message came in. It was the leaked document. Jason opened it up.

"Bowde. Thank you for letting me know. I'm going to look into this. I'll talk to you in a bit. Stay safe," Jason said.

"Any time, my man. And you too, stay safe. Let me know if you need anything," Bowde said just before they both hung up.

Jason read the entire document. What Bowde told him was true. Miles was clearly setting up a big deal with one of the largest producers of smart phones in the country. He was going to use the Morabito patents and resources to enhance the lithium that Mango would need to power the next line of phones they were planning to release the following year. There was a section in the document about a forest demolition coming up that could cause damage to the area of the source. But the location was not disclosed, nor the time when the demolition was supposed to happen. Jason soaked up all this information like a sponge before he opened the door to their motel room.

"Hey, Sal. I gotta step outside for a second. Need some fresh air," said Jason.

"You want me to come?" asked Sal.

"Na, it's okay. Stay here. I'll be right back," said Jason. "Call if you need me. I won't go far."

He walked outside onto the deck and down the hall. Jason went down the stairs and walked past the cars in the parking lot and into the small section of trees behind the motel.

Jason found a maple tree in the wooded area and leaned up against it. He felt a connection as soon as he touched its bark. He could not stop wondering what he had to do next. He slid down the trunk to the ground and dug into the soft dirt until he found the mycelium network of fungi fibers.

As soon as his fingers touched the fibers, he felt a connection. It was like a mild electronic jolt as the tree began to send a message through Jason's hand.

I need to find out where this demolition was going to take place and to stop it, thought Jason.

He always had a feeling that Miles was up to something, and this was it. This would be the biggest deal Morabito had ever signed with another company, and the first of its kind. Once Evergreen Smart Phone was able to utilize the Frankenplant DNA with the lithium, they would make billions more, maybe even trillions, when all was said and done. The profit margin for the smart phone conglomerate was enormous but the market for lithium batteries to power electric vehicles could be even greater.

The push in the last few years for Americans to stop driving gasoline-powered cars and instead buy electric or even hybrid vehicles that ran completely or partially on lithium batteries had passed an inflection point. At least one major car manufacturer had already proclaimed it would no longer manufacture gasoline engines in favor of EVs to help bring down the cost of owning an electric vehicle. The other auto makers might not be far behind. And one state had already announced it was banning the sale of gasoline powered cars in just seven more years.

But the question was, what effect would this have on the planet? Would this be the chain reaction that it would need to begin the final destruction of the planet? For some reason, that was the feeling that the maple tree was giving Jason. That this was the moment he would have to do something to stop it from happening. If he could not get Miles to stop him from signing the deal, he would have to stop the demolition. But how would he do that? He had no clue where or when it would be. It could be across the world for all he knew. He had some more work and research to do. However, Jason knew that this was a big revelation in his mission that the plants had been sending him on. He was beginning to understand his purpose.

Jason pressed his forehead up against the maple tree. He felt so connected he did not want to leave it. But then, he remembered that Sal was still waiting in the motel room. He said goodbye to the maple tree and headed back to the room.

Chapter 24

Because of the deal he had negotiated with Evergreen Smart Industries, it only took the Board of Directors twenty minutes to approve the naming of Miles Walsh as the new President of Morabito Labs. This was what Miles had been aiming for all along. He had been climbing up the corporate ladder at Morabito ever since he joined the company as an intern fresh out of college twelve years before. To celebrate his promotion, he had bought a new, fully electric, four-door convertible Tesla and was just pulling it into his driveway when he noticed a package on the front doorstep.

Miles parked his Tesla in front of the three-car garage at his 10,000-square-foot brick McMansion off of Mulberry Street. He picked up the package and, using his remote-control key, unlocked the door. He carried the package inside and set it on a table just inside the doorway.

He attempted to see who had sent it, but the return address was too blurry to read. He picked up the package again and estimated it weighed about ten pounds. He shook it a couple of times as he walked into his kitchen and placed the package on the marble countertop.

Miles opened his refrigerator and took out an ice cold can of beer, flicking the sides to make sure no bubbles would make the can overflow with foam when he opened it.

"Ahh," he said to himself as he walked back over to the package. He retrieved a pair of scissors from the kitchen drawer and cut the tape on the package. Once he finished cutting it open, he tore the side of the package open. This caused the mechanism inside that Jason had configured to shoot the Frankenplant DNA into the Corpse Flower that was sitting inside the package. Miles could feel something move, so he threw the package on the ground.

"What the fuck is that?"

Whatever was inside the package appeared to be pushing against the sides.

Miles watched as the package tore open. Soon the cardboard box scattered in every direction and an Amorphophallus Titanium, also known as the Corpse Flower, popped out. The lime green, funny looking plant struggled to grow rapidly right in front of Miles. He could not believe what he was seeing.

The plant grew until it stood six feet tall in the middle of the kitchen. Miles was quite startled by the huge plant and hid behind the sink. He was not sure if it would attack him or not.

After Miles hid for two minutes, he looked back and saw that the plant had grown to be about ten feet tall, nearly touching the ceiling.

When he realized that it was not getting any larger, Miles tiptoed toward the Frankenplant sitting in the middle of his kitchen. It was quite an impressive sight. He just was not sure how he would get it out now that it was the size of a small tree. He still thought it could attack him, so he was cautious. He put his hand up against the green leaf. He touched it. Nothing happened. Sweat poured down his forehead until he realized someone must have been messing with him.

"Jason, that son-of-a-bitch," Miles muttered. "It had to be that shmuck."

Miles pulled out his phone and took several pictures of the first-ever Corpse Flower Frankenplant before looking for Jason's number in his contact list.

Jason was sitting on his bed inside the seedy motel room watching television while Sal sat on the other bed, playing mobile games on his smart phone. Jason felt his phone in his pocket begin to vibrate. He sensed that this call was not from a friend. He looked to see that the call was coming from a private number. It was probably just another telemarketer, one of the dozen or so that seemed to call him throughout the day. It appeared that whoever was calling was now leaving a message. He waited until the message light came on before he clicked on voicemail.

"Screening your calls I see," said the voice in the voicemail, "Well, I'll just keep calling until you pick up."

"Who the hell was that?" Jason asked himself.

He pressed the delete button, erasing the call from the voicemail call log.

No sooner did the call disappear, that his phone began vibrating again. It was the same number. Jason hit ignore. But the phone buzzed again.

"Ugh," said Jason as he pressed the button to answer the call.

"Hello?"

"Jason Woods. How have you been?" asked Miles.

"I should have known it was you."

"Very funny prank you pulled there, sending that god damned Corpse Flower and having that mini–Gene Gun shoot it just as I was opening it up, pretty fucking clever there, Woods," said his former boss.

"What the hell do you want from me, Miles?" asked Jason. "I know you guys broke into my house. You already took my job. What the hell else do you want?"

"I want to know where you are. Just so we can have a...chat," said Miles.

"Not a chance in hell Miles. You can go fuck yourself!" Jason exclaimed.

Sal looked over at his father, wondering who he was talking to.

"Whoa, calm down there, slugger. You don't need to get your panties in a bunch, I just want to talk. I was quite impressed with the contraption you made. I thought about it for a while and realized we need you back here at Morabito, man."

"Screw off. I know what you're trying to do, Miles. I'm not stupid, you know. I'm not falling for that crap," said Jason.

"Falling for what? I'm telling you, we really do want you back. I don't think I put things into proper consideration after the accident. It was my bad. I'm sorry we let you go. It was a major mistake on my part. And if I could take it back, I would. But all we can do is change the future. And we want you back at Morabito. What do you say?" Miles asked, sincerely.

Jason was not sure if his former employer was yanking his chain or not. Something inside of him was telling him not to trust him. He looked over to Sal, who shook his head and mouthed the words "Don't ask me," before going back to playing his game.

"I don't think so, man," said Jason. "After everything that's happened, I'm not sure if I can work with you guys ever again."

"Come on, Woods. After all we've been through. Come back to us, man. Morabito needs you. I never appreciated how great of a genetic engineer you really were until it was too late," said Miles. "You know they just made me President of the Lab. You know what that means? I can hire you full-time. No more of this contingent bullshit. You'll get a raise, plus full benefits. Even a pension if you work longer than ten years. Come on. I know now that you weren't responsible for what happened."

"I read about that Evergreen Smart Phone deal," said Jason.

"Isn't it something?" said Miles. "It'll put Morabito on a whole new level. I mean talk about growing into the future. You want to be a part of that, Jason."

"I don't think so."

"Smart phone, electric vehicles. One day lithium batteries will be providing energy for our homes, our hospitals. We'll make a fortune. You'll be a very rich man."

"See, that's the problem. I don't want to be rich. I just want enough to be comfortable. But people like you, there's never enough. I'm sorry, Miles. I can't work for a morally corrupt company, or man, who only thinks about how much money he or it can make."

Sal threw his phone down and started clapping in the background. "Go, Dad!"

"Okay, you listen here you little prick. I was trying to play nice, but nice time is over. You stole from us, you sonofabitch! You took our genetically modified plants as well as our intellectual property and DNA from the lab. Who the fuck do you think you are? Did you think I was just going to let you get away with it? You're going to spend the next twenty years in a federal penitentiary for what you did!" Miles yelled into the phone.

"Now you listen to me, Miles. I'm going to give you one chance to save your ass as well as Morabito Labs. If you call off the deal with Evergreen Smart and get them to stop this upcoming demolition I've been hearing about, I'll stop what I'm doing and forget all about this crap. I may even come back and work with you," Jason affirmed.

"What are you planning to do, Jason? Send me some more Frankenplants? Send me all you got. This deal is bigger than both of us. And how did you even find out about it anyway? We haven't announced it publicly."

"I saw the internal email."

"What did you do, hack our system? That's going to cost you another ten years."

"I don't think so, Miles."

"I actually thought you were smarter than this," said Miles. "What's your problem with us working with Mango Industries? This is just filling a need. It's what consumers want, affordable electric vehicles."

"Who says that's what they want?"

"Have you been living under a rock? Fossil fuels are dead or they soon will be. Nobody wants gas guzzlers anymore."

"Yeah, well I do. And I bet I'm not alone."

"You and the rest of the dinosaurs. You have to get with the program, Jason. The climate changers have won."

"I wouldn't be so sure," said Jason.

"No more drilling. That's what the President said. No more drilling. No more digging for coal. No more fracking for natural gas."

"There's only a couple of problems with your thinking, Miles."

"What's that?"

"China and India. Make that three. Russia. In fact, I would bet that most of the world still depends on fossil fuels, especially coal and gasoline fueled cars and trucks."

"That may be, but we're the USA. We're leading the world out of the dark ages," said Miles.

"No, we're not leading anyone anywhere. Europe has already tried depending on solar and wind and it doesn't work. France got smart and went nuclear, but China is just laughing at us."

"China is producing the batteries for our electric vehicles," countered Miles.

"I didn't say China wasn't profiting from our misguided policies," said Jason. "In fact, China will be the big winner here. While they continue building coal plants for their energy needs, they'll be making a fortune off us because they monopolize the market when it comes to lithium and cobalt, the minerals used in EV batteries."

"Not if this Evergreen Smart Phone deal goes through," said Miles. "We'll be mining our own lithium once that happens."

"How many forests are you going to have to destroy to get access to that lithium?"

"Sacrificing a few trees to save the planet sounds like a good decision to me," said Miles.

"That's the problem, Miles," said Jason. "You and most of the world think we're in danger of global warming because of carbon emissions, but you're wrong."

"Not according to most scientists."

"Consensus science isn't science. It's politics," answered Jason.

"What difference does it make? This deal has been in the works for too long to change anything now. And besides, it is going to take our company to the next level. A deal of this caliber, with a company as big as Evergreen Smart Phone, is going to put us on the map globally. Either get on the train or get run over, Jason. You gotta work with us or this is simply not going to go the way you want it to, pal," Miles explained.

"I'm not going to let you get away with it," warned Jason.

"Tell me where you are, and I promise nothing bad will happen. You'll have your old desk back by next week. In fact, this time, you are going to get your own office. With your name on the door and everything. And I'm promoting you to senior engineer for the company. You will oversee all of the Frankenplant projects going forward. I just gotta know we are on the same page."

"Same page? We're not even in the same book," said Jason as he hung up the phone.

He realized that Miles would probably try tracking him so he told Sal that he would be right back. He went outside the motel room door and down the stairs towards the woods. In the woods, Jason removed the SIM card, broke it in two, then smashed his phone on a rock before stomping on it. He threw it as far into the woods as he could. Then, he went back inside.

"Come on Sal. We're leaving."

"Already?"

"We need to find another place to stay. We also need a new set of wheels, and I need a new phone."

Chapter 25

Across several states in Boise, Idaho, Maurice Jenkins, the founder of Shinua International, was taking a stroll with his two children and wife in Sunrise Park down the street from their luxurious mansion. Maurice told one of his sons to go long for a pass as he cocked back the football he had been carrying. His son ran out into the path just before turning around and catching a bullet from Mr. Jenkins. "Good catch!" he exclaimed.

His son yelled back, "Your turn!"

Maurice started running as fast as he could. He must have gotten about thirty yards away before his son threw the football. As it soared in the sky, Maurice looked back, but as he did, the sun pierced his eyes. This blinded him for a moment as he tried to cover his eyes. But before he realized what he was doing, he tripped over a large rock in the middle of the trail. That caused Maurice to go flying, tumbling into a giant bush that was covered in White Snakeroot, one of the deadliest plants in the world. He was wearing shorts and a tank top, so a good deal of his body was exposed to the poisonous plant.

Maurice picked himself up and continued playing with his son until his skin began to itch like crazy. By the time he got home, his arms, shoulders, and legs were covered with huge blisters that not only itched but burned. His head was on fire and his wife took his temperature: 107 degrees. Standing over the sink, Maurice weaved from tremors and then seizures before he collapsed to the kitchen floor, unconscious.

His wife called 911 and ten minutes later, EMTs were performing emergency procedures to restart his heart. After a half hour of unsuccessful defibrillating, they called it. Maurice was pronounced dead of heart failure brought on by an extreme reaction to a highly toxic White Snakeroot plant.

News of the founder's death made it online and on the message boards before the end of the day. And while it wasn't the most talked about news story, people in the sustainability community were all talking about what was going on.

If he had not been busy packing up, one of those people could have been Jason, under the guise of an anonymous username he had chosen, GreenMachine550. For years, Jason had been communicating with different folks in the know on various anonymous message boards. He was constantly commenting on numerous threads about Frankenplants and other posts that even exposed his old employer, Morabito.

One person who was online at the time and who received an alert about any "plant related deaths" was FBI Special Agent Carter Wiseman.

The number of deaths Carter could connect to plants was now over half a dozen. He checked Google maps to see how far away Boise, Idaho was. Too far to drive. He checked the airlines. No direct flights. Even flying, it would take him an entire day to get there.

Agent Wiseman wondered how long he could continue investigating these plant-related deaths before he had to issue a report along with his assessment about why these were happening and what could be done to stop them. What really bothered him was the lack of evidence that any humans were involved, which ruled out eco-terrorists. He thought back to his conversations with Dr. Julie Green, the botanist and professor. Was there anything she had shared with Wiseman that might help explain these unusual plant-related deaths of high-level corporate executives?

Chapter 26

Jason and Sal finished packing and checked out of the motel. They drove Jason's car to a used car lot and bought a bright yellow Dodge Caravan.

"You couldn't have bought a less conspicuous vehicle?" asked Sal sarcastically, as they drove west on Interstate 80.

"It was the only thing I could afford," snapped Jason. "Besides, who would expect anyone who was trying to keep a low profile to be driving something like this?"

"Good point. Except people have been staring at us whenever they pass us."

"Okay. Look. I'm not thinking that clearly right now," admitted Jason.

He looked over at the teenager he had just recently met and said, "I can't stop thinking about what a weird time this is for you to come into my life."

"It's not like I had a say in it, know what I mean?"

"I'm really sorry about what happened to your mom."

"Yeah, well, I mean. I gotta admit, you're cooler than I thought you would be," said Sal.

"Ha. I guess I'll take that as a compliment. Listen, Sal, if you ever need to talk, I'm here for you," said Jason.

"I appreciate that, Dad."

"I really wish your Mom hadn't kept you away from me for all these years. I mean, I'm sure she had her reasons, but it would at least been nice to know I had a son out there. This is just such a shock. I never really thought I'd be a father. Crazy to think I could have been one all these years if only I knew you existed."

He looked over at Sal. "I guess what I'm trying to say is that I wish I could have been there for you. For her, too."

Sal started to get a bit teary eyed before he said, "Well, she's gone. So, you're stuck with me now. Get used to it. I loved her. I hated that she kept you from me and never let me know you were even alive. When I asked her once where my real father was, she said you had died. I didn't even think this would ever be a possibility. It wasn't until she was dying that she told me the truth. So, I don't care that you weren't there before, at least you're here now."

Jason began to get a bit sad as he looked over and said, "I'm not going anywhere."

Just then, he swerved the van around a large pothole, causing all the boxes of plants to fly around in the back of the van.

Jason took Exit 87 on Route 80 when he saw a road sign for a gas station. The van was nearly out of gas, and they were getting hungry. Jason pulled up next to one of the fuel tanks and put the car into park. The two of them got out and went inside.

He went up to the cashier and gave him some cash. "Forty on pump five."

"You got it," the clerk responded.

Sal was looking around the store, grabbing random munchies like chips, nuts, and beef jerky. He then headed to the cooler section and selected several energy drinks and cans of cola.

Jason also looked around for anything they needed, like an extra toothbrush and some toothpaste. Then he saw a burner phone for sale for thirty dollars. *This way no one will be able to track me through GPS,* he thought to himself. Little did he know that they could still track him if they were able to find out where he bought the phone. However, it was still a better idea than using a smart phone.

"You almost ready?" Jason asked as he brought the phone to the register.

Sal brought over all his drinks and snacks and placed them on the counter, too. The cashier rang everything up.

"Your total is seventy-five dollars and seventy-three cents," he said.

"Jeesh, how many snacks and drinks did you get?" Jason asked Sal.

"I'm a growing boy. What do you want from me?" he responded with a smirk.

Jason started to laugh. He reached into his pocket and pulled out four twenty-dollar bills and placed them on the counter as the clerk took it to make change. Jason was trying to avoid using his credit card, so nobody could track their whereabouts based on their purchases. He had a feeling that Miles would do whatever it took to find him.

Jason and Sal left the store and returned to the van. Jason placed the nozzle into the gas tank and filled it until it stopped at forty dollars, giving the van roughly three quarters of a tank of gas. The two got back into the van and hit the road.

Jason drove what felt like hours, not knowing where to go, but the trees along the sides of the highway continued to guide him.

The faint sense of green grew stronger and stronger in the air and atmosphere. The dark night glowed bright green as the yellow minivan soared down the highway.

Sal fell asleep as Jason kept driving. After about an hour or so, something in the woods to the right of Jason caught his eye. It looked as if a tree was lifting its branch like a hand telling him to stop. He was not sure if he was seeing correctly so he rubbed his eyes and tried to get a better look. He rolled down the passenger window and decided that yes, the tree was telling him to stop the car. Although he had zero clue as to why, he listened. Jason pulled over.

His son stayed asleep as Jason got out of the van and slowly walked toward the woods that lined the road. He felt like the trees were calling to him. He hopped over a barricade and wandered into the dark forest.

As he got closer, he could hear the trees murmuring back and forth with one another. He could barely make out anything they were saying, but he knew they were communicating. At first, he thought they were just talking to each other. But as he got closer, he felt like they were trying to tell him something. Something important.

Jason came face-to-face with one large oak tree in particular that seemed to want his attention. This tree hovered over the rest that surrounded it. Jason got closer and put his hands up against it before pressing his right ear onto the dark brown bark. He listened closely as he could almost feel the vibration of communication, which felt like a heart beating inside the monstrous beautiful oak. He knew that the tree had no heart, but at that moment he was not sure. It felt like a thump, thump, thump. Every four seconds. Then he could feel a message make its way through.

"Sequoia," the tree proclaimed.

"Sequoia Redwood?" Jason asked. He continued to press his head against it.

"Go to the Sequoias," the giant oak tree reiterated.

Jason looked around at the other trees in the forest and it appeared that they were all nodding in agreement.

"This is fucking bizarre," he said to himself.

217

Then Jason backed away from the tree as he remembered Sal was sleeping in the van on the side of the road. He waved the trees goodbye and headed back.

He hopped into the driver's side and started up. "*Go to the Sequoias? What the hell does that even mean?*" Jason asked himself as he merged into the left lane of the highway and began to accelerate.

Chapter 27

A few hundred miles away, Agent Carter Wiseman escorted Dr. Julie Green to his black government-issued sedan that was parked on the corner of Pine Street.

"Please get in," he said as he opened the passenger door.

Julie did so and buckled her seatbelt. She seemed to be in a state of shock because she did not know what was happening. Carter was acting stranger than usual.

Carter shut the door and ran around to the other side of the cruiser. He looked around before he opened the driver-side door and jumped inside. He started the car and turned on his sirens before driving through a red light at the Morgan Street intersection.

"Whoa!" Julie exclaimed. "Where are we going?"

"I just got some major intel—that some powerful people may want you dead. I don't know how this is all connected, but you, and apparently Richard Adler are possible targets in all of this. And I've been told you have quite the history with Mr. Adler, am I correct?"

Julie paled as she held onto the handle on the top of the patrol car. Agent Wiseman cut a left onto a nearby street and zoomed down it with his siren blaring.

"Why me? And Richard Adler might be next?" Julie asked. "I highly doubt anything will happen to that man. He is worth like two hundred billion dollars."

"Well, it's hearsay until proven otherwise. But it's what my sources are telling me," Carter replied.

He stepped on the brakes before they came to a red light with multiple cars flying through the intersection. Then he said, "The hell with this," and Carter turned the volume on the sirens even louder and pulled out in the middle of the intersection with red and blue lights flashing from the roof of his cruiser. This made a few cars swerve around him, almost crashing into one another.

"And they think I'm involved in this somehow, or that I'm in danger?" Julie asked as she gripped the handle even tighter.

"Well, I'm not saying directly. But you do have a history of speaking out against the use of lithium, and the impact lithium mining is having on the rainforest, if I'm not mistaken," Carter said as he looked over at her.

"Yeah, me and millions of other folks online!" Julie exclaimed.

"Right, but most of them didn't talk about it during lectures at college campuses around the country. I'm just saying, I'm going to have to keep you safe. That's all."

"I didn't do anything wrong! I was only telling the truth. The truth is the one thing that can't be bought by these evil corporations and political entities. And the people deserve to know the truth, especially what the biggest tech companies on the planet are doing to harm our ecosystem and our very own environment in the name of climate change!" Julie said in a heat of anger.

"I wish that was true, but while they may not be able to buy the truth, they can pay spin masters to manipulate it to fit their agendas," said Carter. "I'm on your side! I'm just telling you where we're at and why at this point it seems you may be important in helping us solve these plant-related deaths."

"How the hell am I important? I'm just somebody with enough guts and courage to tell people what is really going on! Actually, I .... Just let me out. I want to get out."

"Chill. First of all, I'm not doing that. It's not safe. And plus, I still need your help. You are crucial to helping me find out how to stop all of this."

"And how is that?" she asked.

Carter's car radio cackled, and a voice came over the car's speaker. "Carter. Pull over."

"What? Who is this?"

"Agent Briscoe. There's been another one."

Carter pulled to the curb and picked up the phone. "Another what?"

"That list you started circulating, about plant-related deaths. We just got word that a fella named Maurice Jenkins died of a heart attack after tangling with something called snakeroot plant."

"Jenkins?" said Julie. "Maurice Jenkins? They got him?"

"See?" said Carter. "You were right. Somehow. Some way. Somebody is using the plants as a way of fighting back and taking out all these company figureheads strategically and calculatedly. We are not sure how or exactly what is going on, but it does appear to be connected. It seems they may be killing off all the CEOs whose companies have in some way destroyed wilderness. It's ridiculous to think that the plants themselves are doing it, but someone is using the plants to do it. That's what must be going on. That's the most logical explanation."

He checked for cars, then pulled back out onto the road.

"That's what she does," said Julie.

"She who?"

"Mother Nature. She's fighting back, as she always does," said Professor Green as she stared out of the window. Everything that she had been adamantly saying for years was correct.

"But why now? What's triggered this kind of response?" asked Agent Wiseman.

"That's the sixty-four-million-dollar question, isn't it?" Julie responded. "Humans have been destroying the planet for centuries. Something must have happened, or at least the world of plants thinks something's going to happen that is making the plants react the way they have."

"Like I said, we believe there may be someone out there who's helping them to do it," said Carter. "Now we can neither confirm nor deny anything at the moment, but there was an accident at the Morabito Lab that involved a former employee. We've gotten an anonymous tip that he may be disgruntled and trying to get back at his former boss, Miles Walsh. Mr. Walsh has been cutting deals with a bunch of these companies, promising them ten times profit growth margins with these new Frankenplant genes, or whatever they're called. Either way, he has some big deal going through that involves Richard Adler, Evergreen Smart Phone, and the rainforest resources," Wiseman explained as the cruiser sped down the busy main road.

"I've heard rumors about this for a long time, but I never thought it was actually a thing," said Julie. "I always thought it was conspiracy theories spewed by crazy people on the internet."

"What kind of rumors are you talking about?"

"There are various theories about how the planet's atmosphere was being depleted of oxygen. Most say this isn't going to happen for a few million years, but some folks think it's more like a couple of hundred. And one or two believe it's more like twenty or thirty because we don't need to run out of oxygen, the oxygen in the atmosphere just has to drop by about twenty percent to make it hard for mammals, and that includes us, to breathe."

"How would that happen?"

"I'm not sure," said Julie. "Human expansion, deforestation, anything that depletes the planet of wilderness. The fewer trees and plants producing oxygen, the less oxygen there'll be in the atmosphere. At the same time, less carbon dioxide is being removed so that can't be good, either. Well, this time they may have been correct. The deal has been finalized, and the Evergreen Smart Phone/Morabito partnership means about three hundred new lithium mines are about to pop up around the globe and you know what that means, right?"

"What?"

"A hell of a lot of trees are about to become lumber."

"What has the internet been saying?" asked Carter.

"That there's going to be a large catastrophic event, perhaps in the rainforest, but no one seems entirely too sure just yet. Even if it's true, what in God's name are we supposed to do about it?" Dr. Green asked with her hands up in the air.

"If there is a chance that this former employee of Morabito is actually involved, then we have to get a hold of him somehow," said Carter.

"Do you know who it is, or where he lives?"

"I got my boys back at the station working on that. His name is Jason Woods. He's not at his apartment. We put a trace on his phone but lost it somewhere in the woods about a hundred miles west of Chicago. I suspect he got rid of his phone so he couldn't be tracked. We've been told that during his accident, he may have ingested plant DNA. Afterwards he stole some top-secret and deadly plants and top-notch tech from Morabito that could be very dangerous in the wrong hands," Carter went on.

"Do they have a suspicion that he plans to use it for terrorism or something?" asked Julie.

"We have no clue. At this point we must assume so. But we are going to have to find out if he is one of the good ones, or one of the ones we have to stop, before it's too late."

"I'm just going to say this, but if he is doing anything to help stop greedy executives like Richard Adler from destroying our planet any more than they already have, then I have a feeling he's one of the good ones. I wish I could do more myself to help, just saying."

"I believe you," said Carter.

Chapter 28

After a bit of convincing, FBI Agent Carter Wiseman talked Professor Julie Green into taking a short-term break from the University and joining him on the next nonstop flight from Austin to Chicago. At first, Julie was hesitant to leave her students. But she was completely enchanted by Carter. So, she decided to go with him on the trip. While Carter's charm may have been her deciding factor, more importantly she felt close to the case, as she had been studying the effects done to the plant world by humans her entire career. She felt like this was her calling even if she was somewhat scared for her life. It was like her research prepared her for this moment since she entered the emerging field of forensic botany.

After the two-and-a-half-hour flight, Carter arranged for two local agents to escort them from O'Hare Airport to the Chicago field office where they would be picked up and driven directly to Jason Woods' apartment in nearby Evanston, thirty minutes away.

After checking their badges and credentials, the superintendent at Jason's apartment complex reluctantly unlocked the door to Jason's apartment.

"He's a good tenant, Mr. Woods," said the superintendent. "Always pays rent on time. Never any complaints."

"I'm sure he is," said Carter. "We just want to talk to him, and we couldn't reach him by phone. We wanted to make sure he was okay. But it looks like he's not here. We're just going to take a quick look around to see if we can figure out where he may have gone."

Carter and Julie stepped into Jason's apartment and the first thing they saw was that someone had already ransacked the place. All the furniture was torn apart, and everything was flipped over.

"I guess we're not the only ones looking for Mr. Woods," said Carter.

The FBI agent turned to the superintendent.

"Any idea who could have done this?"

"No, sir," said the superintendent.

After a bit of searching, they found zero clues that would help them figure out where Jason had gone. They left the scene with nothing but confusion.

Carter and Julie went to a nearby hotel, where they could contemplate their next move.

At the receptionist desk, Carter presented his badge and identification. "I believe the Chicago FBI office has reserved a room for me," said Carter.

"Yes. Here it is," said the receptionist.

"Great, we'd also like to add a room for my colleague here."

The receptionist did a quick search on her computer.

"I'm afraid we're fully booked. I can recommend another hotel if you'd like?"

"Look, I don't know about you, but I'm beat," said Julie. "I know we're on this big manhunt to find this Jason Woods guy, but we don't even know for sure if he's involved."

"What are you saying?" asked Carter.

Switching the topic back to the issue at hand, Julie asked the front desk clerk, "Does his room have two beds?"

"Yes, two queen-size beds."

"Terrific," said Julie.

She turned toward Carter.

"We need to take a breath and re-energize. You might get off on the rush, but it's wearing me down. Can we just relax for a night and get back to it in the morning?"

"Sure," said Carter.

Julie added, "We'll need two keys."

Once they got into their room, Carter put his jacket on the chair next to the table in their oversized room.

Julie looked around the room which had a large desk, a sofa, small refrigerator, coffee pot, and a flatscreen TV.

"I'm going to use the facilities," said Julie. "Why don't you see if you can learn more about what happened to CEO Maurice Jenkins while I freshen up."

"Good idea," said Carter, turning on the TV and tuning into an all-news channel.

He settled down on one of the beds as he heard the shower coming from the bathroom. As he channel-surfed searching for anything about the latest plant-related death, his mind fantasized about what Julie looked like on the other side of the door, soaping her nude body in a hot shower. Although the FBI frowned on fraternization among agents and their assets, they were both consenting adults. He just hoped Julie was having similar fantasies about him. She had yet to show anything other than professional interest in the case they were pursuing. Maybe she already had a romantic partner? They'd never discussed their personal lives. How could he expect things to jump so many steps closer?

These days he had to be extremely careful. Any unwanted sexual advances could lead to charges of harassment or worse. Even hinting at such a possibility could lead to a reprimand at the very least. He had to be patient and let her make the first move, or at least provide some kind of clue that she was as interested in taking their relationship to another level as he was.

Not finding any mention of Jenkins' death among the major mainstream media channels, Carter stopped searching just as he heard the shower turned off behind the closed door of the bathroom. Now he started to envision

Julie drying herself. He closed his eyes and imagined the door to the bathroom slowly open, letting a cloud of steam spill out into the room followed by the naked form of Professor Julie Green, emerging from the mist.

"It's all yours," said Julie standing next to her bed wrapped in towels from head to toe. "You might want to call the front desk to get some more towels sent up. I used all the large ones. Also, you should ask for more shampoo, conditioner, and body wash."

Carter immediately stood up and began going through his overnight bag. "Maybe you're right," said Carter. "Tell you what. Why don't I just run down to the front desk and get some additional toiletries myself?"

He started for the door when he felt a hand grab his as he turned himself around. Professor Green had dropped her towels and stood naked before him. She grabbed him by his tie and pulled him close to her. "You're really going to leave me alone like this?"

"Ah," but that was all he was able to say before she put her mouth over his and began as deep and passionate a kiss as Carter had ever had. With their lips pressed together, Julie pushed him down on the hotel bed and climbed on top of him. Wiseman was not sure if what was happening was real, or if he was still fantasizing. Slowly, Julie moved her mouth to his ear and neck, tearing open his shirt in the process.

"I'm sorry if I'm moving too fast for you, Agent Wiseman," said Julie between kisses to his neck and now exposed chest. "But I figured the FBI probably has you guys trained to suppress your sexual urges during periods of close contact with someone you find attractive."

"They absolutely have very little tolerance for this sort of thing," admitted Carter.

"Which is why I decided to make the first move," said Julie. "We're two red-blooded adults and since neither of us are wearing a wedding band, I'm assuming we're also both unattached, or at least single, and we're together in this one hotel room and I for one haven't made love in so long I can't even remember when. So, unless I'm mistaken, and I rarely am when it comes to the male species, you've also been wanting to do this with me for quite some time."

"Since the moment we met," said Carter.

"Well then, we agree on something. So, how about a little help then? asked Julie.

"Huh?" said Carter.

"For starters, you'd better put your gun in the safe in the room."

"Okay."

After Carter took care of that, Julie smiled and said, "Now your belt. I can't quite reach it."

Carter quickly undid his belt and slid down his pants.

"We still have to be cautious," said the special agent.

"Don't worry about that," said Professor Green as she started to slide down his chest. "Outside this room, no will ever know. But for now, let's just enjoy the ride, okay, and let me take you places you've only dreamed of going."

Chapter 29

Meanwhile, at a roadside restaurant/bar in Waterloo, Iowa called Spartan's, Sal and Jason were sitting in a booth. Jason ordered himself a beer and he got Sal a soda.

"Why don't you make that two beers," Sal said.

He figured that drinking beer wasn't a big deal compared to everything they had been going through since they met recently.

"Don't worry, Jason. I mean, Dad. This obviously isn't my first beer," said Sal.

"Yeah, that doesn't make me feel better about it," Jason said, laughing. "But you're still just getting a soda."

"I can't remember the last time I had this much fun, but you gotta tell me what's going on. Where the hell are we going?" Sal asked.

"I'm not sure, just yet," Jason admitted as he had another drink from his mug.

"Are we just gonna drive around, running from your old boss forever?"

"I don't plan on it. Look, all I know is that where we're going has something to do with the Sequoias."

"You mean those giant trees?"

"They're a kind of redwood, but a special breed. That's all I know. And I'm trying to figure out what the hell that even means," said Jason.

"Well, I don't know if this will help but for one of my projects for science last year, I did a report on the Sequoia National Park, which holds the largest and oldest trees in the world. It's in California," Sal explained.

Jason thought about it for a second and said, "You're a genius. I need to make a call."

He pulled out his new phone and walked over toward the bathroom. He dialed in a number that he had memorized. The phone rang and rang. Finally, Bowde answered.

"Hello?" he sounded confused.

"Howard!" Jason exclaimed.

"Woods? Is that you, bro?"

"Yeah, man. Sorry to call you from a burner phone. Shit's been going sideways for a while now. I was being tracked by Miles and his guys, but I don't think they know where I am now," said Jason.

"I'm glad to hear from you. I tried calling your phone for days. I thought you were dead meat," Bowde said.

"Nah, but I do need your help. It's crucial."

"What's going on, partner?"

"Listen, I need to know, do you know of any work or deals Morabito planned to do in the Sequoia Forest out in Cali?" asked Jason.

"Hmm, now that you mention it, I believe I did hear about some sort of deal to use Morabito-magic on some redwood that a company out in Hollywood uses to build multi-million-dollar mansions for the super top one percent elites. I thought it was just a rumor, but I guess the deal went through. So what?" asked Bowde. "What's that even matter?"

"I'm not exactly sure why it matters. But it does."

"You safe out there? You with your boy?" asked Bowde.

"Yeah, we're good. Thanks for asking. How are you doing?"

"Hanging in there, brother. Getting by, I suppose."

"All right well look, I gotta run. I'll keep in touch," said Jason. "Thanks for always being there for me. You're a good friend."

"Same, bro. You've always been there for me too," Bowde replied. "Call me later this week. Good luck."

They both hung up as Jason returned to sit with his son. "How about some buffalo wings? What do you say?"

"Hell yeah!"

The two ate as many wings as their stomachs could handle and had a couple more drinks before they got a room at the local Bed and Breakfast.

Their room had two twin beds and a nightstand. After lying in his smaller than usual bed, Jason turned out the lights and said, "Good night, Sal."

Sal looked over and said, "Good night, Dad."

The two of them passed out quickly, after traveling for days and only taking short naps in the van.

The next morning, they both awoke to the scent of sizzling bacon coming through the crack of their bedroom door.

"Damn, that smells banging," said Sal as he hopped onto his feet.

It took Jason a bit longer to roll out of bed, but he finally did and joined his son downstairs with the other two guests and their hosts, Bob and Mandy, who had run that Bed and Breakfast for over thirty years. They were very nice and friendly hosts.

After a delicious breakfast, Jason asked Bob and Mandy if they had a computer that he could use, which they did. Jason spent about an hour searching the web and reading recent threads on the botanical message forums. There was more and more talk about the recent deaths of founders and CEOs of companies responsible for deforestation. The list had gone viral already and people were even placing bets on who they thought would be next to see their demise. Many had been talking about the possibility of Richard Adler being the next to see his untimely death caused by plants.

One story online was about a man who'd sent a Venus Flytrap to a politician responsible for getting a major sustainability bill passed through Congress. And while the congressman did not die, he did lose a limb, including a piece of his right ear, to the vicious and insatiable carnivorous creation.

Jason looked up from the computer when he realized that the green in his sight had begun to fade, and that he felt less connected to nature. *Oh no, what's happening?* he thought to himself.

The green was still there but now very dim. He remembered he had some more magic mushrooms stored for a rainy day. He'd figured he could do them later and they could go into town, maybe he could find some plants that might have more messages for him. He still was wondering if this was all just a crazy dream or not. But he was not waking up.

He decided not to wait. He went back to their room and pulled out a couple of mushroom caps from a small jar in his computer bag. That left about a half dozen caps. He ate them before chasing them down with a glass of fresh orange juice that Mandy had squeezed herself.

Within minutes, the green hue returned to fill up his sight. He rushed outside and hurried to the first tree he could find. Jason dropped to the ground and plunged his hands beneath the damp soil until his fingertips touched the sinewy fibers. He knew immediately that there was more to do with these newly gained insights as a rush of information poured into his fingers, up his arms, and into his mind.

Whatever the plants were doing was not having any impact to stop the oxygen-obliterating trends. Companies that were destroying forests all over the world were continuing to do so at a rapid pace.

"What can I do?" asked Jason of the tree.

"Go see the General," came a reply.

"The General? Who the hell is that?"

Chapter 30

Several hours later, Jason was driving west on the interstate when he got a call on his burner phone. He recognized the number and immediately picked up.

"Howard?"

"Hey, man" Bowde whispered. "How are you holding up?"

"I guess I'm okay," said Jason as he looked at the palms of his hands closely. It appeared the effects of the magic mushrooms had not worn off completely as the swirls and lines on his palms looked like deep crevices and pathways of roads not taken. He tried to remember which of those deep canyons was his life line when Bowde's voice interrupted his contemplation.

"I think I'm being followed," Bowde whispered.

"Really?" said Jason. "And why are you whispering?"

"I'm pretty sure that Miles is listening in on my conversations. I have a feeling that he may have bugged my house. I don't know, maybe I'm just being paranoid."

"So, you thought you'd call me?" asked Jason. "With Miles listening?"

"I'm outside my apartment. He shouldn't be able to hear me out here."

"What makes you think you're being followed?" Jason asked.

"I did something stupid," said Bowde. "After I got fired, I posted some stuff on the internet, on FacePage, about what a piece of shit Miles is and what he's been doing at Morabito. Ever since then, I see people looking at me, and cars I never saw before seem to be driving by my place again and again."

"If he knows you helped me, he could be hoping you'll lead him to me," said Jason.

"You might be right there. He's really very angry at you, to put it mildly. Where are you, anyway?"

"Sal and I are on our way to California right now. I'm not sure what I'm going to do when I get there, but I know I need to head to the Sequoia National Forest."

"That's like a twenty-four-hour drive!" said Howard.

"More like thirty-one hours," Jason replied.

"That is what I'm calling about. I may have a location you need to check out. I got word from a source close to Miles that there is a giant project out in Kirkwood, California that Miles is involved in. I guess there's something going on over there. And it's going to be big. It's super-secret and barely anybody outside of the inner circle has any clue what it is, but we know Miles is involved and it pertains to the Sequoia National Forest somehow," Bowde explained.

"I knew we were on the right path," said Jason.

"Why don't you fly? It's faster."

"It would be too easy to track us," Jason explained. "I'm only using cash to buy gas or pay for our motels."

"You're right. Makes sense."

Jason continued, "We've got to get to California because that's where the plants told me to go. So we're heading there in the morning. I figure we should be there by Friday."

"If I were you, I would keep a look over your shoulder. Miles most likely has some goons looking for you. I wouldn't be surprised if they're already close. The guy is evil, man. And he can find anyone anywhere on God's green Earth," Bowde whispered.

"We'll keep an eye out," said Jason.

"Ya know, now that I'm not working, I could maybe take a trip to California too," said Bowde.

"I appreciate that, I really do, but you've done too much already. I already cost you your job. I'd really feel bad if I was responsible for you getting hurt, or worse."

"I know you think you can handle yourself, Jason, but you don't want to underestimate Miles. He's got resources that are just too overwhelming, man."

"I've never felt this strong in my entire life," said Jason. "And truthfully, I don't think the plants will let anything happen to me."

Sal looked over at his father from across the room and said to himself, "Damn, this man is crazy."

He then continued to read his Mothman comic book.

"Right, well, just be careful. I'm not sure what Miles is up to, but I know once he decides on something, it's not going to be that easy to stop him. I was getting ready to quit when he fired me. I just couldn't work there anymore. Look, I'm still here for you. So just let me know what I can do."

"Well, thanks for still having my back through all of this," said Jason.

"What are friends for?"

"You're a real one," Jason said as he looked up at the popcorn ceiling above him in the historic Bed and Breakfast room.

"I gotta run," said Bowde. "Take care of your son, and whatever you're planning to do, be good to yourself. You're a good man," said Bowde before he hung up the call.

"You take care too, old friend," said Jason.

Chapter 31

The next morning, Sal and Jason ate a big breakfast with the other travelers that were staying at the latest B & B. Jason had decided to use B&Bs instead of motels and hotels because they were each independently operated and therefore harder to track.

Before the clock struck 9 A.M, the two packed their belongings and brought them outside to fill up the yellow van before their departure.

That morning, Jason used the computer and printer in the B&B's office to look up directions to Kirkwood, California. He printed them out and bought an old map of the country, considering he did not have his smartphone anymore with a GPS application on it.

"What are you doing?" asked Sal.

"Buying a map," said Jason.

"Why not use the GPS on your phone," asked Sal.

"Because I don't have it anymore, remember?"

"You could use mine," said Sal.

"I want you to keep yours turned off, just in case."

"Okay."

Jason put the key into the ignition as the van started up. The engine hummed as the two strapped in their seatbelts. He put the car into reverse and pulled out onto Hillcrest Drive. He headed down the street until he turned onto the highway ramp heading west.

"I have something I have to say to you," Jason said to Sal.

"What's that?"

Sal was afraid Jason would drive him back to his grandparents.

"I'm thrilled that you've come to live with me and it's even great that we're going on this road trip to California together. But when we get home, I'm registering you in the local high school. You don't want your old man getting arrested for causing you to be a truant, do you?"

"Agreed," said Sal, relieved.

"It's been quite a long time since I've had to use a map," said Jason as he shook it open and handed it to his son. "You're going to have to help me navigate and make sure we don't get lost. We need to get to California as soon as possible. Also, keep a look out for any cars that you think may be following us."

Sal took the map and studied the different roads as he compared them to the printed-out directions.

"This shouldn't be too hard," said Sal as he took his finger and moved across the highway that they were on all the way until he pointed to California on the map.

"We'll probably be there in a couple days, if that, maybe in two days, depending on how often we stop," said Sal.

"Looks like we're going on a good old-fashioned road trip!" Jason shouted as he rolled down the window. He looked outside to see the trees on the side of the highway appearing to be leaning west. This validated Jason; he knew he was on the right path.

The directions they had printed out said that it would take roughly twenty-six hours to get to their destination. Jason figured that if they only stopped one time to rest, then they should get there by Friday.

About three hours into their trip, Jason pulled into a gas station so they could fill up their tank. The two went into the mini-mart next to the gas pumps, and Sal bought about twenty dollars' worth of drinks and snacks for the trip. Jason went to use the bathroom. When he got out, he gave the cashier fifty dollars for gas before exiting the store. He went over to the van, grabbed the nozzle and put it into his fuel tank to fill it up.

After about a minute, Jason had the eerie feeling that he was being watched. It was as if something inside him was telling him to be cautious. As the gas pumped into the van's tank, Jason looked around at the other vehicles parked at other pumps and in front of the mini mart. He was looking for out-of-state license plates when Sal walked out the front of the store and over to his father.

"What's going on, Dad?" Sal asked. "Everything all right?"

He could tell his dad was troubled about something, as he looked around the parking lot.

"I have a feeling somebody is following us," Jason said.

Sal looked around and all he saw was an elderly lady smoking a cigarette in front of the store and a family getting out of their pick-up truck at the pump next to them.

"Hmm, I don't think so. But what do I know?" said Sal as he looked around some more.

"Just to be safe, let's get the hell out of here," said Jason as he shook the last bits of gas into the tank before putting the nozzle back on the pump. The two hopped into the van and sped off. Jason adjusted his rear-view mirror and looked back to make sure the coast was clear. His senses were still telling him to stay vigilant.

As Jason drove down the highway, rock and roll blared through the van's speakers. Sal rolled the passenger-side window down and stuck his head out, his face into the wind and his hair blowing out at the sides.

As Jason looked out the driver's side window, it appeared that the trees were waving to him as he drove by. It was if they were guiding him along the two-lane blacktop that Jason had decided to take instead of the faster and more popular inter-states. He figured it would add a day or two to the trip, but he was more likely to avoid any followers on these state and county roads. Besides, he had the trees to keep him on track. He felt like he didn't even need a map, like the forest that surrounded him was leading them to where they needed to go.

Sal kept his head out the window as the breeze blew his long bangs across his eyes. After a while, Sal sat back in his seat. He looked at Jason and said, "So, I get that we are traveling across the country to stop your old boss from doing something bad? Is that right?"

Jason sighed and said, "Yeah, maybe. I suppose so. Only it's a little more complicated than that. I'm not sure exactly what I'm supposed to do."

Jason reached in the back seat and grabbed a can of cola out of a bag. He cracked open the pull-tab and took a swig.

"Well, why do you hate him so much?" Sal asked as he opened a bag of sour cream and onion potato chips. He took out a handful and began to munch.

"You know what? I didn't always hate him. He was a decent boss at first. He believed in making sure the combinations we were using to create the hybrid plants made sense. And he did good. Then, over time, we all started to see what Miles was up to. The deals he was making had more to do with making money than creating something people wanted or needed. The shady people he was working with had no scruples whatsoever. They thought nothing about threatening a competitor's family if they got in the way. I turned my head for a long time, ignoring all the bullshit that was going on behind closed doors. But now, it just seems like my calling to put a stop to whatever he is planning next," Jason explained.

"Well, what was it like working at Morabito?" asked Sal as he ate another handful of chips and drank from his cola.

Jason thought back to a couple of years prior as he continued to drive. The question sent him down a journey on memory lane. One date specifically came to mind.

It was a rainy Tuesday afternoon. Jason was working on a secret project inside the Morabito lab with his co-workers, Theo, Rhonda, and Howard Bowde. They were tasked with experimenting on Beaver Tail Cacti looking for different benefits it could apply to a new hand cream. Or at least that is what they were told they were doing.

"Hey Jason, would you pass me the thermometer?" asked Rhonda as she slid her rolling chair across the room and began jotting some numbers on her notepad.

"Sure thing," said Jason as he grabbed the thermometer off the lab desk and brought it to Rhonda's workstation.

"Thanks, Sugar," she said as she placed the thermometer inside the bottom of the cactus after boiling it for a few minutes.

"Man, when are they gonna give us some real assignments?" asked Bowde as he filled out a report.

Theo walked over with a couple more of the Beaver Tail Cacti in a box and placed them next to the workstation. "For real, they got us out here playing with cactuses and shit."

"It's pronounced cacti, and you know that," said Rhonda.

"Listen, I heard we got some sweet projects coming up in the next couple of months. We just have to be patient," said Jason.

He wasn't even sure what his function was at Morabito most of the time, but he was just happy to have a job in a field he was passionate about. "Miles appreciates what we are doing, even if he doesn't show it all of the time."

"A huh, sure," said Theo. "All that mother fucker cares about is money, that's it."

"Watch your mouth," said Rhonda. "You know they're always listening."

"I don't care, let them. They already know what I think. I'm just too good of a genetic engineer for them to fire my ass. I'm one of the best they got," Theo said with confidence.

"You are pretty good, but don't get cocky," said Bowde.

Just then, an alarm sounded throughout the Morabito building and into the lab. Lights began flashing as the four lab workers evacuated through the back door exit.

"What the hell is going on?" asked Rhonda as she followed the guys out the back.

"Probably just another drill," said Jason as they all made their way through the hallway and out the building.

When they joined the rest of the departments in their assigned muster area in the parking lot, they found that most everyone had no clue what was going on. But it appeared everyone had left the building.

"What a great waste of our valuable time," said Theo as he rolled his eyes and lit up a cigarette.

"It's all right. I have a feeling that the cacti can wait," said Bowde.

They all waited in the parking lot roughly fifty yards from the front of the building. Theo inhaled the smoke from his menthol cigarette, held it in before finally exhaling it out. Rhonda coughed as the cloud of smoke washed over her like a wave.

"Do you mind?" she asked as she covered her mouth.

"It's a free country," said Theo, and he took another puff.

"All right, all right, go over there if you need to smoke," said Jason as he pushed Theo away from the group.

Finally, the alarm stopped. Moments later, employees began to make their way back inside of the building. One supervisor stood on a boulder and yelled out, "Great job! This was just a test! You all passed!"

Jason and the rest of the lab crew headed back inside. Theo took one last puff from his cigarette before he dropped it to the floor and stepped on the ember.

As they made their way through the front of the building, Jason's phone pinged with a text from a friend.

"Go ahead, you guys, I'll catch up with you," he said as he stopped in the hallway to text his friend back.

As the rest of the employees swarmed back into their respective department rooms, Jason finished his text and headed back to his lab.

As he walked down the hallway, he could hear a weird noise coming from a room to the right of him. He had never been in there before. The windows were tinted. But this time, the door was cracked open just a bit. Jason's curiosity arose, as he put his ear to the door to get a better sense of what he was hearing. It sounded like a toilet was flushing loudly, but it wasn't a bathroom. Jason leaned up against the door, opening it up slightly.

He saw three men in lab coats with a machine hooked up to a bunch of exotic looking plants. Sparks were flying and liquid was splashing in every direction. Jason had no clue what he was looking at, but it appeared as if the plants were not happy with what was going on. "What in the world?" Jason whispered to himself. Then, he was spotted as the three men both looked over to see Jason staring at them.

One of the men yelled, "Get the hell out!"

Jason quickly shut the door and made his way back to the lab. He had no clue what he had just witnessed. But it made him feel uneasy.

When he got back to the lab, Theo was writing a formula on the white board. Theo looked over at Jason as he walked in the room. "Where the hell were you?"

"I…I don't know. I just walked by the weirdest thing. I don't know what I saw, but it was some weird shit going on," said Jason as he scratched his head.

"We don't know a tenth of the crap that goes on here, my friend," said Bowde.

"I realized Bowde was right," Jason told Sal. "There were things going on that none of us ever knew about. And that was the first day I started to question the company I worked for."

"Whoa. Well, it sounds like you had a cool job when you were still there," said Sal as he finished his bag of chips.

"It had its moments. But the longer I spent there, the more I could see the writing on the walls. Miles was up to some bullshit."

"So, let me ask you something, Pops. Why did you wait until they let you go? Why didn't you just leave?"

"I guess I got comfortable. The money was good. I was there for a long time. I never thought I would end up working for a monster. But I guess that is what he is. My boss was a monster. And now I have the chance to stop him. I just wish I knew what he was up to. And now I know where we must go, I just need to know what I must do."

"I'm sure we'll figure that out soon enough," said Sal.

"I think you're right," said Jason.

Jason decided to get back onto the highway, to save some time. The two flew down the highway at eighty miles an hour, the speed limit in Wyoming. The highway signs seemed to be getting further and further apart from one another.

After about ten hours of driving, Jason stopped for the night at a seedy motel in Rawlins, Wyoming. It was called the Blue Dream Inn but it looked like a bad dream to Jason and their room had a musky, moldy smell, which is why it only cost them thirty-nine dollars for the night. Jason figured they could use some sleep before they drove the rest of the trip. He was getting really tired and didn't want to fall asleep at the wheel.

It was almost 3 A.M. when they checked in, ringing a bell to wake up an unpleasant woman in a housecoat who was quite thin.

Once they got to their room, Jason lay down on one of the beds and almost immediately drifted off to sleep. Sal hung out for a little bit while his dad slept. He rolled up a little bit of weed that he had hidden in his sock into a skinny joint. He went outside onto the porch of the motel room and lit it up.

Sal was tired but did not feel like sleeping. As he dragged on the joint filling his lungs with some of the strongest weed west of the Mississippi, he considered his good fortune. First, he could not believe he was seeing so many new sights and states that he never thought he would ever visit in his lifetime. His mother never took him anywhere except the store to buy clothes for school. Even though he was still shocked and hurt from the loss of his mother, he was glad he was able to now bond with his father. It was filling a void and something he had missed his entire life. He just wished his dad wasn't so batshit crazy. He felt so embarrassed by him whenever he went on and on about talking to plants. Sal wanted to say something to him about it, but he kept quiet and just went along with it. Maybe when they got to California, he could talk his father into seeing a shrink. Little did he know, his father was already seeing a therapist.

Chapter 32

Special Agent Carter Wiseman and Dr. Julie Green were at the Chicago FBI headquarters, discussing their next move. They were back to acting as if their relationship was completely all business between agent and expert in case anyone was watching them.

"So here is what we know," Carter began. "Multiple CEOs have been victims of untimely and mysterious deaths that appear to have involved some kind of plant, and all have died in the span of the last three weeks. All of them also worked at companies that appeared on a 'Top Ten' list of firms responsible for the destruction of forests around the world. The next big name on the list is Chance Wilder. And somehow, this guy Miles Walsh is involved."

"Who is Chance Wilder?" asked Julie.

"The founder and owner of Wildwood Homes Incorporated. He's an old-school real estate guru who builds houses for the rich and famous. He makes mansions for all the Silicon Valley big wigs," said Carter.

"Apparently, he has a big operation in the Sequoia National Forest in California coming up this weekend."

"Interesting, so he builds the houses with lumber from sequoias and redwood trees I'm guessing?" asked Dr. Green as she took a drink of her diet cola.

"Bingo. He specializes in homes built from redwoods. These mansions are selling for twenty to forty million dollars."

"So, what's the extent of Miles Walsh's involvement?"

"We're not sure. Redwoods tend to be large trees so it wouldn't make much sense to make them larger. So, if it does involve Morabito's DNA splicing technology, then there must be another reason," said Carter as he walked around the office.

"Right, and you're thinking Chance may see his untimely death any day now," said Julie. "So, we must get over there and protect this redwood forest destroyer. What are we still doing in Chicago?"

"We're booked on a morning flight to California," Carter replied. "If I didn't know better, I might think you'd like us to leave Chance to his own devices."

"I guess it's because I know the damage companies like his are doing to the planet's biodiversity through massive deforestation," said Julie. "These forests are responsible for creating the oxygen in the air that we breathe. These bastards are literally smothering the planet." She looked thoughtful.

"You know, I was thinking. Let's assume the plants really are working together to take out all of these powerful figures. What if we take the position that the plants are doing the right thing? What if these people are supposed to die if it means protecting this planet by any means necessary? Wouldn't we fight for our survival as well? And truthfully, the plants are fighting for our survival, too. Working together, stopping the ones that need to be stopped. Something that maybe we should be doing for them," Julie went on.

"Well, as much as that sounds like a fantastic science fiction movie, it's going to be a hard sell on my side," Carter responded. "The FBI takes murder seriously no matter what the reason. I cannot—we cannot—condone it."

"You sure about that?" she asked.

"I have to be," said Carter. "But we are beginning to believe this may all be the evil plan of a mastermind. Perhaps, this Jason Woods character. The one that used to work for Morabito. I'm thinking he might show up at this upcoming Wildwood Homes operation going on in California. Our Intel still says he may have orchestrated some or all these attacks," said Carter.

"It just doesn't make any sense. How in the hell would one man be able to pull that off in so many different places around the country?" asked Julie. She walked across to the other side of the room and gazed out the window.

"Julie, c'mon. You know that human beings are capable of insane amounts of madness. And if this Jason

Woods guy is capable of a third of these heinous attacks, then he has to be stopped at all costs!" Carter exclaimed. "Plus, he may have help. We just don't know."

"I have a hunch that he's not the one to blame. But if you think he has something to do with it, and if you trust your gut, then I trust you. Just don't make us do something that I won't be able to live with myself after," said Dr. Green.

Chapter 33

The next morning, Jason fell out of his bed around 8:30 A.M. The impact of his body hitting the floor woke him up. He jumped onto his feet. At first, he was not even sure where he was. He looked over at the other bed and saw Sal was still asleep. He was in a motel somewhere. He peered outside the window and saw a nearly empty parking lot. Across the street was a strip mall containing a laundry mat, next to a Chinese takeout, a check cashing operation, and UPS store.

Closing the curtains, Jason crossed the room and entered the bathroom where he turned on the shower. He turned the level all the way up until it was as hot as it could get. He stripped off his underwear and climbed into the shower.

As the steaming hot water drilled into his head, he began to remember consuming a few more mushrooms before falling into a plant world dream. In the dream, he could feel the plant cells multiplying within his body and his blood which now contained rejuvenating powers that still coursed through his body. The redwood DNA had been multiplying inside of his body ever since the accident and that combined with the effects of the psilocybin in the mushrooms produced an unusual state of consciousness that could only be described as someone who was steadfast, sturdy and determined to make a difference by protecting his newfound family of flora. He also felt a sense of euphoria in that his previous state of low-level depression seemed to have lifted. The melancholy he usually felt was now replaced with a sense of duty and purpose.

Jason did not just see the world through a green-tinted lens, his entire being embodied a new greenness. He smiled at the thought that he had discovered his own personal green new deal. Only in his deal, the greenness was all inclusive which meant he bore no animosity toward such things as fossil fuel, which he never could understand, since it was supposed to refer to such things as oil, natural gas and coal, none of which were derived from fossils, but rather the earth's steady supply of lubricants that allowed the planet's crust which is made up of plates of rock that form the earth's surface.

The green hues seemed to stand out stronger than all the other colors on the spectrum combined. He also had a hunger for more greens than ever before. A burger-and-fries man forever, he now had a craving for multiple sides of different green vegetables. His favorite were peas, French green beans, broccoli, and spinach. But he grew to love all of them. He had never been a salad guy, but now he craved salad every day.

He got out of the shower and was drying off when Sal finally awoke. Jason entered the room with a towel wrapped around him. "Ready to hit the road, son?"

"Sure thing, Dad," Sal yawned.

"You might want to grab a shower. No telling when we'll have time for another one."

"What do you mean?" asked Sal as he wiped the sleep from his eyes.

"The plants have been talking to me again," said Jason. "I know that sounds kind of crazy son, but believe me, we have a chance to do something great."

"Sure, Dad. Whatever you say," Sal said, turning his face away so Jason could not see him roll his eyes.

The two cleaned up their room before they left the motel. Jason wanted to make sure they left nothing behind in case someone was on their tail. After storing the plants and equipment back in the van, they pulled up to the front office to drop off the room key to the front desk.

As Jason turned out of the motel parking lot, an all-black tinted sedan pulled out of a parking spot down the street from the motel and followed the yellow van out onto the service road from a distance. The car continued to follow them as they made their way onto the highway.

Jason and Sal were back on the interstate, I-80 when they left Wyoming and entered Utah. In the dream, Jason felt the plants were concerned he was taking too long to get to Sequoia National Park, so he decided they could

261

no longer have the luxury of taking the so-called blue highway routes to California because it was taking too long. Blue highways was a reference to the blue roadways on those triple "A" maps, indicating the route was either a state, or county road rather than a U.S. or interstate highway.

By taking the interstates they had about fourteen hours left on their journey to the Golden State, if they did not hit traffic snarls along the way. So far, traffic was not too bad. The two had made an early start and planned to hit the road first and get breakfast a little bit later. Jason decided that this trip provided an excellent opportunity to get to know his son better.

"So," said Jason. "What's your favorite TV show?"

"TV show? I don't really watch TV that much. Most of the shows are too lame for words. There are a couple of Netflix shows I like. *Stranger Things* and *Umbrella Academy*."

"I think I've heard of them," said Jason.

"How about you?"

"Hmm. I guess maybe *Dr. Mars*? That was probably my favorite show growing up. I didn't watch too much television either really."

"What the hell is *Dr. Mars*?"

"It's this great sci-fi show. Every episode is different and has some crazy plot intertwining different current events and pop culture references. We need to watch it sometime," Jason said.

"You mean like *Twilight Zone* or *Black Mirror*?"

"I suppose."

"As nerdy as that shit sounds, I'd be cool with it. Let's watch it when we get back home," said Sal.

"Yeah, when we get back home. That sounds like a plan."

"Speaking of plans," said Sal. "What's the plan once we get to Sequoia National Park?"

"Guess we'll know once we get there."

"So, you don't really know what we're getting into here, do you?"

"No clue."

"What are the plants telling you?"

"Just that there's something about to happen and I have to do whatever it takes to stop it."

"That's a little vague," said Sal. "What's it like, talking to plants? Do they have their own language?"

"It's hard to explain," said Jason. "It isn't really talking like you and me talking. It's hard to put into words because, well, there are no words. It's just a kind of knowing."

"Knowing? Like in knowledge? That kind of knowing?"

"Sort of. Only different."

"Different how? In what way?"

"With knowledge you learn something and then you know it. With plants it's just…

"Just what?"

"There. One minute you aren't aware of something, and then you are."

"That's whack."

"Yeah, whack."

"Cool."

Jason couldn't shake the feeling that they were being followed, so he decided to use a maneuver he once read about in a spy novel. He put on his right turn signal as they neared an exit and entered the lane on the right. He looked in the rear-view mirror to see if any of the following vehicles did the same thing. A truck he had passed a while back did the same thing, as did a pitch-black tinted sedan a few cars back.

He felt a tingle down his neck. Jason looked in his rear-view mirror as he passed the exit without getting off. The truck got off and the black sedan continued to follow them. He could not tell for sure if they were following him, or just behind him on a highway heading west. But his senses were telling him to be cautious. The trees to the right and to the left of the road continued to point him in the direction they were heading on the map.

The yellow van flew down the highway at more than seventy, closer to eighty, miles per hour. Jason cracked open a can of orange soda just as the foam inside began to overflow. He sipped it before it spilled all over him.

He looked at the rear-view mirror and the black sedan was gone, replaced by an 18-wheeler. Jason smiled with relief and finished his soda. He decided to continue learning more about his newfound son.

"So, like, what do you want to be when you grow up?" asked Jason.

"Hmm, I'm not really sure," Sal replied as he ripped open a bag of barbeque chips. "I used to want to be a pro football player, but I'm not all that fast or strong or anything. I tried out for the team last year, but I wasn't picked. So, yeah. Doubt that will ever happen."

"You're still growing," said Jason. "Don't give up so easily. I think you're going to be taller than me, and the rest is just a matter of exercise to build up those muscles. You can do anything you set your mind and heart to."

"I think I might actually want to be a scientist when I grow up, like you."

"Oh yeah?" said Jason as a smirk grew on his face. He placed his can of soda in the cupholder. "Science covers a lot of ground. There's biology, zoology, botany, geology, psychology, sociology, meteorology, political science, physics, rocket science, medicine, pharmacology, forensics, genetics, anthropology, computer science. What kind of science would you like to work in?"

"Well, I don't know. Your life seems pretty good," said Sal. "What you do with creating new plants and stuff. That sounds like fun."

"I don't know if 'fun' is the right word. I mean yeah, things have been wild as of late. However, most of my career was not this exciting. It was quite boring when I think back on it. So many years wasted on bullshit experiment after bullshit experiment. If I could take it all back, I think I would have been a doctor. Maybe tried helping people more. Something like that."

"I don't think you've wasted any time. You're way cooler than I ever expected you to be," said Sal.

"I'm not sure how I'm supposed to take that."

"As a compliment."

"Then thanks," said Jason. "I'm sorry you're meeting me when I seem to be angry all the time. It doesn't have anything to do with you."

"You can't be mad at me. You didn't even know I existed until last week."

"That, I am angry about," Jason responded. "So, what are your favorite subjects in school?"

"History. English. Biology. But do we really have to talk about school right now?"

Chapter 34

It was nearly seven in the evening when Jason pulled off at a truck stop at exit 117A. Next to the gas station was a country buffet.

"How about we eat here tonight? We have a big day ahead of us tomorrow," Jason asked.

"Sounds great. I'm starving," said Sal.

Jason parked the van on the side of the buffet. The two got out and walked inside and therefore did not see the same black car that had been following them for hours pull into the lot as well and park on the other side of the truck stop so it would not be seen.

Sal and Jason got a table in the back. The waiter took their order for drinks. Sal got a cola, while Jason decided to have a big glass of beer. The waiter offered him some water as well, which Jason responded, "Sure, why not?"

They got up from their table and walked over to the hot food bars to check out the buffet.

Jason noticed a large flat screen television mounted on the wall had the news on. It was very loud, but Jason focused on his hearing senses for a moment. He could start to make out what the newscaster was saying.

"We are live outside of where Chance Wilder, founder of Wildwood Homes Incorporated, will be giving a press conference right here in the Sequoia National Forest," said local reporter Alexander Ruffleson.

The reporter was surrounded by protestors, some of which were holding signs. One of the signs read, "SAVE THE TREES!"

"The demolition of these giant sequoias is angering many activists who believe the company will do irreversible damage if they go through with it," Ruffleson went on. "Other notable names that are in attendance are Richard Adler, CEO of Evergreen Smart Phone, and Miles Walsh, the president of Morabito Labs. It is not clear why these men are here for the demolition, but many users online in the comment section believe it is some sort of big deal that is in the works between the three companies. This is not the first time that Wildwood Homes has been protested. Years before, Mr. Wilder and his company were boycotted for building homes only for the rich while more and more people were becoming homeless every day. He was criticized for being unphilanthropic when asked by many in Hollywood to use some of the money the company generated to build affordable housing and even housing for the homeless."

Jason stared at the screen. "Is this why I'm heading west," he said to himself, "This is all starting to make so much sense. They want me to stop this demolition."

The broadcast went to a commercial.

"Dad, you gonna get some food? This looks amazing!" said Sal as he walked over with a plate stacked with fried chicken, mashed potatoes, green beans, macaroni and cheese, corn, and whatever else was hidden underneath.

"Huh? Oh yeah. Unfortunately, we must eat and run," said Jason. "We have to get back on the road."

"Dad, you're going to give yourself indigestion."

"I have to stop them."

"Stop who?"

"This guy Chance Wilder and my old boss."

"Stop them from what exactly?"

"From killing the sequoias," Jason replied before grabbing a plate.

"How are you going to do that?"

"I don't know yet."

"All right, So, why don't we sit down and eat this great soul food," said Sal. "Maybe something will come to you."

"Sounds good. My soul could use some food," Jason replied as he walked over to the salad bar. It was shining bright green with tubs of leafy vegetables. Jason first filled his plate with romaine lettuce and spinach leaves. Then, he threw some raw broccoli on the plate, followed by peas, and edamame. He looked at the array of dressings to choose from. He chose the one that read, "Green Goddess."

Jason was about to head back to their table when two men walked in through the front door. They were both wearing black suits, white shirts, and dark blue ties. They each looked to be over six feet tall. They wore dark shades, even though it was nighttime. One of them had blond hair, while the other had light brown hair. They looked at Jason getting his food and saw that Jason was staring at them. The blond whispered something to his smart watch. Jason was not sure he heard the man correctly. It sounded like he said, "We got him."

The blond man lowered his wrist and smart watch to his side. He nodded to his partner and then began charging at Jason.

"Oh shit," said Jason as the man got closer and closer. He looked down at his plate, grabbed a handful of greens and shoved it in his mouth. As the man got a few feet away, he dove at Jason. That is when Jason maneuvered his body back just before whapping him in the face with his plate. The man fell to the floor. He immediately propped himself back onto his feet, this time swinging his body to the left just before kicking Jason with a roundhouse across the face. This knocked Jason back, stumbling into a hot tray full of carrots. The ruckus made the other customers run away in fear. This got the attention of Sal who was taking a big bite of his fried chicken.

"What the hell?" Sal said standing up from the table.

The other man in the suit walked over slowly while his partner was throwing punches at Jason. Jason was managing to block most of them. That was until the attacker jabbed him in the throat. This made Jason trip over the soup section, spraying Chicken Noodle Soup and New England Clam chowder through the air like a fountain. Jason laid on the other side of the buffet line. He could not breathe for a moment.

Sal ran toward the salad bar to help his Dad but got clotheslined by the other black-suited man. Sal went down and out cold.

Jason and the blond were sizing each other up on opposite sides of a large puddle of soup.

"Who sent you?!" Jason croaked.

"We both know who sent us," said the blond man in the shades.

Jason reached behind him and grabbed a handful of hot roasted salted edamame just as the blond was stepping across the soup. He launched the soybeans into the air, hitting the suited man in the face. A few of them hit him directly in the eyes, blinding him for a moment. This gave Jason a chance to hide behind one of the counters.

After rubbing his eyes, the blond man crept around the corner of the buffet line, but Jason was nowhere in sight. His partner joined him. They looked around but could not see where he went. That is when the two men turned around to find Jason with a cooking tray full of green beans. The beans were piping hot out of the kitchen. The brown-haired man reached into his pocket, but before he could pull out his gun, Jason had flung the entire pot of steaming green beans into their faces.

Both men screamed as they fell to the ground. Jason saw Sal lying on the floor unconscious. He ran towards him and grabbed him off the floor.

"We have to get the hell out of here!" Jason shouted as Sal opened his eyes.

Jason stood him up and looked him over.

"Are you okay? Can you walk"

"I think so," said Sal.

"Let's go!" Jason replied before they both ran out of the front door.

Back at the buffet, the two suited men got up dripping with hot water and green beans. They looked around but did not see Jason or Sal anywhere. Then, through a large picture window, they could see them walking quickly toward a yellow van. They wiped down their suits and headed toward the entrance.

Jason and Sal got to the van, Jason unlocked the door, and they both jumped inside. He put the key into the ignition, turning it to the right until the engine started.

The two men in suits busted through the front door of the truck stop. The blond one pulled out a pistol and began shooting at the van as it pulled away and out of the parking lot. The bullets hit the side of the van, one of them knocking out the left rear light.

"Get down!" Jason yelled as he sped off onto the road. Sal ducked.

The two men in the black suits ran over to their car and hopped inside. They pulled out of the parking spot and left the lot. Jason was about fifty yards away, but the men were speeding up to get closer to the yellow van. Jason turned onto the highway ramp heading west.

The tinted black car was gaining on them until they settled in behind them. They followed Jason for several miles as Jason weaved in and out of the lanes, making everything in the back of the van fly around.

"What am I gonna do? What am I gonna do?" Jason said aloud.

"We gotta lose them!" Sal yelled.

They heard a gunshot just before they felt the side of the car get clipped. The tinted car must have been ten feet behind them. The blond man was driving the car as the brown-haired man in glasses shot out the window. That is when an idea came to Jason.

"Sal, listen. I need you to grab my computer bag in the back and bring it up here."

"Okay, Pops," said Sal as he looked back to make sure the guy wasn't shooting anymore.

It appeared the shots had stopped for a moment. Sal unbuckled his seatbelt and jumped into the back of the van. He looked around but could not find the computer bag Jason was talking about. But after a bit of searching, he finally found it. He brought it back up to the front of the van. He gave it to his father.

"Grab the wheel," said Jason.

Sal grabbed the wheel as Jason unzipped the computer bag. He pulled out a tiny Golden Barrel cactus that he had stolen from his old job. Then, he grabbed one of the Gene Guns he had left.

"What are you thinking about doing?" asked Sal as he held the steering wheel making sure they didn't drift off into the other lane of the highway.

"I'm going to try something stupid, but it just might work. Keep holding the wheel."

Jason rolled down his window. He reached into a box on the floor behind him and pulled out a cactus the size of a soccer ball. He put it up to his ear and listened. A smile appeared on Jason's lips as he heard a steady hum coming from inside the cactus. Jason looked over at his son and said, "Here goes nothing. You keep steering while I slow them down."

Sal continued to steer the car. Jason lifted the cactus up and held it just below the window opening. It did not take long before the black sedan pulled alongside the van. A window on the passenger side came down and a man holding a gun looked up at Jason.

"How you doin?" said Jason.

"Pull over," said the man with the gun.

"Sure thing," said Jason, as he took his foot off the gas. At the same time, he lifted the cactus up so it would clear the window and then, while still smiling at the man with the gun, tossed the cactus through the window of the black sedan and saw it land in the lap of the man with the gun. He immediately floored the gas pedal as the van sped off down the road as the gunman took a shot at Jason.

Jason was able to dodge the bullet even though it ripped through a piece of shirt sleeve and left a red welt on his left arm. He thought he might have been hit, but his adrenaline was pumping so fast he did not think much of it. He looked at the side-view mirror and saw that the sedan had started to catch up with them again.

"Three...two...one..." Jason counted to himself just before he saw the van start to swerve.

Sal looked at the rear view and saw the van veering back and forth across the highway. "What did you do?"

"Gave them something to take their mind off of us for a while," said Jason. "You see each one of those cacti back there are filled with about a million little scorpion eggs, and when you can hear a humming sound that means those eggs are about to hatch."

The gunman in the sedan looked down at the cactus lying on his lap. "What the..." Suddenly the cactus exploded like a grenade hurling thousands of tiny scorpions in every direction covering both the driver and gunman with angry eight-legged Arachnids aching for something to sting.

"Jesus Christ!" yelled the driver. "Get these things off of me!"

As the driver tried to fight the onslaught of a thousand stingers, he lost control of the sedan as it hit a side rail causing it to rise into the air and flip on its side.

Looking through the rearview mirror, Jason saw the black sedan skidding on its side until it came to rest at the side of the highway. The passenger door flew open as the gunman crawled out, covered in scorpions, his hands covering his face.

Damn!" yelled Sal as he watched the action out the back window. "That was savage, Dad!"

"I guess I kind of overdid it," said Jason as he pulled into the lane next to him.

He looked back in the mirror to make sure that no more cars were following them. It appeared that they were safe for the time being.

"Okay, you're right. I agree, that was savage. But you know what son? Sometimes nature is savage to survive."

Chapter 35

The two continued to drive through the night. They had to make it to the Sequoia National Forest by the next afternoon before the demolition would begin. Jason knew that if he kept driving, they should make it there before sunrise.

Jason drove on the highway for hours and hours. After a while, Sal fell asleep in the car. The night sky turned cloudy by the early morning. It was as if they were driving through the clouds. Jason followed the guidance of the trees that surrounded him. They pointed west.

Finally, the van passed by a sign on the highway that read, "Welcome to California."

About two miles down that road, Jason spotted someone with a backpack trudging up a steep incline. As he got closer, he could see it was a woman, and she had her thumb out.

Jason pulled up next to her and stopped. Sal was still asleep in the back seat.

"Where you headed?" asked Jason.

"To Sequoia National Park," said the young woman. "The Save the Planet Club, of which I'm a member, has asked us to go there for some kind of demonstration."

"You're in luck," said Jason. "That's exactly where I'm going too."

"Awesome," said the woman. "Name's Sara by the way, but my friends call me Gypsy, since I'm a bit of a nomad, they say."

"Gypsy, I'm Jason. That's my son, Sal, in the back. I'll introduce you when he wakes up. It's been a long, strange trip, to say the least."

Gypsy opened the door and put her backpack on the floor in front of her seat and climbed in.

"Where are you coming from?" asked Gypsy.

"Just outside of Chicago," said Jason.

"Wow! That's around two thousand miles away! How did you hear about the demonstration," asked Gypsy who looked to be around thirty years old.

"I'll tell you when we get to know each other better," said Jason.

"You'll tell me now or I'm getting out of this van," said Gypsy.

"You're not gonna believe me."

"You won't know unless you tell me," said Gypsy.

"Well, the trees told me," said Jason.

"I believe you," said Gypsy.

"You do?"

"See," said Gypsy. "You gotta learn to trust people, Jason. Now let's go. We have about another hundred miles ahead of us."

Jason put the van in gear and pulled back onto the highway.

"So, Gypsy, where are you coming from?"

"Vegas."

"Always wanted to go there," said Jason.

"What's stopping you?"

"Nothing. Got caught up in my job. Just some place on my bucket list, ya know."

"Yeah. You gotta go one day. But Jason, I've been walking for the past few hours. You mind if I get some shut eye?"

"Go ahead. I'll let you know when we get there."

"Thanks," said Gypsy, as she put her head against the door. She was asleep in seconds.

As he drove, Jason kept glancing over at his new passenger. Although she wore practically no make-up, she was naturally beautiful. "She's out of your league, pal," Jason thought to himself. He told himself to just keep his eyes on the road and his hands on the wheel.

Chapter 36

The sign on the side of the state highway 198 read "Three Rivers, 2708, Gateway to Sequoia-Kings Canyon National Parks."

Jason pulled off the road, just past the sign, and stopped the van. He turned off the engine.

"I think we're here," Jason said.

Gypsy stretched out and wiped the sleep from her eyes. Sal was waking up to find the sun coming up in the distance. The air felt different.

"Wow, we're here," Sal said as he stepped outside of the van. Suddenly, he realized someone was sitting in the front passenger seat. "Hey, who are you?"

Gypsy opened her door and stepped out to stretch some more.

"Gypsy," she said holding out her hand. "You're Sal, right?"

"Dad?"

Jason got out and joined his son and his hitchhiker by the side of the van.

"You were sleeping when I picked Gypsy up hitch-hiking. She's going to the same place we are. Isn't that amazing?"

"I guess," Sal replied unenthusiastically.

"Remember what I said about 'Do what I say, not what I do,' so please, Sal, don't ever pick up a hitchhiker. I made an exception for Gypsy."

The three of them looked down into the village of Three Rivers, nestled into a patch of land divided into three of the five forks of the Kaweah River in the foothills of the Sierra Nevada Mountains.

"I don't know about you guys, but I could get something to eat," said Jason.

"Sounds good to me," said Gypsy.

They piled back into the van and continued up State Route 198 into the village of Three Rivers. "There's the place," said Gypsy. "It's called the Sequoia Coffee Company and it serves breakfast and brunch."

Jason pulled into the gravel parking lot and stopped the van.

They took a table outside under a large umbrella. A waitress appeared from inside and stood by their table.

"Coffees?"

"Black," said Jason.

"Black," said Gypsy.

"You got Mountain Dew?" asked Sal.

"Just coffee, tea, or hot chocolate."

"Hot chocolate," said Sal.

"Be right back. The menu's over there on the stand," said the waitress.

They all looked at the stand and saw a chalk board with three columns, one said Sky Bowl, one said Mountain Bowl, and the third said Sunrise Bowl. Each column contained a variety of breakfasts, from granola and oatmeal to eggs, sausage, French toast, corned beef hash, and avocado toast.

The waitress returned with their coffees and hot chocolate. "Know what you want?"

"Are those our only choices?" said Gypsy.

"No, but that's what most folks order. We can make you anything you want, honey. We also got griddle donuts, which if you've never had, you ain't lived yet."

"I just want a cheddar cheese omelet with an English muffin," said Gypsy.

"Okay, how about you, big fella?" she asked, looking at Sal.

"I'll have one of those griddle donuts and can you make pancakes?"

"Blueberry, raspberry, banana, pecan, plain, buttermilk, or whole grain?"

"Pecan buttermilk," said Sal. "Sausage on the side."

"And you?" she asked Jason.

"Can you do a western omelet with just the vegetables?"

"Got it. Be back in a few," said the waitress as she walked back inside.

Gypsy was reading a text on her phone.

"From looking at the map, I figure we're about fifteen miles from the actual park," said Jason. "Can I ask you something?"

Gypsy looked up from her phone. "What?"

"What is it you're demonstrating against?"

"Stop the Chop. Isn't that why you're here?"

"I guess it is," said Jason.

"You guess? You drove all the way here from where'd you say?"

"Evanston, Illinois. Just outside of Chicago."

"You drove halfway across the country, and you don't know why?" asked Gypsy.

"I sorta knew. I knew it had something to do with trees. And that it was probably something bad. That I had to do what I could to stop it."

"That's a bit random."

"You have to forgive my Dad," said Sal. "He's been under a lot of pressure lately. He lost his job a few weeks ago, after getting hurt in some kind of bio-chemical accident. Plus, he just found out he has a son, me. And he's been eating these strange mushrooms and talking to plants and well, you get the picture, right."

"Not really," said Gypsy.

"When I told you I was coming here because the plants told me to, you said you believed me," said Jason. "Were you just kidding?"

"No, I believe you. I just figured they told you the whole story."

"Well, if you've ever talked to plants, then you'd know they sometimes leave shit out."

"Okay, I get that," said Gypsy. "So, you just need me to fill in what the plants didn't tell you, is that it?"

"That's it," Jason replied.

"Well, I got this email from the Save the Planet Club that some assholes were planning on chopping down trees in Sequoia National Park so they put out a call to all members to show up and stop them. You know there are ten million members to our club? It goes back fifty years. Can you believe our Commander in Chief is even allowing this to happen? These are our parks."

"Actually, the federal government controls what goes on in the parks," said Jason.

"Whose side are you on?" asked Gypsy.

"I'm on the side of the trees," said Jason. "When is this chopping supposed to occur?"

"This weekend is what I was told," said Gypsy.

"Where are you supposed to meet the rest of your club members?" Jason asked.

"At the foot of General Sherman," said Gypsy.

"General?"

"It's a tree. I'm sure you've heard of it. It's the oldest tree in the park, I believe."

"I'm not sure if it's the oldest, but it's the largest. It stands some two hundred seventy-five feet tall," said Jason.

"Wow," said Gypsy.

"That's tall!" said Sal.

"That's what they were trying to tell me," said Jason. "They told me to see the General. I should've figured it was a tree."

"So, how long have you been talking to trees?"

"Ever since the accident," said Jason. "I'm a biogenetics engineer, and one day the Gene Gun I was using exploded, and my body absorbed some radioactive plant DNA. Maple tree to be exact. Ever since that happened, I've been communicating with the plant world."

"My friends are gonna love you," said Gypsy.

"We'll see," said Jason. "Here comes our food."

The waitress who took their order appeared at their table holding a giant tray piled with steaming plates.

"Hope you're all hungry," she said, handing out their orders.

After breakfast, Jason, Gypsy, and Sal got back into the yellow van and followed the signs to the Sequoia National Park. They knew they were getting close when they had to drive through a giant notch in an even larger tree that had fallen across the road leading into the park. The roof of the van nearly didn't clear the top of the notched opening.

There was a $35 vehicle fee collected by a young man in a guard shack. They drove in and parked.

As they emerged from the van, the three of them looked out into the forest of giants, trees as tall as skyscrapers as far as the eye could see. The park was made up of forty separate Sequoia groves.

"Guess we're here," said Jason. "Why don't you see if you can find your friends."

"What are you gonna do?" asked Gypsy.

"Go see the General."

"That's where I'm supposed to meet em'," said Gypsy. "Might as well go together."

"What am I supposed to do?" asked Sal.

"Just hold down the fort," said Jason. "I just need a couple minutes, Sal."

"Why can't I come too?" Sal asked.

"I just need a moment to myself with the trees," said Jason. "I won't be long. I promise."

"No problem, Pops," said Sal. "I'll be right here."

Jason and Gypsy walked off toward a trail leading up through the giant sequoias. As they continued up the trail, they could see a large sign ahead announcing the "Giant Forest," which is home for General Sherman and four more of the largest trees on the planet. These were the war council of the plant world.

He reached into his jean pockets and felt a few more loose magic mushrooms in there. "What the hell. Why not?" Jason asked himself before taking a bite.

"What are you doing?" asked Gypsy.

"Magic mushrooms," said Jason. "They help me communicate with the plant world. Don't ask me why or how, they just do."

"I'm not judging," said Gypsy. "If you have any to spare, I'd like to try some."

"You ever do shrooms?"

"Once or twice," said Gypsy. "Though I never tried to talk to plants. I did do some serious introspective contemplation."

"Knock yourself out," said Jason as he handed her a couple of mushrooms.

"I'm gonna go talk to the General now," said Jason.

"I'll see if I can find my friends," said Gypsy.

Jason turned toward the General, and looked up. By now, Jason's body reacted to the shrooms nearly instantaneously. He placed his hand against the General's bark. He let his senses connect to the giant living being. He could feel the General's pain. The gigantic tree felt frightened. It was not alone. They all were. All the trees in the park's forest shared a fear that had been growing greater by the day.

The other redwoods all seemed to be leaning in towards Jason, like they were hanging their heads down in grief. Jason put his ear up against the General to see if he could hear anything that went along with the grimness he sensed. As he did that, it began to block out all surrounding sounds of human chatter, birds chirping, and wind rushing. Then, Jason started to hear something that sounded like a whisper. It said, "Stop them."

Jason felt so connected to the General as well as all the other surrounding trees. He felt as if they were transferring life to him just by the touch. He knew how important they were, all the oxygen they produced, and what killing them would do to the atmosphere. Jason could feel their sadness. But also, their anger. It was overwhelming.

He continued to press his hand up against the bark, but he had to move his ear away as the voices got louder and louder. Jason could hear different trees trying to communicate with him all at once. He looked down at his watch. It appeared to be ticking slower than ever. *It must be the shrooms*, Jason thought to himself.

Jason then slid down to the base of the huge trunk and felt the moist ground. He stuck his fingers into the grass and soil, as if he was putting on a glove. He pushed deeper until the tips of his fingers connected with the mycelium strands and a jolt of awareness entered his body.

That awareness was very troubling. If he understood correctly, it meant he was too late.

"Don't worry General. The Cavalry has arrived," said Jason, although he was not sure that mattered any more.

As he stood back up, Jason felt unsettled over this latest communication. He looked around at the trees. There did not seem to be a problem or any threat that he could detect. Jason finally made his way back to Sal who was waiting near the car.

"How'd it go?" asked Sal.

"It was…intense," Jason replied.

"Do you know what you have to do?"

"Not entirely, but we're here, and that was the first step," said Jason.

Just then, Gypsy joined them.

"Did you find your friends?" asked Jason.

"They were here, but apparently they already left," said Gypsy.

"You mean the demonstration is over?" asked Jason.

"I'm not sure what happened," said Gypsy. "I talked to a few folks who were hanging around and they said whatever was supposed to happen got cancelled. I don't get it. Last I heard, some fool had threatened to chop down a bunch of these sequoias to build mansions for some rich folks. Apparently, it was all a joke."

"Or a distraction," said Jason.

"Why a distraction?" asked Gypsy.

"I have to make a call," said Jason and he got out his mobile and punched in Bowde's number.

"Are you there yet?" Bowde asked.

"We're here," said Jason. "But something strange is going on."

"Yeah, well, Miles is the personification of strange. You must know that by now." Bowde replied.

"No, I mean, everything seems fine."

"Fine? What are you, nuts? It's been on television for hours. How these giant earth moving vehicles have been tearing down forests on the sides of mountains to clear the area for lithium mines."

"I'm telling you Bowde, we're right here in the Sequoia National Park and everything's fine."

"Yeah, well that's because you're in the wrong place, asshole. Who said anything about Sequoia National Park? I said Kirkwood, California. It's in the northern Sierra Nevada mountains."

"That's what he meant?" Jason asked in a much louder voice.

"What *who* meant?" asked Bowde.

"The General. He said I was too late. He just didn't give me enough information, that I was in the wrong location. How far is Kirkwood from the Sequoia National Park?"

"Let me check Google maps," said Bowde. "Looks like about three hundred twenty miles."

"I gotta go," said Jason.

"Go where?" said Bowde. "By the time you get there, all the trees will be gone."

"I gotta try," said Jason.

Jason put away his phone and turned toward Gypsy and Sal.

"What is it?" asked Sal.

"They tricked us," said Jason. "They're destroying a forest in Nevada over five hours from here."

"Then, they tricked me too," said Gypsy. "You mind if I come with you?"

"Fine by me," said Jason. "What about it, Sal? You okay with Gypsy coming with us?"

"Of course."

Chapter 37

Jason, Sal, and Gypsy got back into the van and Jason used *an* app to find the fastest route that would get them to Kirkwood in more than five and a half hours but included some tolls.

After they were on their way, Gypsy looked over at Jason and said, "I get the feeling you know something that you're not telling me."

"Only that the people involved, the ones we need to stop, are a nasty bunch," said Jason.

"How do you know these folks?" asked Gypsy.

"I used to work for them," said Jason.

"I knew there was something," said Gypsy.

"I guess I'm ashamed about that," admitted Jason. "I just want to make it right."

"Why are they destroying the forests?" asked Gypsy.

"Lithium," said Jason. "They've got this deal to dig about two dozen lithium mines around the world and most of them involve the destruction of large areas of forest land.

It's one of them Green New deal initiatives our misinformed former President signed off on a while back."

"That's fucked up," said Gypsy. "How come I never heard about this?"

"Cause the media was covering it up."

"Why?"

"It goes against the whole climate change narrative that administration was pushing, that we're facing this existential crisis of global warming, blah, blah, blah."

"Aren't we? Don't tell me you're one of those climate change deniers," said Gypsy.

"No, not at all. I believe climate change is real," said Jason. "It's just not something we need to be that concerned with right now. Plus, ironically, destroying forests only makes the problem of carbon dioxide in the atmosphere that much worse since it's the trees and forests that remove it during photosynthesis to create oxygen in our atmosphere. It's this fallacy that everyone has to stop driving gas engine cars and go electric or the world is going to end that led to the push to mine lithium which is used in electric vehicle batteries. Only unfortunately that push is going to do more harm than any possible good by depleting our atmosphere of oxygen."

"So, all this money, these trillions of dollars we're spending on climate change is actually doing more harm than good?"

"Afraid so," said Jason. "Even the United Nations, which has hosted many of these climate change conferences, just put out its list of top priorities for the world related to its Sustainable Development Goals. There are sixteen things on the list and guess which one has moved to the bottom of that list?"

"Climate change?"

"Yep. I figure if the U.N. isn't that worried about it anymore, I shouldn't be either. Look at China, India, Russia, most of the industrialized world, as they continue to build coal powered factories and drill for oil. But we stopped but that is going to change. We had this ridiculous war on fossil fuel that was a major factor in causing inflation and supply chain disruption and recession. And the people who were suffering the most were the poorest because they could no longer afford a decent meal," Jason explained.

"Why don't more people know about this?" Gypsy asked.

"Clicks and greed. The media gets more clicks from telling scary stories and frightening people than by telling the truth. Then politicians pick up horror scenarios and promise to save us by building more electric cars and solar panels. Armageddon is big business. Have you noticed lately that every time there's a hurricane or fire, somehow climate change creeps into the story as the villain responsible, or at least a contributing factor?"

"So, the media is responsible, is that what you're saying?"

"Not completely, but it's a contributing factor. The media is among those responsible for letting itself get manipulated for ratings. But there's something else driving all this and it all boils down to whoever stands to gain the most, be it power, wealth, or whatever. It's basic human greed, I'm afraid, and it's going to destroy us all."

"The plants told you all that, huh?"

"No, I sort of figured it out myself by watching what my old boss was up to. Miles doesn't do anything that doesn't benefit Miles. If he's involved in this destruction of forests, then he must be getting something out of it."

"I should send some texts," said Gypsy. "Maybe I can get some of my friends who got fooled into going to Sequoia National Park, like me, to join us in Kirkwood."

"Guess it couldn't hurt," said Jason.

"So, Gypsy," asked Sal from the back seat, "What's your story?"

"My story?"

"Where do you come from, what do you do, who are you? That sorta thing."

"Like I told your Dad, I came here from Vegas, to join up with other members of the Save the Planet Club. It's an environmental group."

"What do you do in Vegas?" asked Sal.

"Whatever it takes," said Gypsy. "A little dancing, a little dealing. Cards, not drugs. How about you Sal. What's your story? You talk to plants, too?"

"Nah. That's just my Dad's thing."

"What's your Mom do?"

"She's dead. That's why I'm with my Dad. Why are you here?"

"Oh, sorry. Look kid, maybe we should start over, okay? I don't know you; you don't know me. We got a long trip ahead, so let's try to keep it friendly."

"Yeah, well, I was just getting to know my Dad when you showed up out of nowhere, and ever since then, he hasn't said two words to me."

Jason looked in the rearview, "Sal, hey. I'm sorry. I've got a lot on my mind, and it doesn't have anything to do with Gypsy, so don't blame her, okay? We're heading into a major shitstorm and I still don't have a clue about what I'm gonna do once we get there."

Chapter 38

Special Agent Carter Wiseman and Dr. Julie Green landed on a small private airstrip on the outskirts of Kirkwood, California, courtesy of the FBI. They deplaned and were escorted to a black electric SUV before being driven to a temporary job site built in the forest against the side of a mountain. As they got closer, they could see a large chunk of the mountain and forest range had been removed and all that remained was rock and soil, and several earth digging machines. It was the same location being broadcast on the news.

"Now that we're here, we need to get in contact with Mr. Wilder and Miles. We must let them know they could be in immediate danger," Agent Wiseman said.

"I have a bad feeling about this," Julie responded. "I don't know why, but I'm starting to feel sick."

"Are you okay?" asked Carter. "Here, Julie, have some water," he said as he unscrewed the cap of his water bottle and handed it to Julie.

She took the bottle and had a sip.

"Just breathe," said Carter.

Julie took a deep breath.

"It's going to be okay," Carter continued. "We're doing our duty here."

"Are we? You realize one of those assholes we're trying to save is about to destroy one of our national treasures? And they won't be happy to see us," Julie said.

The car they were in hit a speed bump, increasing Julie's tension.

Julie continued, "I say you just arrest the sons of bitches under the guise of protective custody and shut this shit down."

"You know I can't do that," said Wiseman. "The President of the United States previously signed an executive order allowing federal land to be used for lithium mining."

"Did that order give these assholes the right to destroy thousands of acres of forests?"

"I'm afraid it did," said Wiseman.

"Then the order has to be revoked or Congress has to pass legislation invalidating that order," said Julie. "That order put the planet in jeopardy thereby putting the country in danger."

It turned out that it took Jason, Gypsy, and Sal a little over six hours to reach the outskirts of Kirkwood, California. They got off the highway and were driving the minivan through the backroads of forests and campgrounds, edging closer to where large sections of forest were being leveled to clear the area for mining.

Jason stopped the van on a dirt road, miles away from any main roads. He could see the work site from a distance through the trees. He saw many men in orange jackets.

Jason ran his right hand through his beard. It had grown almost three inches in the past few weeks, faster than it had ever grown before.

He pulled out his burner flip phone and dialed Bowde's number. The phone rang, until Howard finally answered.

"Woods?"

"I made it," said Jason. "We're in Kirkwood."

"No way," Bowde said. "You're a lunatic."

"Guess so," said Jason as he rubbed his thick beard.

"I can't believe it. I'm guessing you've seen the news. Miles is out there in full force with this Chance Wilder guy? I see there are a few protests going on," said Bowde.

"Yeah, I saw that. We picked up a hitchhiker named Gypsy who called in her Save the Planet Club friends to make an appearance."

"So, I guess you're not the only one trying to stop them," Howard said.

"That's true," said Jason. "But what if I'm the only one who *can* stop them?"

"Listen. The truth is you gotta get them to agree to cancel the plans altogether. Miles is a madman and all he cares about is the money these deals are gonna bring to him and Morabito. But Richard Adler and Chance Wilder might be able to be convinced if they think their personal safety is at stake. You just gotta get to them," Bowde explained.

"Well, I'm gonna do what I can. I'm sure Miles is gonna be there, expecting me," said Jason.

"Screw Miles. You can do this," Howard said. "I know you can."

"I appreciate your faith in me," said Jason. "I'm gonna try my best."

"I'll be here for you if you need me. Just call any time," said Bowde.

"Thanks. I'll be in touch," said Jason before he hung up the phone.

Then, he threw the burner phone into the woods.

"Let's go. It's time to get over there," said Jason.

"I'm ready," said Sal.

"Me too," added Gypsy.

They filled a couple of backpacks with drinks, some snacks, some exotic plants Jason still had that he'd stolen from the Morabito labs, and a loaded Gene Gun.

"What the hell is that?" asked Gypsy, as Jason strapped the box holding the helium and DNA pellets onto his back, along with the Gene gun into a holster originally designed to hold a revolver.

"This is a Gene Gun," said Jason. "It's what we use to create new forms of plant life. Primarily vegetables and recently hard wood."

"What do you expect to do with it out here?"

"I don't know," said Jason. "I just know I will feel better having it than not."

"If you say so," said Gypsy.

"Better to be prepared for anything," said Jason.

Once they were all packed up, Jason, Gypsy, and Sal headed for the center of the action, through the forest of redwoods toward the Wildwood Homes job site. They were hiding behind trees and making their way through the woods as stealthily as they could.

A little less than a mile away, Julie and Carter were elbowing their way through the small crowd of protestors outside of the temporary job site Wildwood Homes Incorporated put up to prepare for the deforestation of that large area of the Kirkwood National Park. Protestors were chanting in unison things like, "Leave the trees alone!" and "Save the Redwoods."

It did not look like the protestors were having any effect on the work as dozens of workers continued to prepare to cut the redwoods. There were large sawing machines around certain sequoias that looked so sharp they could cut through anything on earth.

Carter and Julie saw Miles Walsh climb out of a large SUV. They hurried over to him.

"Mr. Walsh. We need to have a word with you," said Agent Wiseman.

"Yes, how can I help you?" asked Miles. "I have a meeting I need to get to with Chance Wilder in just a minute."

"Mr. Walsh. My name is Special Agent Carter Wiseman with the FBI. And this is Dr. Julie Green."

"How can I help you folks?" asked Miles.

"Well, we traveled a long way to get here. First from Texas to Chicago, and now here. We are very concerned that you, as well as Mr. Adler and Mr. Wilder, are all in danger. I don't know if you've heard but as many as half a dozen CEOs in your field have died under mysteriously circumstances recently. We suggest you both leave here immediately and get your crews to shut down," Carter pleaded.

"What do you mean?" the president of Morabito asked.

"We don't think it's safe for you to be here," Julie said sincerely.

"You think these protestors are gonna try to harm us? They don't seem that violent," said Miles.

"No, we don't think the protestors are the problem. We had an anonymous tip about a Jason Woods, a former employer of yours actually," said Wiseman.

"You think my former employee, Jason Woods, is gonna show up and try to ruin things for us or to harm us?" asked Miles with a grin on his face. "Honestly, I don't think the guy has it in him."

"We heard that he tried to threaten you once before. Is that true?" agent Wiseman asked.

"The guy sent me a package. He was just messing around. Disgruntled that he lost the job that he loved. I got over it. I don't think that he will try anything. However, just in case I'll give the order to have beefed up security here.

But the deal between Wildwood Homes and Morabito will be crucial for both companies going forward. And it is a big part to do with what we have going on with Evergreen Smart Phone. So, this must work out. We can't cancel anything now. Plus I promised Richard as a special reward for our lithium partnership, we'll be using the trees we cut down to build his perfect redwood sequoia home by next summer. We need to make that happen if we ever want this Evergreen Smart Phone deal to turn into reality. So, will you help ensure that this all goes down without any problems, Special Agent Wiseman?" asked Miles.

"We understand the importance of this deal to you, but we are very concerned about your safety, and especially Richard Adler, who is quite a powerful figure in big tech. We will stick around and make sure nothing goes wrong. But I am telling you, sir, I would get Mr. Wilder to postpone operations until we get everything under wraps. At least until we take Jason Woods into custody so he's not a threat. However, it's your call. We are just here to warn you and for support," Carter explained.

Dr. Green added, "With all these recent deaths we're hearing about with CEOs around the country, we don't want y'all to be next in line. Which brings me to my next point. It may not be Jason you should be worried about."

"There's someone else?"

"Not someone," said Julie.

302

"What then?"

"We don't know how to explain it without sounding crazy," said Carter.

"It's the plants," blurted Julie. "You need to be worried about the plants."

"What's she talking about?" asked Miles.

"Each death of a CEO involved some sort of plant," Carter added.

"You're right. You do sound crazy. Listen. I appreciate your concern. And I appreciate your support. Now, we got some work to do. And I have a meeting I must get to with Mr. Wilder and Mr. Adler. But we will talk again soon, Agent Wiseman," said Miles before shaking the agent's hand. He waved to Julie with an eerie smile, then he turned around to walk away.

"We tried," Carter said. "If they don't believe us, if they don't want our help, there isn't much else we can do."

"That man gives me the creeps. I don't like his vibe," said Julie.

"We're doing our job here. We're doing what we are hired to do," said Carter. "Even if that means protecting those we may not totally agree with. Even if you 'don't like his vibe,' as you put it."

"I don't know. I told you, I had, and I still have a bad feeling about this," said Julie as she looked around at all of the redwoods that surrounded her.

"It will be over soon," said Carter as he put his hand on Julie's shoulder. "By tomorrow, we'll be on a plane heading back home. And when we land, I'm taking you out for Korean BBQ."

"How can you even think about food at a time like this?" said Julie. "Look around you. These beautiful trees that have survived hundreds and some of them thousands of years of fires, drought, floods, are being destroyed because some billionaire wants to build a home out of them. This isn't right and you know it."

"You know there's more to it than that," said Wiseman. "They need to clear the trees so they can get to the lithium. It's the new oil. It's what's going to give us back our energy independence."

"I've read the former administration's talking points," said Julie. "What they didn't tell us was the cost and the damage lithium mining was doing to the environment. See what's going on here? How much land is being ravaged to mine for lithium? It's nothing like drilling for oil, Carter. Lithium requires hundreds of acres of land to extract the lithium from the minerals within it because it can't exist on its own. It's too unstable. It's why lithium batteries have been known to catch fire when left on too long. Whoever thought lithium was the answer didn't think things through.

"You know some cars can't even park in certain garages because their lithium batteries are unstable? Check it out. The cost of extracting lithium from the earth is a hundred times higher than mining fossil fuels like oil, coal and natural gas. Destroying this land does more to contribute to global warming than all the carbon emissions in all of the cars and factories in the world. So no, my friend. You've been sold a bill of goods by industrial thugs who have been panicking the world for decades just so they can make money."

"If that's how you feel, why are you even helping me?" asked Wiseman.

"It's not how I *feel,* it's just the truth," said Julie. "I also don't feel that murder is the answer and that's why I'm helping you. But if you want to stop the murders, you need to understand the motives behind them."

"And they are?" asked Wiseman.

"Isn't it obvious?" answered Julie. "Survival of the planet."

Chapter 39

Jason, Gypsy and Sal were making their way through the redwood forest in the job site in Kirkwood National Park when Jason's computer bag was beginning to weigh heavily on his shoulder. So he led the others to a fallen tree and sat down.

"Let's rest here," said Jason. "Sal, grab me a water from your backpack."

Sal took out two plastic bottles of water and handed one to Jason and the other to Gypsy. "Thanks," she said

"We're getting close," said Jason.

He felt an intimacy with the plant world that he had never felt before, a powerful closeness and sense of family walking through the redwood forest with his son and his new friend. The forest made him feel safe. And the closer he got to the site that was being protested, the angrier he got. He could hear chants from more than a half mile away, "Leave! Leave! We need trees to breathe!"

The three started walking again. And as Jason got closer, he realized that he started to see more and more red.

He still saw some green, but the red hues were becoming stronger. He figured this had something to do with being amid a redwood forest that was being demolished to create a desert-like environment in order to extract lithium from the ground where the trees once stood.

Jason also felt a sense of helplessness over what to do. Even if he figured out a way to stop the destruction here, he knew there were hundreds of other locations around the world including the rainforests of South America that were experiencing the same destruction. He was just one person. What could he possibly do to stop this forest deforestation before it was too late?

It was nearing eleven in the morning and workers in hardhats and giant machines were tearing down the beautiful, tall, cinnamon-colored trees. A large section of forest had already been cleared as huge logging trucks hauled away the trunks of these ancient warriors.

Jason approached a redwood that was still standing. He leaned closer and pressed his hands against its rough bark.

"What can I do?" Jason asked out loud.

Just then a leaf drifted from above and landed at Jason's feet. Jason knelt down to retrieve the leaf, and as his hands touched the ground, he could feel a vibration coming from beneath the soil. He dropped the leaf and plunged his hands into the ground at the foot of the redwood.

As soon as his fingers connected to the tiny network of mycelium fungi a communication came through. "You need to stop them."

Jason looked down at the ground as tears filled his eyes.

How? was all he could think.

"Show them the consequences" came the answer.

"How do I do that?" asked Jason.

"You have the tools and the wisdom. Use them."

Jason stood up and returned to Gypsy and Sal.

"C'mon, we need to keep going," said Jason.

He picked up his computer bag and powerwalked to the area where the workers were tearing down trees.

Jason, Gypsy, and Sal got closer to the jobsite. They crept around the corner where the Wildwood Homes Inc. huts and portable containers were set up. It appeared that there was an office with caution tape around it. Jason could see these contraptions around many of the larger trees containing the largest and sharpest sawblades he had ever seen.

"We need to blend in with the workers," said Jason. "Otherwise, we'll never get close to the leaders."

Jason looked through a window of one of the trailers and saw lockers and orange vests, along with hard hats similar to ones the workers chopping down the trees were wearing.

"In here," said Jason as he led Gypsy and Sal into the trailer where they found a box of orange vests. They put them on as well as hard hats. Then they stepped outside and followed a group of workers toward a crowd near a larger trailer.

"What's the plan, Dad?" asked Sal.

"Right now, the plan is to get close to the people running this disaster."

"Then what?" Sal asked.

"Talk to them."

"Talk? Dad, I think we're beyond the talking stage."

"I'm sure you're right, son, but I figure I gotta give them a chance. Then, if they still don't get it, well, then I use this," said Jason, holding up the Gene Gun.

Jason, Gypsy, and Sal joined a group of workers as they walked in a group to a large trailer, like the kind movie production companies used for their top talent.

The group stopped in front of the trailer until the entire area in front of the trailer was filled with men wearing orange vests and hard hats.

Jason looked around at the crowd and decided to find out why everyone was just standing around.

"Excuse me," Jason said to one of the workers. "Why are we here again?"

"Beats the shit out of me," the worker responded. "My supe tells us to gather by the boss's trailer at noon, so we gather in front of the boss's trailer at noon."

"Yeah," said Jason. "Thanks."

Just then, the door to the trailer opened and out stepped Miles and another man who approached the crowd of workers.

Miles stepped up to a podium and a microphone. He tapped the mic to make sure it was on. Then he stepped back and the other man walked over and took the mic from Miles.

"How's everyone doing?" he asked. "For those who don't know me, my name is Chance Wilder and you all work for me. I just wanted to take some time out of your busy day to say thanks and to tell you all how proud I am of each and every one of you. You are blazing a trail into the future, the tip of the spear in this energy revolution. By clearing this land, you are on the front line of helping us regain our energy independence by allowing us access to a valuable mineral used in virtually every electric vehicle being manufactured today. This is just the beginning, too. We've located sites within the U.S. for another twenty-five lithium mines that will require your services. You know what that means, right? Long-term employment. That's right. I would say you have ten more years of job security. How great is that?"

Jason looked around at the group of workers who looked under-whelmed by what they heard. Around the edges of the clearing, protestors continued to chant and shout. But they had even less effect on the men in orange vests and hardhats.

One of the men stepped forward and raised his hand. "You know what would be even greater?" asked the hardhat.

"What's that?" asked Chance.

"If we got paid on time, once in a while," said the worker.

"Yeah," shouted a few others.

"That's all being taken care of," said Chance. "We just signed a multi-billion-dollar partnership with Morabito Labs. So, I can pretty much guarantee that not only will we be paying you on time, but there's going to be a little bonus in your next pay checks, especially if we finish this job on schedule. So, let's get back to work, and turn these trees into lumber."

The crowd of workers quickly dispersed, leaving Jason, Gypsy, and Sal standing by themselves. But Jason felt his connection to the plants in the area growing stronger. He saw that work was about to start up again. He looked down at his watch. It read 11:33.

"Let's go," he said as he headed toward Miles and Chance, who were just about to go back inside the large trailer.

Chapter 40

"Miles!" Jason shouted.

Miles spun around.

"Jason Woods, holy shit, in the flesh," said Miles. "I hear you've been looking for me."

"That's funny. It's come to my attention that you've been looking for me," said Jason.

"Yeah, well I guess we're both a couple of hard guys to get ahold of these days," Miles responded.

"Is this the guy you were telling me about? The lunatic that used to work at Morabito?" asked Chance.

"Yep, this is him," Miles said. "Jason Woods. Genetics engineer extraordinaire. Jason used to be a pretty good scientist. Not bad with a Gene Gun, either. Made me and Morabito a ton of money creating different kinds of hybrid plants and vegetables. But then, something happened, and he went rogue on us."

Miles noticed Gypsy and Sal. "And who might you folks be?"

"Listen, Miles," said Jason. "You guys have to put an end to this."

312

"What are you talking about? Put an end to what? What do you think is going on here? This is just business," said Miles.

"Yes, I get it," said Jason. "Everything is just business to you. But I am telling you, and you, Mr. Wilder, that you can't do this. There will be consequences."

"Save it, fella," said Chance. "You think you're the first dipshit activist that's tried to stop me? You're not the first and you won't be the last."

"Sir, with all due respect. This is much bigger than you and I. And I'm afraid of what will happen to you if you proceed," Jason continued.

"What's going to happen?"

"People are going to get hurt. And, not just you, but everyone here," said Jason.

"You threatening me? Did you hear this clown? You think I'm afraid of you?"

"It's not me you have be afraid of."

"Oh, you think that army of tree huggers out there are going to do something?" Miles asked.

"Not them, either."

Chance looked at Miles. "You got any idea what this guy is talking about?" asked Chance.

"I got messages," Jason blurted.

"Messages? What do you mean, messages?"

"From them, the trees. I know it's hard to believe. But the trees spoke to me. They told me to stop you. Or they will retaliate."

313

Both Chance and Miles began laughing hysterically together.

"Man, this asshole is crazier than you made him out to be," said Chance.

"Hey! Just…just…shut the fuck up! And listen to my dad!" Sal shouted.

The two men continued to laugh until Chance stopped and said, "All right, the fun and games are over. Get these two buffoons the hell out of my face already. We got work to do."

"I tried," said Jason, as he pulled the Gene Gun out of its makeshift holster. "If you don't believe me, maybe you'll believe them."

"What's he rambling on about?"

Jason aimed the Gene Gun at Chance and fired a pellet of redwood DNA into his chest. He then turned toward Miles and did the same thing.

"What the hell!" shouted Chance. "The son of a bitch just shot me."

"You'll be fine," said Jason. "It's just a little tree DNA."

"Woods," said Miles, "you just got yourself a felony assault charge. I figure it'll be good for about ten to fifteen years, minimum. And hey, look, it's the FBI, right on cue."

Special Agent Carter and Dr. Julie Green approached Sal, Gypsy, and Jason.

"Jason Woods, I presume," said Carter.

"That's me," said Jason.

"I'm Special Agent Carter Wiseman of the FBI. I'm afraid you're going to have to come with me. I have some questions I need to ask you."

"Questions?" yelled Miles. "You have to arrest him."

"That's not the way it works," said Carter. "As of now, Mr. Woods is considered a person of interest in an on-going investigation. So, until we have any evidence directly connecting him to a crime, we'd like to just question him, okay?"

"You got your link right here," said Miles. "He just assaulted me and Chance Wilder. Shot us with that Gene Gun he's carrying."

Carter turned toward Jason. "Is that true?"

"Technically, yes, although I'm not sure it rises to the level of assault," noted Jason. "If you'd just give me a couple of minutes to explain what's happening here, and you still feel like a crime has been committed, I'll gladly surrender and you can arrest me on charges of assault, although I doubt they'd hold up in court."

"First, remove that Gene Gun, or whatever you call it, and then tell me what you want to say," said Carter.

Jason unstrapped the Gene Gun and put it on the ground. "This device, the Gene Gun, is used in genetic labs to create new lifeforms, typically plants and vegetables, by combining their DNA at the molecular level. The so-called assault in this case involved microscopic particles of redwood DNA, as well as mycelium fungi, and psilocybin to help speed the process. It took me a couple days before I could…well, you'll see soon enough."

"Speed the process? What process?"

"The communications process."

Carter looked at Julie. "Do you know what he's talking about?"

"I think he's talking about communicating with plants," said Sal.

"The only reason I used the Gene Gun was because they weren't listening to me," said Jason. "So, they need to hear it from the source. Although I'm not sure 'hear' is the right sense."

"You're still not making much sense to me," said Carter.

"Let me go back to the beginning," said Jason. "It all started after the accident at Morabito Labs when I was hit with a dose of plant DNA. Maple tree to be exact. This was about four weeks ago. After that, I began getting messages from the plant world, communications, that something bad was going to happen."

"Bad? Like what?"

"Like a major extinction event."

"He's nuts," yelled Miles. "Extinction event, my ass. We're just cutting down a few trees here."

"I'm inclined to agree with Miles on that one," said Carter.

"You're making a mistake," said Jason.

"Maybe, but for now, why don't you and your friends just come with me and let these men do their jobs," said Carter as he placed his hand on Jason's shoulder.

"Please take your hand off my shoulder," said Jason as he nudged himself away.

"Don't make this difficult," said Carter. "I've had a long day, and I don't feel like using force. Just come with me."

Jason looked at Gypsy, who had fear in her eyes and then at Sal, who looked just as frightened.

"Okay," said Jason, "but let's not go too far because you're going to witness something that unless you see it, you may not believe it."

"Let's just move over there so we're out of the way," said Carter.

Jason, Gypsy, and Sal followed Agent Wiseman and Professor Julie Green as they walked away from the trailer and to the edge of the work area.

"Okay, fellas. Showtime's over," said Chance. "Let's wrap this baby up."

On Chance's command, men in orange vests returned to their machinery and resumed their work.

Chapter 41

Julie and Carter escorted Jason and Sal over to a nearby bench. Jason and Sal sat down. FBI Agent Carter began grilling them, first asking Jason, "So, where were you the night of August 3rd?" This was the same night that Cecil Lyons was killed.

"What?" said Jason. "I have no clue. How am I supposed to remember?"

"It was just four weeks ago."

"That was soon after my accident, so I was probably high on psilocybin and communicating with the plants. I have no idea where I was on any specific day during that time. Why do you ask?"

"We have reason to believe you may have had something do with the deaths of various CEOs around that time," said Wiseman.

"What in the world? Of course not!" Jason shouted. "I've never killed or had anyone killed in my entire life!"

"Why did you come all the way here?" asked Julie.

Turning toward Julie, Carter said, almost in a whisper, "Let me do this. I got it."

"Agent Carter, I've been researching this topic my entire adult life. Let me speak to him," Julie said with confidence.

"Okay. Fine. Have a go at him," Wiseman said.

"What made you travel all of this way from a suburb of Chicago?" she asked.

"You're going to say I'm batshit insane."

"Try me," said Dr. Green.

"Well, the trees told me to be here. That I needed to stop all of this, before it's too late," Jason said.

"How do you understand the trees?" Julie asked with a confused look on her face.

"Like I said, it started with an accident with a Gene Gun in a genetics lab," said Jason. "Oh, and a little bit of mushrooms. But long story short, I speak to them, and they speak to me. And I know they, meaning Miles and, in this case Chance, need to be stopped. I'm not sure what will happen, but I really don't think it will be good for any of us."

Julie stopped to think for a moment. She looked at Jason dead in the eyes. She thought for a few moments, then she looked over at Carter and said, "Maybe he's right. I believe him."

"What are you talking about? This man is insane, at the very least," said Carter.

"You don't know shit about me!" Jason shouted.

Just then, the giant saws came to life. One of them was set up at the largest redwood in Kirkwood National Park. A middle-aged man in a hardhat had wrapped the giant saw mechanism around the tree. He lifted a box that exposed the button that would begin the sawing process. Then he suddenly pushed the giant red button.

This prompted the blade to come alive. It sliced into the two-inch-thick bark on the side of the magnificent redwood. All around them, saws sputtered and buzzed as other workers began to work on their trees. The destruction was well underway.

"We're too late," said Jason, reluctantly.

But then, he heard shouting coming from the large trailer. It was Miles and Chance, and they were yelling, "Stop!" It appeared that they both may have begun to see in green as well.

The two men ran among the sawing machines, waving their arms and yelling. "Stop sawing. Stop! Turn off your machines!"

Miles had tears streaming down his face. He looked like a changed man, not to mention more than a little deranged. Chance jumped up on a large sawing machine and pulled the operator away and turned it off himself. He then looked up at the giant redwood and bowed his head.

"Please forgive me," he pleaded to the redwood.

One by one, the sawing activities stopped.

"What the hell?" asked Wiseman.

Chapter 42

As Miles and Chance moved among the giant sawing machines, urging each one to shut off the saws, Carter and Julie turned in unison toward Jason.

Gypsy pulled Jason toward her and gave him a passionate kiss on the lips. Sal hugged his father from the side.

"As amazing as it sounds, it looks like Mr. Woods' plan worked," said Julie.

Gypsy stopped kissing Jason and leaned her head against his chest.

Jason turned toward Julie and Wiseman and said, "But will we be able to replicate this around the world? There are another one hundred sites just like this one, destroying forests all over the planet."

"Maybe you won't have to," said the FBI agent.

"If what you're about to say involves certain governmental three letter agencies taking control of the mass and social media to spread information, then you should just remember how well that has worked out."

"I know," said Carter. "It was terrible. But this time it will be different. This time we won't try to hide it. Plus, this time we'll be on the right side."

"So why not let the media decide that for themselves?" asked Julie.

"Because they might not get it," said Carter.

Jason explained, "When enough scientists like me stop being sheep and speak up about how politics and greed have corrupted the ESG —Environmental, Social, Governance —movement, we'll be able to put our priorities regarding climate change, clean water, and all the other environmental, social, and governance issues into a more realistic perspective. Once we remove panic and fear from the conversation, we can have a serious discussion on how to use fossil fuels responsibly until alternative forms of energy are able to replace them. Right now, we're about fifty years away from that happening. This rush to totally eliminate fossil fuel now was what was going to contribute to our extinction. And since we aren't smart enough to see that, nature took action to get our attention. Well, I'd say they have, wouldn't you?"

By now, all the sawing had stopped, and Miles stood next to Chance, each man covered with sawdust from the machines they had just shut down.

The clouds seemed to suddenly open up and rain poured down. Just then, lightning struck one of the redwoods that had been cut deeply by a saw.

Jason jumped at the sound as the tree cracked loudly and the redwood fell over toward Miles and Chance.

Jason raced across the clearing and tackled Miles and Chance, pushing them out of the way, just before the tree came falling to the ground, right where they had been standing.

Jason, Miles, and Chance were covered with mud from the rain as they stood up and looked at the huge fallen redwood.

"You saved my life," said Miles.

"Mine too," added Chance.

"It's the least I could do," said Jason. "You stopped the sawing and saved the forest. Or at least what's left of it."

"But the trees are obviously still angry at us," said Chance.

"You were about to wipe out an entire forest," said Jason. "Apparently not all of the trees got the word you're no longer the enemy, which by the way, still exists and still needs to be stopped."

"What can we do to help?" said Miles.

"Yeah, now that we know what's going on, I can definitely begin spreading the word among my contacts," said Chance. "Getting them to believe me, however, might not be so easy though."

"Look what I had to do to get you two to see the truth," said Jason. "I can't go around the world shooting CEOs with a Gene Gun."

"Let's get out of this rain and figure out what we have to do," said Miles.

Jason, Chance, and Miles ran toward the large trailer. Before going inside, Jason stopped.

"I'll be right back," said Jason. "Just let me tell my son and my new friend what I'm doing."

"Invite them in," said Chance. "The FBI agent and his botanist as well. We'll put on a fresh pot of coffee."

Jason rejoined Gypsy and Sal, who found shelter under a nearby maple tree.

"My hero," shouted Gypsy, who threw her arms around Jason and kissed him again.

After a moment, Jason pushed her back and said, "Hold that thought. We have more work to do. Miles and Chance have agreed to help us get the word out to all the other sites. But we may need some authoritative institution to provide enough incentive to get them to do what we're asking. We're dealing with billions of dollars in potential profits, salaries and payoffs, so those incentives must be worth more than money."

"How about freedom?" asked Gypsy.

"I'm listening," said Jason.

"We've got the FBI here. Let's use them," she added. "They can threaten to lock up whoever refuses to stop destroying the forests."

"I don't know," said Jason, looking over at Agent Wiseman who had found a similar shelter under another tree with Julie, his botanist partner.

"Can't hurt to ask," said Gypsy.

Jason ran through the rain and joined Carter and Julie. "Hey, Miles and Chance want us to join them in the trailer to devise a plan to stop the other mining sites from destroying forests in those locations," said Jason.

"This should be fun," said Carter sarcastically.

"It's the least we can do," said Julie.

Carter, Julie, Jason, Gypsy, and Sal all ran toward the trailer where Miles and Chance were waiting with a fresh pot of coffee and a table full of pastries.

Jason looked out the window and saw the rain had stopped, allowing the workers to complete their shutting down of the equipment, while those who had nothing else to do began to leave the area.

The few protestors left at the edge of the clearing rejoiced as the machinery was shut down and all sawing stopped.

Jason, Sal, and Gypsy cautiously approached the table where Miles and Chance were huddled in their own private meeting.

Miles turned toward Jason. "Chance and I have reached out to anyone we know who are involved in deforestation activities, but we're not sure how to reach all the others."

Jason looked down at the table and saw a copy of the *Financial Times*, which had the headline, "Davos World Economic Forum Pledges to Escalate Climate Mitigation."

He looked up, and said to Miles, Chance, and everyone else assembled in the trailer, "We follow the money. Or at least go where the money is."

"Where's that?" asked Miles.

Chapter 43

Jason picked up the popular pink financial publication. "Anybody know where Davos is?"

"Switzerland," said Chance. "I was invited to attend a couple of years ago. A lot of movers and shakers, Wall Street CEOs, movie stars, business journalists, and academics go there."

"If we can convince the people funding deforestation to stop paying for it, I bet those who are doing it will halt the devastation," said Jason.

"You might be on to something," said Miles.

"So how do we get to Davos?"

"You have to be invited," said Chance. "Fortunately, once you get invited, the invitations keep coming. Who wants to be my plus one?"

"We can take the Morabito Jet," said Miles.

"Can I come?" asked Gypsy.

"Me too?" said Sal.

Jason turned toward Miles and Chance. "It's gotta be the three of us."

"No problem, although it will just be you and me at the forum," Chance said to Jason.

"We can handle that."

Jason looked out a window of the trailer and saw a forest at the edge of the clearing. "I must step out for a couple of minutes. Gypsy and Sal, you stay here. I won't be long."

With that, Jason stood up and left the trailer. Outside the rain had stopped and a rainbow appeared on the horizon. Workers in hardhats were getting the machinery ready to move out.

Jason walked across the clearing and around fallen trees. He reached the edge of the forest and felt a beckoning. Slowly he moved in among the redwoods and other trees. He knelt next to the tallest tree he could find. The ground at its base was still damp as Jason plunged his hands into the moist soil, pushing deeper until his fingers touched the tiny strands of mycelium that connected all the plants of the forest.

A rush of overwhelming mixed feelings of gratitude and sorrow poured into his fingers and up his arms and through his body. The trees were grateful he had stopped the sawing and saddened by the trees that had already been cut down.

"I wish I could have gotten here sooner," said Jason. "I went to the wrong park. But I have a plan to get Morabito to combine redwood DNA with a faster growing plant that will help replace the trees we lost faster than usual. I know there's a lot more work we need to do to stop what's happening. That's why I'm flying to Switzerland to hopefully convince the powerful people who are behind what nearly happened here that they're making a horrible mistake. I may need your help while I'm there, so send word to the forests and plants near Davos, Switzerland, that I'll be in their area. It's a long shot and one that may not amount to anything. But we must try."

Chapter 44

Morabito's private jet was a Gulfstream 650, which had a seating capacity of sixteen. On this flight from California to Chicago it carried two pilots, a flight attendant and seven passengers—Jason, Gypsy, Sal, Chance, Miles, Dr. Julie Green, and FBI Special Agent Carter Wiseman.

"We're lucky they scheduled this Forum during the summer," said Chance. "Usually, it's in January and cold as hell there. But since climate change is so much of this year's agenda, they must have figured it would be more impactful to talk about global warming when it was warm out. Anyway, it's good for us. Timing wise that is."

"We have a two-and-a-half-hour flight to Chicago and then another eight hours and forty minutes to Switzerland," said Miles. "We'll layover in Chicago for the night and leave for Zurich first thing in the morning. There were airports closer to Davos, but so many attendees were using private jets to attend the Economic Forum there was no more room for any other flights at either the Samedan St. Moritz Airport, or the Thal St. Gallen-Altenrhein airports. So, we'll have to land in Zurich and then take ground transportation to Davos, which I'm told will take us just under two and a half hours."

"Hopefully, that'll give us enough time to come up with a plan about what to do once we get there," said Jason.

"According to the program, the climate change panel isn't for another couple of days," said Chance. "The keynote speaker is the premier scientist in the world when it comes to global warming and all things related to climate change."

"If we can convince him that the world is taking a tragically wrong approach that will lead to another mass extinction event, then we may have a chance," said Jason. "But how are we going to get to him before his speech?"

"You leave that to me," said Miles. "These guys may think they're the smartest people on the planet, but they all have their weaknesses."

"I don't like the sound of that," said Agent Wiseman.

"And I don't like that you're coming on this trip," said Miles, "but I was outvoted."

"He's the only real authority figure we have," said Jason. "We need his credibility."

"But that doesn't extend to extortion or anything illegal," said Wiseman.

"We're trying to save the world here, Carter," added Julie. "If we have to bend the rules a bit, I'd say it's worth it, wouldn't you?"

After thinking about it for a few moments, he responded, "I guess, when you put it that way," said Carter.

Just then Gypsy came running from the rear of the jet, and grabbed Jason by the hand. "Come on, I want to show you something," said Gypsy.

Jason let himself be pulled behind a curtain and into another section of the jet. They passed a few more seats and then behind a second curtain, they came to a private bedroom, with its own shower."

"Time to join the mile high club, Jason," smiled Gypsy.

"What are you talking about?"

"I was planning on waiting until Chicago to reward my hero. But when I found this it's just too good to pass up," said Gypsy. "Besides, what else are we going to do for the next two hours?"

"What if someone comes back here?" asked Jason.

"Jason, nobody's coming back here," said Gypsy. "Your son is playing video games on his tablet, that agent and his botanist buddy, maybe, but only because they want to do the same thing that we're going to do but we got here first, and I doubt Chance and Miles give a shit."

"Gypsy, you don't have to do this," said Jason.

"Who says I have to do anything," said Gypsy, as she removed her jacket. "I've been wanting to do this since you shot those two knuckleheads with your Gene Gun. Don't tell me you haven't wanted the same thing. I see how you look at me."

Gypsy removed her top and began to undo her jeans.

"Wait," begged Jason.

"For what," asked Gypsy, as she pulled down her jeans.

"I don't know what's going to happen."

"Don't tell me you're a virgin. You have a son."

"Remember? I was in an accident, and absorbed some plant DNA," said Jason.

"What kind?"

"Maple tree."

Gypsy smiled, "Sounds like if anything, it's going to be an enhancement."

"Just give me a second," said Jason.

He found a piece of paper and a magic marker. He wrote "Do Not Disturb" on the paper and taped it to the other side of the curtain.

"And they should call it the 'eight-mile club' by the way," said Jason

"Get over here," Gypsy replied.

Back in the front of the jet, Julie and Carter were discussing with Chance and Miles options for getting the movers and shakers attending the World Economic Forum to move away from their Net Zero carbon emissions mission that was driving the world's industrial nations into a rabid production mandate for all things powered by electricity. A recent survey had found that over half of all American car owners said their next car or truck would be an electrically powered vehicle, or a hybrid, if they could afford it. Half of the-major cities in the U.S. and Europe were about to ban the use of gas heated stoves and ovens, replacing them with electric appliances. Billions of dollars had been earmarked for more offshore windfarms, despite recent evidence that such farms were having a deteriorating impact on both plant and animal ocean life. The most spectacular were the beaching of a dozen humpback whales along the northeast coast of Labrador.

"We need to get to the most vocal climate activists speaking at the Forum and get them to stop alarming the world with their dire predictions of death and destruction unless everyone stops using fossil fuels," said Chance.

"What about Al Gore," said Miles. "He had those two movies that scared the shit out of me. Plus, he was a vice president and almost a president. How about him?"

"He's not going to change his tune," said Chance. "He's made too much money by selling his end of the world scenarios."

"Didn't that used to be us, before Jason shot us with his Gene Gun and we started to see in green?" said Miles.

"You have a point," agreed Chance. "And how are we going to get Jason close enough to someone like Al Gore to shoot him with plant DNA? He's going to be surrounded by security."

"Who else, then?" asked Miles.

"There's that kid, Hedda somebody," said Chance. "The activist who made the covers of *Time* and *Rolling Stone* magazines."

"Gerber," said Miles. "Hedda Gerber. She does get people riled up."

"Is she going to be there?"

"We need to get a guest list," said Miles.

"Or we can just check her website," said Chance, who got out his smart phone and Googled Hedda Gerber.

"Yep," said Chance. "She'll be speaking there on Friday, the last day."

"Does she say where she's staying?" asked Miles.

"No," said Chance. But wait. She has an Instagram account. There she is, standing in front of the Spengler's Inn. Looks like one of the less expensive places."

"Which means there won't be as much security," said Miles.

"Looks like she got there early," said Chance, who used his mobile phone to check Google news for recent news stories about Davos and Climate Change.

Chance continued, "She's protesting the hypocrisy of so many attendees arriving in private jets that burn up tons of fuel and leave behind tons of carbon dioxide in the atmosphere."

"She was on every news channel," said Miles, who did a quick search of the Drudge Report. "She's perfect."

"Maybe," said Chance. "There's just one problem. She may be the face of Climate Change, but I doubt she's controlling any of the companies leveling the forests to mine lithium. We need to convince the ones investing in extracting all that lithium and using it for lithium batteries."

"The Chinese," said Miles. "They have the monopoly on lithium batteries."

"Are they even going to be at Davos?" asked Chance.

"You can bet they'll be there," said Julie. "They stay in the shadows, though. And by Chinese, I assume you mean the Chinese Communist Party and those it controls."

"Of course," said Miles.

"You'll never see the CEO of a China-based company on a panel, or as a keynote," added Julie. "But if you scour the audience, there will be several Asian faces. Of all the countries invested in sustainability and ESG-dominated firms, China is the largest. Ironically, it's also the planet's largest polluter and has no plans whatsoever to stop using fossil fuels itself as its primary energy source. Meanwhile, it makes a fortune selling all its China-made renewable energy products to the rest of the world. When it comes to energy, we're China's useful idiots. It's a pure economics play. China uses cheap energy while the rest of the world except for India uses more expensive electric and renewable energy. It's the cost of energy that's behind the forty-year rise in inflation, which weakens our economy like a cancer, while China's economy thrives and grows stronger."

"If what you're saying is true, then we are unlikely to achieve our goals," said Chance.

"Not necessarily," said Julie. "We just need to find the right people to convince we're heading toward a mass extinction event. The Chinese aren't stupid, nor are they suicidal. Look at what they've achieved in the last fifty years? They've grown from the eighth largest economy to the second. Their goal is to be number one within five years and at this rate, they'll beat or achieve that goal provided we're all still alive by then. So, I say the answer is that if we can convince the Chinese, you save the world."

"Hey," said Chance. "Look at this. It just appeared in the British newspaper, *The Guardian*."

On Chance's tablet, was the headline: "U.S. Transition to Electric Cars Threatens Environmental Havoc."

"It's exactly what Jason was carrying on about, how the demand for electric vehicles will require huge amounts of lithium for their batteries, causing damaging expansions of mining," said Chance.

"Maybe we don't have to fly to Davos, Switzerland after all," said Miles.

"One headline isn't going to make much difference," said Chance. "We still need to get to the money people who are driving the climate mitigation movement. These folks have sunk billions of dollars into electric vehicles and renewable energy. They're going to want a return on those investments, so this isn't going to be so easy to stop. Plus, the Chinese have built all of this into their goal of global domination, and they've paid off quite a few useful idiots around the world to let that happen. It's all about control and they want to control it all."

Chapter 45

Gypsy said, "I want to do it," as she lay with her head against Jason's still heaving chest following what Jason would only describe as the best sex he'd ever had.

"Can you give me a few minutes to recover first," asked Jason. "I'm still coming down from what we just did."

"Not that," said Gypsy. "I want to do what you do. I want to talk to plants."

"You don't need me for that," said Jason. "Just talk to them."

"You know what I mean," said Gypsy. "Can't you just shoot me with that Gene Gun, like you did with Miles and what's his name?"

"Chance, his name is Chance. And I was desperate. I didn't even know if it would work."

"Well, now you know, so what's the problem?" she asked.

"For one, I don't have many of those shots left. I think I'm going to need as many as I can get when we get to Davos if that's what it takes to convince the money people that what they're investing in is going to destroy life as we know it."

"Then when we get back from Davos?" asked Gypsy.

"Okay," said Jason.

Suddenly the curtain separating the rear compartment of the plane was yanked open and Chance was standing in the doorway, grinning.

"Wondered where you two went," said Chance. "New plan. We're not staying over in Chicago. We're flying to Teterboro in New Jersey where we'll refuel and then go straight on to Davos. We just heard a major influencer is speaking tomorrow so we must get there before he takes the stage."

Early the next morning, when they landed, it was a cool 62 degrees at the St. Gallen-Altenrein airport, just 30 miles from Davos, Switzerland. Usually, room rates during the summer were cheap except whenever the Economic Forum was underway. During those busy times, the hotels doubled and tripled their prices. Money was not the issue. Everything was booked up. But fortunately Chance was able to find a private house that he could rent that could accommodate the entire group and booked it for the next few days.

While most of the group began taking their bags into the Victorian house and choosing their rooms, Jason headed off in search of the closest forest.

"Where are you going?" asked Gypsy.

"I need to talk to some trees," said Jason.

"I'm coming with you."

"Suit yourself," said Jason.

"Hey Dad," shouted Sal. "Where are you going?"

"Just taking a walk," said Jason. "Why don't you grab us some rooms?"

"How many?" asked Sal.

Jason turned toward Gypsy who gave him a look. "I think two ought to do it."

Gypsy smiled.

Jason and Gypsy did not have to walk far before finding themselves in a forest of Norway Spruce, a tree that only grew to a few hundred feet and were all about three hundred years old. Still, Jason figured a tree was still a tree and if his understanding of the plant communication system would be the same worldwide, then these trees should be plugged in to what their elders back in California were communicating.

He found a moist spot in the soil beneath a two-hundred-foot-tall Norway spruce. Jason knelt down and pushed his hands beneath the surface deep enough to find the nest of mycelium fibers. Gypsy knelt next to him, watching closely.

"What are they saying?" she asked.

"I'm not sure," said Jason. "I should have taken some mushrooms before coming out. They enhance the experience."

340

"We are at the epicenter of the church of climate change worshippers," said Gypsy. "Davos is to climate change fanatics what the Vatican is to Catholics. Maybe some of that thinking has soaked into the soil."

"That's not what I'm picking up," said Jason. "It's almost as if the plant world has accepted the notion that there's nothing they can do to stop another mass extinction event. It's like they've given up."

"That's not good," said Gypsy. "So, this trip was all for nothing?"

"We don't know that yet," said Jason. "We still need to try."

"And if we can't change their minds?" asked Gypsy.

"Then we'll have to come up with something else," said Jason.

Jason could feel one of the Norway spruces place a branch on his back. It was as if it wanted to say, "Thank you."

"Don't thank me yet," said Jason. "We need to find some mushrooms."

"The Davos Premiere Club!" said Gypsy.

"What's that?"

"AN underground rock bar," said Gypsy.

"In Davos?"

"Near Davos. I'm just not sure it's still open. It's been almost ten years since I traveled around Europe. All I remember is that if you needed to score, The Davos Premiere Club was the place."

"Or, we could just find the shamans."

"The who?"

"The shamans. They're supposed to be putting on a symposium at the World Economic Forum," said Jason.

"What's a shaman?"

"Sort of a witch doctor."

"And they're going to be at the Forum?"

"They're putting on a program about Medical Psychedelics," said Jason.

"Okay," said Gypsy, "but if that doesn't work, we'll hit the bar."

Just then, Jason's phone vibrated, and he took it out of his pants pocket.

"Hey Sal. What's up?"

"Where are you?" Sal asked.

"Went for a walk with Gypsy."

"Well, get your ass back here. The U.N. just released some kind of doomsday report and the Economic Forum folks have called an emergency session. Miles thinks we need to be there."

"We're on our way," said Jason. "Sounds like things are heating up."

The Congress Hotel and Convention Center in the heart of downtown Davos was made up of several different buildings, with a main hall that seated over 3,000 attendees. It had hosted the week-long annual economic forum for the past fifty years.

Outside in the square, in front of the main entrance, a group of protestors gathered to demonstrate their anger at the corporations they held responsible for most of the world's environmental and social problems.

Jason, Miles, and Chance pushed through the mob to reach the entrance, where Chance handed Miles and Jason badges on lanyards to be worn around their necks. That would give them access to the meeting which was already underway.

As they entered the massive auditorium, a group of men and women were presenting a PowerPoint about a United Nations report.

"Because of this upward revision, we predict climate disasters will become so extreme that people will not be able to adapt and that basic components of the Earth's system will be fundamentally and irrevocably altered," said the man behind the podium.

"What does all this mean, you may ask," he continued. "I'll tell you. It means heat waves, famines, and infectious diseases will claim hundreds of millions of lives by the end of the century. And this time, it won't just be the poor who are impacted but people in all economic levels, from the poorest to the wealthiest. In other words, no one will be safe."

Jason turned to Miles and Chance. "Now they'll probably escalate the war on fossil fuels and speed up the mining of rare earth minerals used in the batteries of electronic vehicles," said Jason.

"What do you want to do?" asked Chance.

"I need some mushrooms," said Jason. "Somewhere in these halls there's a session on psychedelics involving some shamans. We need to find it."

Miles pulled out his Forum guidebook which had the agendas and locations for all the sessions.

"I found it," said Miles. "Three buildings away."

It took them about ten minutes to fast walk to the Psychedelic sessions being run by the shamans. And less than one minute to find that the session was all talk and no show, meaning there were no actual mushrooms on display or available for consumption.

"Looks like it's the Club, then," said Jason.

"Club?" Miles and Chance asked in unison.

"It's this place Gypsy found. An underground club. Supposed to be able to get anything there."

"Let's go. Where is it?" Miles asked.

"We must get Gypsy. She'll know."

The trio took a taxi back to the rental and found Gypsy playing video games with Sal.

Jason explained the situation to her and asked her to get ready to go with him to the Club.

"We could go there now, but it wouldn't do much good," said Gypsy.

"Why not?"

"Nobody goes there before midnight."

"That's several hours from now," said Miles.

"I need to get some sleep. And now sounds like the best time to do that," said Jason. "Miles, you and Chance

344

probably need some sleep as well. Let's all regroup around 11:30 tonight."

Chapter 46

Just as Jason's head was hitting a pillow, Agent Wiseman and Julie were getting out of the taxi in front of the World Economic Forum.

"Are you sure this is a good idea?" asked Carter.

"No, but I was starting to feel useless back there. I know most of the people in this panel, and I just might be able to open their eyes to other possibilities when it comes to the imminent threat of climate change due to carbon emissions."

"I don't know," said Carter. "These are the die-hard gloom-and-doomers. They've been preaching the evils of fossil fuels for so long, it's become part of their DNA. Not to mention their financial investment in that belief."

"I don't expect it to be easy," said Julie. "I just have to try. The fact that I used to be one of them could provide the leverage I need to at least get some of them to listen."

The sign on the door of Auditorium 10 read, "The Unintended Consequences of Climate Change".

Carter and Julie entered and took seats in the last row just as the moderator began his slide show.

"Everyone knows about the major ramifications of global warming, more violent weather patterns, rising ocean levels, melting ice caps, etcetera. What we're going to discuss in this panel are those little-known consequences that have been detected so far," said a bearded man identified as Dr. Rand Morrissey.

"Slide one please," said Dr. Morrissey. As he said that, on the wall behind the panel a photo of an ugly lizard appeared.

"This is the Bearded Dragon of Australia. Can anyone guess how global warming affects this beautiful creature?" Morrissey waited a beat or two before he answered, "When it gets warmer, the sex of the lizard's embryos undergo a sex change usually from male to female. Trans at birth. Eggs with male sex chromosomes end up developing as females."

"Next slide please."

The dragon slide was replaced by a photo of a frog.

"Is that one of your three-legged frogs?" asked Carter.

"I don't think so," said Julie.

"This is the Coqui Frog of Puerto Rico," said Morrissey. "It's named after the loud call that male frogs make at night to attract a female frog. When the planet gets warmer, the Coqui Frog gets smaller. And this causes the frog's pitch of their croaks to be higher, which in turn makes it sound louder. You may wonder what the problem is in that. Well, it seems the females don't respond as well to these high-pitched calls. They're a turnoff, so to speak, so there's less copulating. The eventual result is that the coqui species could become extinct all because global warming has made the male mating call ineffective."

Julie Green stood up and raised her hand.

"Yes, ma'am," said Morrissey. "You have a question."

"How do you know it's due to global warming?"

After a brief pause, Morrissey responded, "What else could it be?"

"I'm a botanist who's been studying the effect of plant life disruptions on the animal kingdom, frogs in particular, and we've determined there is a direct correlation between stress among the plant eco-system and anomalies in animals, in this case frogs. They appear to be more susceptible to such disruptions. For example, in certain swamps we've seen extreme shifts in algae production that seemed to impact the frog community's birth cycle. Newly hatched frogs are being born with just three legs and sometimes no eyes. Such defects are typically related to radioactive generated situations, but there was no radioactivity detected and the only change in the eco-system was in the make-up of the algae. The algae definitely showed changes in DNA with the removal of specific deoxyribose strands containing certain proteins necessary for the survival of some species of frogs. And it had nothing to do with global warming or temperature variations of any kind, actually."

"Perhaps you're right, but that has nothing to do with what we're talking about here, which is the impact of climate change on …."

Interrupting him, Julie continued, "But what I'm trying say is that not every bad thing that happens can be tied to climate change. In fact, most of those extreme weather patterns being tied to climate change have actually nothing to do with global warming but have been occurring in the same or sometimes even greater frequency in the past than they are now. We're just hearing about it more because the media is fixated on turning every bad weather story into a climate disaster when hurricanes, tornadoes, earthquakes, or whatever have been happening since forever."

"That's your opinion," said Morrissey.

"That's not an opinion, that's a fact," responded Julie.
"Consider that on September 17th, 1928 a hurricane known as the Okeechobee made landfall near West Palm Beach in Florida resulting in an estimated 2,500 deaths in the United States. And yet, climate change was blamed by some for Hurricane Helene which made landfall on September 26th, 2024 near the panhandle of Florida, devastating parts of another six states as well, resulting in at least 227 deaths."

"What's your point?"

Dr. Green continued. "Don't get me wrong, Dr. Morrissey. There are reasons to move away from fossil fuels, such as pollution. And the earth may be getting warmer, but it has less to do with greenhouse gas and more to do to with its orbit around the sun pulling us ever closer to that burning star. That is the true cause of global warming."

"Are you saying we should just give up?"

"I'm saying we're looking in the wrong direction," said Julie. "I've recently come to believe we can do something to stop what could be another mass extinction event, but it has to start here, at this meeting, and all the nations of the world and their governments and corporations have to participate. Otherwise, we may not make it."

"Please, share with us. What should we do?"

"We have to stop destroying the world's forests and wildlife," said Julie. "I believe global warming is real, and needs to be addressed. But we're going about it all wrong, and people, perhaps all of us, are going die if we continue on this course. By focusing on climate change all the time, we ignore the greater and more impending threats to life on this planet. Right now, we can live with climate change. But we can't live without clean drinking water, or enough nutritious food and, eventually, if we continue destroying the forests, unfortunately oxygen will no longer be created in the amount needed to sustain life as we know it."

In the rear of the auditorium, a young man who had attended Dr. Julie Green's Kyoto presentation appeared from the shadows. As people were streaming out, he kept his eyes on Julie and Carter before making a call on his cell phone.

350

"She's here," said the young man. "In Davos."

"A denier at Davos," said the voice on the phone. "Lots of luck."

"She's not a denier," said the young man. "She's more in that 'false alarm camp.' They believe in climate change. They just don't see it as the impending threat the media is making it out to be."

"They're the most dangerous," said the voice on the phone.

"What do you want me to do?"

"Follow her. And, if you see a chance, take it."

Chapter 47

It was dark outside when Jason woke up with a start. He'd been dreaming of being back in Sequoia National Park, kneeling at the foot of General Sherman. He was sinking his hands deep into the damp earth at the base of the tree's giant trunk, until the tips of his fingers connected to the strands of mycelium. The connection was like a jolt of lightning, illuminating giant earth-moving equipment plowing canyon-sized groves into the rainforests and fields of wildflowers, upending all that stood in their way.

Jason looked at the clock on the bedstand. The digital face said it was 11:30 PM. Jason nudged Gypsy awake.

"Is it time?" she asked.

"I think so," said Jason.

"Then let's go shroom shopping," said Gypsy as she climbed out of bed naked and slipped on a T-shirt that said "Save the Whales. They're what's keeping the casinos alive."

From the outside, the Davos Premiere Club and Hotel didn't look like anything special. It was just a large gray painted box-like building with a string of black limos lining the street in front.

"Look at that," said Gypsy. "If we're too stoned afterward, we can just crash in the hotel.

"You sure this is the right place?"

"Supposed to be the hottest club in town, and during the Economic Forum, this is where all those uptight corporate types come to unwind."

Inside the club section, strobe lights danced in time with the music that was so loud the walls were vibrating.

Gypsy took Jason's hand and pulled him through the throng of a dancing mob moving to the beat of an electronic bass and drum.

Once past the dancing floor, Gypsy found the restrooms and pulled Jason inside. Over the door was a sign that read: "All Genders Welcome."

Inside the restroom, a cloud of marijuana and hashish smoke hung from the ceiling like a psychedelic pillow. One deep breath and you were floating on air.

"The dude in the corner," said Gypsy. "He's gotta be the one."

Jason saw a young man, so thin he almost looked translucent. He had a short brush cut hair on one side and long dreadlocks to his shoulders on the other. He was sort of a cross between Bob Marley and Joe Friday.

"Let me handle this," said Gypsy.

"Be my guest," said Jason.

Gypsy waited until the young man was free and then she stepped up in front of him.

"We're looking for some shrooms," said Gypsy. "Or if that's not possible, any form of psilocybin will do."

"No problem," said the young man. "Any favorite? We have five varieties from the strongest to the mildest. All depends on your tolerance, my friend."

"We can go heavy here," said Gypsy.

"Then I recommend the flying saucer caps. I've got one ounce bag left. Three hundred Euros."

"That's a little more than we've got. What will one hundred Euros buy us?"

"I've got some Blue Meanies. Not as powerful but they'll give you a trip for sure. I have a half ounce I can sell you for one hundred and ten Euros."

"All I have is one hundred."

"Okay, just don't tell anyone how much you paid me for them, okay?"

"No problem, brother," said Gypsy as she turned to Jason. "One hundred Euros."

Jason pulled out his money and gave her five twenty Euro notes.

"Let's get out of here before I lose my hearing," begged Jason.

Jason and Gypsy made their way back outside where Jason's ears were still ringing from the thunderous music blaring away inside the club.

"Hey, are you hungry?"

"I could eat," said Jason.

"We passed a pizza place on the way up the hill. Let's see if it's still open. I hear pizza with mushrooms is great."

"Anything to bury the taste of fungi is fine with me," said Jason, as they started down the hill from the hot Davos nightspot.

Fortunately, the pizza restaurant was still open as Gypsy and Jason arrived and ordered a large pizza with everything on it except mushrooms, since they planned on using their own.

While they waited for the pizza, Gypsy took out the Blue Meanie mushroom caps and started to grind them up into a pile of small pieces.

"I figure I'll just sprinkle the entire pizza like this was oregano or something," said Gypsy.

"It doesn't really matter to me," said Jason. "I just have this feeling the plants are planning something, and I need to know what it is."

"Tell you what," said Gypsy. "I'll put all of yours on one piece. How's that sound? That way it'll get into your system faster."

"Okay," said Jason. "I don't really know all that much about mushrooms. The ones I bought at that Botanica are the only ones I've ever had."

"Let me be your travel guide then, my friend," said Gypsy. "Blue Meanies are one of most potent shrooms you can take. First off, don't ask me why they're called blue because they're light gray and pack a double punch because they contain both psilocybin and psilocin, two separate hallucinogens. Ah, here's our pizza."

"Can you bring us a couple beers?" asked Gypsy.

As soon as the waiter went off, Gypsy began sprinkling the pile of ground mushrooms on to a large slice of pizza. Then she sprinkled the rest over the remaining slices.

"Bon Appetit," said Gypsy. "I hear it also works better than Viagra, so save some energy, big boy."

Jason picked up the slice covered with ground blue meanies and devoured it. Gypsy looked wide-eyed as Jason practically shoved the entire slice into his mouth and began chewing.

Their two beers arrived, and he quickly grabbed one of them before chugging down half the glass.

Jason reached for another slice of mushroom-covered pizza.

Gypsy immediately grabbed a piece for herself.

"Don't get too far ahead of me, babe," said Gypsy. "We're taking this trip together, remember."

Within ten minutes, the pizza was completely devoured.

Gypsy ordered two more beers.

"I figure we have another twenty minutes or so before it kicks in," said Gypsy. "What do you think?"

"I think I want to be in the woods when it does," said Jason.

"Have you looked around here? This place is all woods. Don't worry. When it kicks in, the woods will come to us."

Jason picked up one of the beers the waiter just brought and drank it down. "Put yours in a plastic cup or something, and let's go."

"Okay," said Gypsy. "I know you're just trying to save the world and all, and it's a turn on, I'll admit it, but the girl has her needs. You know what I'm saying?"

"One thing at a time okay. I need to connect to them and then after, if there's time, we'll ...."

"We'll what?"

"Have sex."

"What if I want to have sex in the forest?"

"Then we'll have sex in the forest, although I'm not sure how much fun that'll be."

"It'll be fun. I'll make sure of that."

Jason stood up and took Gypsy's hand as they crossed a street and began walking up a mountain that would become a ski slope in the winter.

After walking a few hundred yards, they looked back, and the town of Davos was lit up below them like a Christmas tree in July. It looked like a picture postcard.

Jason spotted a tall tree at the end of the clearing, and it seemed to be beckoning to him.

"Over there," he pointed and started to head for the tree.

As soon as they got there, a feeling of euphoria shot through Jason's soul and the lights from the town below took on different shapes and colors. They also began floating up the side of the mountain like lanterns drifting ceremoniously.

"I'm starting to feel it," said Gypsy. "It's like every cell in my body is laughing."

"Can you feel the presence?" asked Jason.

"The presence of what?" asked Gypsy.

"When I first felt it, I thought maybe it was God," said Jason. "But it's not. Then, I thought maybe it was some great spirit that Native Americans talk about. But then when I connected to the network, I realized it was nature. It's force and power and wisdom. Come kneel next to me."

Jason knelt beneath the tall pine tree and brushed away the cones and needles laying beneath it.

"Just do what I do, okay," said Jason.

"Okay," Gypsy replied.

Jason pushed his hands down into the dirt and dug until he could feel the damp earth extending his fingers as deep as they could go until they touched the mycelium threads making up the fungi network beneath the forest floor.

"Keep digging until your fingers touch these tiny white strands," said Jason, as his eyes began to water, and his face looked awestruck.

"I think I feel them," said Gypsy. "Jesus, what the fuck!"

Jason pulled his hands out of the dirt and looked at Gypsy who was still connected to the mycelium network. Her irises had rolled up under their lids and all he could see were the whites of her eyes. Her entire body was vibrating as if she was in a convulsive state. Jason leaned toward her and pulled her arms out of the ground. Her vibrations stopped as her eyes opened wide.

"Oh my God!" cried Gypsy. "What are we going to do?"

"What is it?"

"The plants. They said it's too late. That the forces driving the destruction are too powerful and widespread. But then they seemed to be mourning me, or us, I guess."

"Mourning as in our deaths?"

"I'm not sure. They seemed to think something bad is going to happen and …Let me just see if I can learn more."

Gypsy plunged her hands back into the soil. Jason immediately did too.

Gypsy looked at Jason wide-eyed and fainted.

"Gypsy!"

"No!" shouted Jason. He quickly checked to see if she was still breathing and then checked her pulse. A smile came to his face when he knew she was okay.

"Sleep tight Gyps. I should have prepared you better for this."

After he made Gypsy comfortable lying on the grass, Jason plunged his hands back beneath the damp earth, until his fingers connected to the underground mycelium network.

"You have to give me more time," said Jason. "I don't care if think it's too late. There must be a way. Well, I'm not ready to give up. I think we can still fix this."

Jason looked over at Gypsy who was just starting to regain consciousness. He then felt another message enter through his fingertips.

"What do you mean I have one more chance? What's going to appear? By opportunity, can you be more specific? What if I miss it? You can't be serious."

Chapter 48

Back at the rental, Dr. Julie Green and FBI Agent Wiseman were briefing Miles and Chance, as well as Sal, about their experiences at the World Economic Forum.

"The problem as I see it," said Julie, "is that they've bought into the Climate Change narrative for such a long time, it's become engrained into their thought processes, and nothing we say or do is going to change their minds."

"What you're saying is that it's up to my dad to shoot them with those Gene Guns," said Sal, demonstrating the stance with a Gene Gun.

"I don't think even that would make a difference," said Agent Wiseman. "There's just too many of them. And they're all collectively buying into that theory."

"So, what do we do?" asked Chance.

"Well, we're due for another Ice Age," said Julie. "Maybe that'll cool down all this rhetoric about global warming. But then, we'll all be living under layers of ice, so it'll be a trade-off."

"You're not serious?" asked Agent Wiseman.

"Half serious," said Julie.

Just then there was a knock on the door. Sal opened it to find Jason holding up a barely conscious Gypsy.

"What are you doing with the Gene Gun?" asked Jason.

"Miles was showing me how it worked," said Sal.

"What happened to her?" asked Miles.

"Her first encounter with the plant world under the influence of magic mushrooms," said Jason. "Wiped her out. She's just stuck in a mushroom-induced trance state."

"Just what we need," said Carter.

"Put her to bed," said Julie. "She probably just needs to sleep it off."

"That's what I planned to do," said Jason. "And as soon as she recovers, we need to get back to California."

"What's in California?" asked Miles.

"I need to see the General,' said Jason.

"The General, what General?" asked Carter.

"General Sherman," said Jason.

"You're talking about that Sequoia, aren't you?" asked Julie.

"I am," said Jason. "He's giving the orders, and it doesn't look good."

"What are you talking about?" asked Miles.

"They, the plant world, and General Sherman, in particular, don't think we humans have gotten the message to stop what we're doing. So I think they're going to escalate."

"And do what?"

"That, I don't know," said Jason. "That's what I need to find out."

"I'm afraid you're going to have to wait," said a voice from the doorway.

They all turned toward around and saw the young man whom Julie immediately recognized as the man who approached her in Kyoto.

"Dr. Green," said the man. "I'm afraid you and your friends won't be traveling anywhere right now."

"And why is that?" asked Julie.

The man produced a very large machine gun. "Because I need you all to come with me."

Chapter 49

"*Excuse me, you do look familiar, but am I supposed to* know you?" asked a visibly-shaken Julie.

"Not necessarily," said the man with the machine gun as he stepped into the rented room.

"How do you know me?" asked Julie.

"Your presentation at the Kyoto COP 27 conference."

"Did I say something that offended you?" asked Julie.

"Not that I can remember."

"Then what's this all about?" asked Julie.

"You'll have to ask my boss," said the gunman. "I'm just following orders."

"Who's your boss?" asked Miles.

"Even if I tell you her name, you wouldn't recognize it," said the gunman. "But why don't we wait until we meet her. I have a large van that should accommodate everyone. I'd hate to have to leave a body behind."

"Body," said Jason.

"I have orders to leave no witnesses behind. So, let's just see if we all fit, okay?"

The "pop" sound came from behind the gunman who spun around to find Sal holding a strange looking contraption about the size of a portable hair dryer.

"What the hell!" said the gunman. "What did you shoot me with?"

"I'm sorry," said Sal. "I didn't mean for the Gene Gun to go off."

"I should kill you right now," said the gunman.

"No!" shouted Jason. "You're not hurt. It's just an assortment of plant DNA mixed with psilocybin. It's relatively harmless and you shouldn't have any lasting effects, but it's important for you to be open to what we're about to tell you before we let you take us to your boss."

"What?"

"How long will it take for us to get to her?"

"Ten, fifteen minutes. She's here in Davos for the Forum," said the gunman as he continued to point the machine gun. That's when he began to see in green. "Whoa," he said.

"Great," said Jason. "We can leave now and fill you in along the way."

"I get the feeling I was expected," said the gunman.

"Well, let's put it this way," said Jason. "I was warned that something like this was going to happen. I just didn't know what. And now I do."

"What are you talking about?"

"An opportunity. A chance to make a difference," said Jason. "Like I said, I'll fill you in once we get moving. I assume your boss is the one pulling most of the strings when it comes to Climate Change messaging."

"You have no idea. But wait, how did you know that?"

"Because you showed up to stop us."

On the van ride through Davos, Jason told the gunman what the plant world had warned him about regarding the escalated destruction of forests around the world to mine the rare minerals required to make lithium batteries to power electric vehicles. He was just finishing his talk when the van pulled up in front of one of the few office buildings in the Swiss mountain village.

The sign over the door read "Swiss Headquarters for Solaris Public Relations."

"Your boss works for a PR firm?" asked Jason.

"She's the founder."

"Terrific," said Jason. "Just what we need to get the word out."

Jason, Gypsy, still half-unconscious, Sal, Julie, Carter, Miles, Chance, and the gunman all crowded into the same elevator as the gunman hit PH for penthouse.

"I want that latest U.N. report circulated to every news outlet on the planet," said Silvia Singh, President, and founder of Solaris Public Relations.

The back wall of her office was covered with photos showing Silvia with several well-known figures and

366

institutions associated with climate change including former Vice President Al Gore, Greta Thunberg, Leonardo DiCaprio, King Charles III and John Kerry, the previous administration's climate czar.

Other photos highlighted her company's clients such as the United Nations, the World Economic Forum, governments of China and India, companies like FacePage, Babylon, and the largest electric vehicle battery manufacturers and media companies in the world, as well as most auto companies.

Silvia was lowering her mobile phone when the intercom on her desk buzzed.

"There are some people here to see you," said a male voice.

"Send them in," said Silvia.

The door to Silvia's office opened and Jason entered alone.

Silvia looked up to see a young bearded man in his 30s holding an unwieldly shaped device about the size of a hair dryer.

"Who are you? I was expecting Dr. Julie Green," said Silvia.

"She's here," said Jason. "I just want you to know that what I'm about to do isn't going to hurt very much."

Jason raised the Gene Gun and shot Silvia in the forehead.

"What the hell!" Silvia shouted.

She pushed a button on the intercom. "Security. I want security in here immediately!"

Silvia touched her forehead where the DNA capsule had entered. "That hurt like hell."

"The pain will pass," said Jason. "But why don't you sit down so we can talk."

Just then, the door opened and the man with the machine gun stepped in.

"That man assaulted me," said Silvia. "I want him arrested."

"I can't do that. Just listen to what he has to say."

"You're fired!" Silvia went to push the intercom again, but her security man pulled the intercom off her desk and unplugged it from the wall.

As he did that, Julie Green, Carter Wiseman, a wobbly Gypsy, Sal, Miles, and Chance all entered Silvia's office and stood behind Jason.

"I don't know what you people think is going to happen," said Silvia, "but I can assure you, you'll all wish you were never born when I get through with you."

"Hey, Dad," said Sal. "Maybe that DNA and mushroom stuff doesn't work on everybody."

"Let's pray that you're wrong, son," said Jason. "Because what we have here is someone who has more control over what many people think than anyone on the planet and if she can't convince the people of the world to change their minds about climate change and stop destroying the forests, we're all doomed."

Silvia suddenly sat down as the expression of rage on her face melted into one of concern and then understanding. She then looked up at the group of people standing in her office as a tear fell from each eye.

Jason was the first to notice the change.

"You're seeing it, aren't you?"

"I don't know what I'm seeing," said Silvia.

"You're seeing what the world's going to look like if we keep doing what we're doing," said Jason.

"And what do you expect from me?"

"To help us change a few million minds," said Jason.

"And you think I can do this?"

Jason looked at the wall behind her and said, "I think you may be the only one who can."

"Is what I'm seeing for real?" asked Silvia.

"If what you're seeing is a planet devoid of life, then yes, that's what's going to happen if we continue on this path of deforestation to mine the minerals needed for electric vehicles."

"And you think I can stop that?"

"If you can't, who can?" asked Jason.

"How about the people making a fortune from it?"

"But it's you who've disseminated the message that what they're doing is for good, when now you know it's going to have the exact opposite impact. There must be something you can do."

"Oh, I can change the message, but if you think that's going to change their behavior, you're just naïve. The only change will be that I'll be replaced by someone who will do their bidding. These people are too powerful.

They control governments. Countries. Billions of people. And they've been at this for too long to change any minds in a meaningful way overnight. It could take years, but I get the feeling we don't have years, am I right?"

"I don't know how long we have but I get the feeling we're getting close to a dangerous point since most of the planet's forests have already been destroyed. It may not take the elimination of much more to reach the tipping point in terms of how much oxygen is needed in the air to sustain life."

"What happens if we can't stop them?" asked Sal.

"Then it will be up to the plant world to escalate what they've been doing," said Jason.

"The plant world? What can they do?" asked Silvia.

"From what we can determine, they've already taken out a half-dozen heads of companies responsible for deforestation," said Agent Wiseman. "There may be more that we haven't discovered yet."

"That's not going to make any difference," said Silvia.

"Why not?" asked Jason.

"Because they're corporations. They'll just pick a new CEO and keep on doing it. You need to get to the policy makers, the ones who control how countries behave. That's who dictate things like climate agendas. And right now, most of the countries on the planet are all signed off on stopping global warming by turning to green energy sources, such as electric vehicles, windmills, solar. Even nuclear in some cases."

"That's why we came to Davos," said Miles. "Don't they all attend the World Economic Forum?"

"Not the ones in charge," said Silvia. "They'll send their Climate Czars, and anyone associated with climate in the media. It becomes somewhat of an echo chamber, with everyone preaching the same thing."

"So even if we convince the people here, it might not make a difference," said Julie.

"I'm afraid not," said Silvia.

"Somehow I think the General knew this all along," said Jason, as he walked toward the door. "Please excuse me, there's something I need to do." And with that he left the room.

"Who's the General?" asked Silvia.

Jason walked deep into the same forest that he and Gypsy had visited and found the tallest tree. He kneeled next to it and pushed his hands into the damp earth until his fingers touched the network of connecting fibers. He looked back up at the tree.

"A need you to send a message to the General for me if that's even possible," said Jason. "I'm praying that it is. Just tell him that I understand why he thought that killing those CEOs would make a difference, but he must know by now that it didn't. Besides, killing people is wrong to begin with and I should have said something about that a long time ago. But I get it. In your world, this was war and what you did you saw as a justifiable killing, but it wasn't murder, and you gotta stop. I know you're planning something big, but please, can you do it without killing anyone else? I can help you get the word out now. , whatever you're planning, we can make sure that this time they, and by they I mean the folks responsible for this mess, understand the consequences of what they're doing. And General, if there's a way to let me know you got this message I'd appreciate it. Thanks. It's Jason, by the way."

Jason blew out some air and then leaned back against the trunk of the tall evergreen. He looked at his hands still buried deep into the soil, sighed, and closed his eyes.

When Jason finally woke up, it was dark out and his hands were still buried in the ground. He moved his fingers to get his circulation going again as he reconnected to the mycorrhizal fungi network. A soon as his finger tips touched the fibrous strands, Jason received a communication, and he smiled as his eyes filled with tears.

Epilogue

The General had already realized that not enough had changed since the first orders had been issued to stop those considered responsible for the deaths of his brothers and sisters in the forests of the world. The time had come to push out the next wave of action with the hope that this time the people responsible got the message.

The message spread like the speed of light throughout the mycelium network of the Sequoia National Forest, and then beyond from one forest to the next in the north and south and east.

The first fires started in Canada where lightning struck the dry underbrush the forestry department had failed to remove even though they knew that every year the same thing would occur. The government would blame this all on climate change, even though it had been going on long before the combustible engine had ever been invented to thin out overgrown forests of dying trees.

The fires spread from the Canadian Rockies to the Canadian side of the Great Lakes and then eastward to Labrador and Nova Scotia.

After days of burning, the cloud of burnt plant life began to drift south and over the United States. The cities of New York, Chicago, Buffalo, and even as far south as Washington, D.C. and Atlanta felt the effects of burning air, which made it hard for everyone to breathe.

The air in New York City turned orange for a few days as people were forced to stay inside and work from home as they did during the 2020-2023 COVID-19 Pandemic.

Despite this, the government continued to blame global warming until Silvia's massive public relations machine began kicking out an alternative theory that something other than climate change was to blame. namely, lithium mining.

Officials immediately debunked the notion, but as more and more media outlets began running articles quoting reputable so-called climate scientists as supporting the idea that this not only had nothing to do with global warming, but was instead, nature's warning to us all of how valuable our forests are and that the clouds of burning embers were a sample of what the atmosphere would be like if too many trees were destroyed—the air would no longer be breathable.

Eventually stories were being published about how the increase in lithium mining had caused a sharp rise in deforestation that posed a greater threat than global warming.

Slowly, over time, the companies mining for lithium and other rare minerals stopped their destruction of forests and looked for other methods to extract the minerals from the Earth.

Fossil fuel, once the evil foe of climate activists, was no longer considered a threat, but a necessary means of survival until alternative energy sources were available. The new administration was able to go back to drilling and the completion of oil pipelines, which caused oil prices to drop significantly. This was followed immediately by the lower cost of almost everything else, and inflation, once on the rise, was now nearly non-existent.

The quality of life began to improve globally as more people had access to affordable energy once again and could then focus their attention on other necessities such as clean drinking water and nutrition. Even crime dropped as more people were able to live within their means.

Gypsy moved in with Jason and Sal, and they opened their own Botanica in Oregon where magic mushrooms were now legal.

Miles, as the new CEO of Morabito, began using his genetic engineers, led by the reinstated Howard Bowde, to produce fast-growing trees to replenish the forests that had been destroyed during the lithium mining boom.

Carter quit the FBI and he and Julie opened a plant store in Austin, Texas that became a part of the Pleasure of Plants initiative started in the UK.

On their monthly trip to the Sequoia National Park, Jason, Gypsy, and Sal gathered around the base of General Sherman. Flying high under the influence of psilocybin, they all plunged their hands beneath the earth until their fingers connected to the mycelium network, and they felt the wave upon wave of plant-generated joy.

About the Authors

Fred Yager, author of six novels, three nonfiction titles, and two poetry collections, grew up in Coeymans Hollow, New York. He served in the U.S. Navy for four years, worked at the Associated Press for thirteen years followed by writing, editing, or production positions at several companies including CBS, FOX 5 (NY), Merrill Lynch, AARP Financial, and Morgan Stanley. Fred graduated from CCNY and lives with his wife, Jan Yager, in Tampa, Florida, where he is a freelance editor and ghostwriter. They have two adult sons, Jeff and Scott, and six grandchildren. For more on Fred, go to: https://www.fredandjanyager.com

Jeff Yager grew up in Stamford, Connecticut, graduating from Westhill High School. He relocated to Florida and graduated Pasco Hernandez State College with an AA degree in English. Jeff is an accomplished author whose published books include three novels and two illustrated children's books. In addition to his writing career, Jeff is also a professional wrestler and rap artist. He and his partner Justyna live with their three sons in a town outside of Tampa. For more on Jeff, go to: https://www.jeffyager.us

Selected Other Novels by Fred Yager

The Asian Queen
ISBN 1938998201
This work of historical fiction tells the compelling story of a war-torn Cambodia following the aftermath of the Vietnam War. Esther Brafford is a young American volunteer for the United Nations who wants to have a positive impact on the lives of Cambodian refugees seeking asylum in U.S. camps. Each day, she witnesses the horrific injuries that many Cambodian natives are left with as she wishes she could do more to help them. Esther decides that she must venture into Cambodia to find proof and bring it to the UN to put an end to the slaughter. With the help of Heng, a former member of the Khmer Rouge, and Monty Tipton, an American Vietnam War deserter manning the riverboat, the *Asian Queen*, Esther must make the perilous trip to retrieve the evidence before it is too late. Will Tipton help her? If he does, will they make it out of there alive?

CYBERSONA
ISBN 978-1938998232

In an extreme case of identity theft, a computer genius who has recently become a quadriplegic when caught in the crossfire of a gang shootout uses an Internet game called "Cybersona" to take over the body of another player, a recently fired science teacher, to get revenge on those responsible for his paralysis. To get his body back, the teacher takes over the body of the next player who signs on; that player turns out to be a middle schooler.

SOUND FROM A STAR
ISBN 978-1889262994
(YOUNG ADULT)

Devon Turner, a junior in high school, thinks he's picked up music from outer space on his satellite dish. He records the sound, takes it to an astronomer who shares it with a musicologist. Within 24 hours, the sound is being played on radio stations everywhere. The music has a powerful vibration that can be used to heal or to destroy. Where is the music coming from?

UNTIMELY DEATH
Available in e-book, print, and audiobook formats.
A psychological thriller that introduces a new sleuth, criminology professor Dr. Kimberly Stone. This acclaimed first novel by the husband-and-wife writing team of Fred Yager and Jan Yager probes the darkest depths of the human psyche. There are translations of this riveting mystery in Swedish and Vietnamese.

Praise for *UNTIMELY DEATH*:
"In their first novel, *Untimely Death*, husband-and-wife authors Fred and Jan Yager achieve the literary equivalent of a rookie who hammers a home-run in his first big-league at bat....The Yagers have written a winner. "
—Associated Press, Charley Morey, AP Special Features

"*Untimely Death* is a riveting thriller that takes the reader on a tour of Manhattan's underground where anything goes..."
—Klausner's Bookshelf 2, *Midwest Book Review*

JUST YOUR EVERYDAY PEOPLE

Available in e-book, print, and audiobook formats.

A suspense novel that deals with the potentially dire consequences of withholding information and practical jokes. What starts out as a night of dining, drinking, and dirty dancing evolves into a twisted and deadly black hole of suspense and terror, showing just how fragile the barrier is between a mundane, everyday life and a macabre nightmare lurking just below the surface of suburbia.

"*Just Your Everyday People* isn't your everyday read. It's a sneaky little thriller that explores the underside of suburban life in a way that contrasts the mundane with the horrible....A walk on the dark side."
—John Lutz, best-selling novelist, *Single White Female*

"The friendship between two married couples begins to unravel when one of the wives seduces a stranger in a bar. Blackmail, betrayal and murder ensue, and the danger seems to come from all directions."
—*Publishers Weekly*, Mystery NOTES

Selected Other Selected Novels by Jeff Yager

SEVEN DAYS IN VIRTUAL REALITY

Available in e-book, print, and audiobook formats.

Reader response: "A page turner"

What would you do if you were offered lots of money to go back in time and relive seven days of your life? What if, for even more money, you were allowed to change what happened? Would you do it, or would you leave everything the same? This is the dilemma that a recently unemployed divorced father of two teenagers, Louis Parker, faces as he explores the challenges of entering the virtual reality world.

Louis runs into an old friend of his brother's and he gets enticed into testing out a new virtual reality videogame. For the first version, Louis will relive selected moments from his life. But in the second version, for more money, he could make changes in the past. If he does make a change, what might be the unintended consequences of those changes? What would you do if you could change your past? Would you if you could?

I LIKE GOD

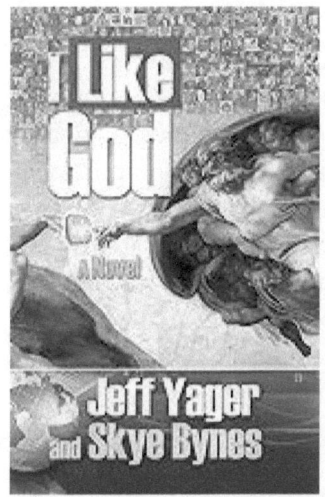

Available in e-book, print, and audiobook formats

Joey Taylor, an unemployed pizza delivery guy, creates a page for God but forgets about it until his girlfriend asks him to activate his page so she can brag about their relationship status. When Joey returns to the page, much to his surprise, he finds that his God page has 30 million "likes." *I Like God* is a powerful and well-written novel that explores how Joey handles – or mishandles – his newfound power. Written by two insightful Millennials, this engaging novel offers fresh insights into the impact of social media

"'*I Like God: A Novel*' is one of those impressively written works of fiction that reveals something of what could really come to pass in today's social media dominated popular culture. A ripping great read from beginning to end, "*I Like God: A Novel*" is very highly recommended for community library General Fiction collections...."

—Micah Andrew, *Midwest Book Review*

ATOM & EVE

Available in e-book, print, and audiobook formats.

Atom & Eve is a prophetic YA novel about a deadly pandemic with no cure, is an example of that. In Jeff Yager's first sci-fi thriller, set several years in the future, sixteen-year-old Ricky Romanello, a college freshman, is playing basketball when he collapses and winds up in a coma suffering from a powerful flu that hits the U.S. population causing deaths and a dramatic economic slowdown. Research scientist Dr. Mandy Fox has been developing an anti-aging drug that she believes might also eradicate the flu. Ricky takes the drug and so does the rest of the population. It stops the deadly pandemic but everyone soon discovers there unintended side effect to the new drug. In this page turner of a sci-fi novel, you'll also discover the first female presidential candidate and a police officer with questionable ethics. The way the author weaves together the plots and subplots of this intriguing debut novel is a memorable read that is appealing to adults as well as teens.

"...a great debut for its author, Jeff Yager. Its mix of suspense, science, romance, and even politics will keep the reader turning the pages to find out what happens next, and there are enough twists and turns to ensure the pace never slackens."

—Alan Caruba, book reviewer, Founding member of the National Book Critics Circle

STUNT DOUBLE

2026

Available in e-book and print formats

This action-packed novel takes you inside the world of a stunt double where Johnny Biggs must stand in for Cole Tillman, a Hollywood star. But will events happen that change Johnny's fate?

A GHOSTLY TWIST

(YA- Young adult)

Forthcoming

Sixteen-year-old Albert is still getting over his father's death three years before. He teams up with his new romantic interest at school, Lilly, as well as his friends Mike, Zack, and Jamal, and Jamal's cousin Terence, and together they create a new online series called *Ghost Squad*. Together, the Ghost Squad investigates haunted places like the Ghost Town of St. Elmo.